Robert and Arabella

Also by Kathleen Winsor

Robert and Arabella

by

Kathleen Winsor

Harmony Books/New York

Published by Harmony Books, a division of Crown Publishers, Inc., 225
Park Avenue South, New York, New York 10003

HARMONY and colophon are trademarks of Crown Publishers, Inc.
Manufactured in the United States of America

Library of Congress Cataloging-in-Publication Data

Winsor, Kathleen.
   Robert and Arabella.

   I. Title.
PS3545.I7575R6   1986   813'.52   85-17680

ISBN 0-517-56078-X

Book design by Ron McCutchan

10 9 8 7 6 5 4 3 2 1

First Edition

for you

"The summer's flower is to the summer sweet. . . ."
WILLIAM SHAKESPEARE

◉ A.D. 1315 ◉

❧ CHAPTER ONE ❧

A
t a swift signal from one of their number the five young women swung their horses in a semicircle and came galloping across the meadow, toward where a brightly painted green and red and blue wagon stood. A young man squatted on his heels beside a campfire, feeding the flames. Two horses, exceptionally fine ones for a gypsy, browsed nearby. Watching alertly as they approached stood a handsome dog, tall, slender of body, with a sleek brown-gray coat.

The young man glanced up as they came careering toward him, hair flying, skirts above their knees as they rode astride and bareback, and presently surrounded him, smiling as if at some joyous secret or discovery, their mounts moving restlessly, foaming from the fast rough treatment they had been given.

He stood and bowed slightly. "Good morning, ladies," he said gravely, while they exchanged glances and laughed with soft surprise among themselves.

Over the fire hung a copper pot, and fumes of cooking lamb and vegetables and herbs rose from it, a ravishing smell upon the air.

They gave him no answer but began a slow amble about his encampment, talking among themselves as if he were deaf, and presently he squatted on his heels and continued his preparations for breakfast.

They talked softly, but not too softly. Clearly they wanted

him to know what they thought of him, his horses, his large silent dog, his wagon.

"A gypsy. I heard there was one in the neighborhood."

"Do you suppose he'll try to steal us?"

One of the girls laughed merrily. "Steal us? More likely, the other way around. Look at him."

"That hair. Like gold with the sun on it. I thought gypsies all had—" She stopped, glancing uneasily at one of the girls, black-haired and black-eyed, who gave her a warning look. "Black hair," she added quickly, "is known to be a sign of royalty. All the Normans, I've heard, had black hair."

"The gold earrings. He stole them, too, of course."

"But his shoulders. His back. His waist and hips—"

His clothes enjoyed their minute attention, although he was dressed like many men of every rank when at leisure: faded blue linen Turkish trousers, close-fitting and pushed to the calf; a faded striped silk shirt opened to the waist, the sleeves rolled to his elbows. A wide belt made of strips of dark red leather was wrapped close about his waist, with three sheathed knives stuck through it. His feet were bare.

"Look at his chest."

He glanced up, narrowing his blue eyes slightly. "You must excuse me, ladies. I was not expecting guests."

"We aren't guests. We are curious observers."

"And censors."

"Let's look inside the wagon. I've always wondered—"

He was on his feet and before the steps so swiftly that all five laughed gleefully.

"What are you hiding?"

"Won't you let us see what's inside?"

"There's no one there. What I'm hiding is—my privacy."

This sent them into joyous laughter again, all but the one girl whose long black hair was tied at her nape with a black velvet ribbon. She had become quieter, observing him with earnest attention and increasing wistfulness. Now she spoke quickly and admonishingly to the others.

4

"Go along. I'll catch up with you. If I don't, I'll ride back alone."

"But if you come back alone what will we—"

The girl made an impatient gesture. "Go along." She clapped her hands. "Quickly!"

The four, startled, galloped away, glancing back only once.

He laughed. "What pleasure to have such authority."

"Shall you help me down, or must I slide down myself?"

"I'll help you, of course."

He stood beside her, waiting. The other girls were now far away. She swung one leg wide over the horse's head and he reached up, spread his hands about her waist and lifted her down. By accident or design, there was a glimpse of curling black hair. Then she stood beside him; the skirt fell about her, spreading upon the grass.

He was looking at her curiously, and she smiled. "You saw me, didn't you?"

"I saw a very little of you."

"And you're wondering if I wanted you to, or if it happened by accident."

"I'm wondering."

"I wanted you to. But that's all I want."

This seemed to amuse him. "I'm not a rapist."

"You're a gypsy. And you are very beautiful. Can I have something to eat? We set out before five this morning. We expected to be back long before now."

"You expected to be back where?"

She raised one arm and pointed to where a castle stood, far in the distance. "There. It's where I live."

"I see. And what do you do there?"

"You think perhaps I wait on the Queen—do her laundry, or bring her a page boy when the King is away?"

Did he think that serving girls went riding in long-trained yellow velvet dresses embroidered with the monarchy's black roses and leopards? Mounted on an animal like Solomon?

"I have no idea what you do. That's why I asked. Excuse

5

me a moment." He disappeared into the wagon and reappeared with two bowls, gold and gem-studded, two gold spoons, and silk damask napkins.

"Where did you steal these?" she asked, for they were as handsome as any she had seen.

He squatted and began to ladle the stew into a bowl, which he set on the grass as he prepared the other. "They are part of my stock-in-trade. I am, you might say, a rather wealthy merchant."

She smiled skeptically, but said nothing. She sat, cross-legged, her skirt carefully covering her, prepared to learn his history. Instead, he inquired about hers.

"You still haven't told me. Your chores at the castle." He was teasing her for her confident arrogance, amusing himself to find how she would answer.

. She looked at him, lowering her head a little, and smiled. Not a smile of ingratiation or flirtatiousness, there was some challenge in it, and an answering amusement. She tasted the stew, hot and good, savory with the fresh-killed lamb and herbs.

"My chores are simple enough, I suppose, provided I never have the ill luck to become Queen. But then I have four older brothers. I had two older sisters, but they died." If these losses had troubled her, she seemed to have forgotten.

She reached out one hand, fingers spread wide, and touched his chest. The touch was brief, and she returned to eating the stew. "You're warm. You're the most beautiful man I've seen. I thought gypsies were ugly. Are you sure you're not an impostor?"

"Quite sure. And so—you are telling me that you are—"

"Her Royal Highness, the Princess Arabella." She glanced sideways, smiling, her eyes shining brightly. "Oh, I have a great many other names. Too many. I've forgotten most of them. Arabella is enough. Or Your Royal Highness. Your name?"

"Robert."

"Robert. You could be of any nation."

He picked up the plates and bowls and spoons, rinsed them in a nearby creek and came back, standing beside her for a moment, looking down curiously, with increasing intensity. He went to the wagon and returned carrying two large gold goblets, extending one to her.

"What is it?" She looked suspiciously into the goblet, which evidently contained red wine. "Is it a fatal potion?"

"Where did you learn your superstitions?"

"Don't gypsies give fatal potions to children and women?"

"Children don't interest me, and with women I haven't needed a fatal potion."

"No," she agreed, sipping the wine, and glanced sideways at him where he squatted beside her. "I can see you."

"You're very beautiful," he said apologetically. "And very provocative."

She drank slowly, looking away, and then, unable to resist, looked again at the bulge between his legs. "I'm a virgin. Literally speaking, that is."

He gave a soft knowing laugh and sat down, extending his legs and crossing them at the knees. "Literally speaking?"

"No man has ever been inside me. Otherwise—" She shrugged.

"I see," he said gravely.

"A castle is not a very private place to grow up in. And royalty and nobility are not much given to modesty. We live in one another's rooms and beds and do almost as we like."

"What have you liked to do?"

"There are pages, many of them handsome. I let them put themselves against me—but when it begins to hurt, I push them away. Sometimes I hold them in my hand. Once, in my mouth—to see what it was like."

"And?"

"I would have to love a man to like that very much." She looked away, silent for several moments, staring toward the castle. "I'm waiting."

"For what?"

"They're not of high enough rank."

He laughed. "You're waiting for your parents to make the choice?"

"I mustn't interfere with the King's plans." She gave him a wise smile. "No one does. And my mother has warned me. A princess—well, a princess is a part of the Crown's property. It must be in good condition."

They laughed, growing easier momentarily. She started to lie backward, but reconsidered.

"How old are you?" he asked.

"Fourteen, eight months ago."

"Isn't that rather old for an unmarried princess?"

"Oh, I've had fiancés, four of them. The first when I was less than a year old, I've been told. There's been Aragon and Catalonia and Burgundy and Lombardy. They were all younger than I, and they all died before I was twelve. I'd never seen any of them." She tilted her head to one side, looking at him with a wise ironic smile. "I was glad when each of them died. I'm not eager to live among strangers."

He looked amused. "It's your duty."

"I'm not eager to do my duty, either. And as I keep getting more beautiful the King becomes more ambitious. I think he must be holding me for ransom." She laughed. "How old are you?"

"Twenty."

"That's quite old, isn't it? But then, think of my father. He's forty-seven." Her large black eyes were solemn. All at once she stood up. "I must go. If my maids-in-waiting get back first, they're too stupid to make up a reasonable lie. I'll come tomorrow. You will be here?"

"No."

"But I want to see you. Don't you want to see me?"

"Are you sure you know what you want?"

"I think so."

"And what about my rank?"

"Your rank. You're a gypsy. Aren't all gypsies descended from the pharaohs of Egypt?"

"That's one myth."

She was standing very near him, and he was much taller, taller than her father or brothers. His face had become gravely serious.

"My mother was brought a gypsy," she confided. "An old woman, I've been told—when I was four months old. She looked at me carefully and pronounced to my mother: 'Let her beware of love.' " She drew a quick breath. "If I come to you tomorrow—what will you do to me?"

"You know what I will do. And if you don't leave soon, I may do it now. We're alone—look how alone—and anyway, you wouldn't want to stop me. You don't want to stop me now. How easy it would be. How easy and how—"

"How easy and—"

"It is glorious."

"I must leave. I must think. I'm becoming a little afraid. You won't make me fall in love with you?"

"I won't try to."

Giving a slight smile over his shoulder he set out to retrieve her horse. When he returned she lifted her arms, he took hold of her waist, and she was astride Solomon, her skirts higher than before. All at once his hand cupped her and two fingers entered, only far enough to determine she had told the truth. He pressed with one knuckle, harder, then harder, and all at once let go and stepped away. "See if any of your pages can do that."

"Oh, my God." She reached toward him. "Do it again—please—"

"Someone may come. Tomorrow, on the south side of the oak grove, there is a quiet place. I'll be there."

"I've never felt that before—please—once more—"

"Good Jesus Christ, get out of here, before you kill me. I don't want to rape you. I want to take you the way a woman should be taken the first time—slowly, carefully, and then—however you want, as much as you want—as long as you want—"

"I won't sleep—I'll feel your fingers on me—and you haven't even kissed me—"

She leaned down, he stepped closer, and all at once gave Solomon a blow on the rump. The animal started forward at a bound, but she recovered quickly and turning, she was smiling, waving gaily. "I'll be there, on the south side of the grove at six in the morning. Goodbye, goodbye—don't make me fall in love with you. And mix another potion—you know the one I mean—"

◎ CHAPTER TWO ◎

She arrived near the oak grove with her maids-in-waiting, having given them instructions to ride for five hours. If she was not there when they returned, they were to wait for her so that they could return together.

They looked at her enviously as she turned aside, and she gave a brief wave, scarcely aware of anything but the heavy beat of her heart. Solomon approached the grove slowly. There was no fire, no wagon, and she began to be afraid that he had forgotten. Perhaps he had gone away. She sternly warned herself that these fears were other signs of incipient love. Staying awake most of the night had been another.

All at once he was there, taking her bridle.

She dismounted quickly, too eager to wait for his help, and caught hold of his shoulders. "Take me into your house—or whatever it is."

She had not noticed that he was not smiling and had not touched her. Now he took a backward step. She gazed at him anxiously, almost grief-stricken to have him out of her touch. When she reached out to him again, he caught her hands gently.

"I'm here," she protested. "Didn't you expect me?"

"No. I expected you would have thought better of it during the night."

"I didn't sleep. All I thought about was what it will be like to have you inside me." She crossed the space between them and placed her fingers lightly against his chest. "You don't want me?"

He smiled, but the smile was serious, and a warning. "Goodbye, Arabella."

"Goodbye?"

"Yes. That's best."

"For you?"

He laughed. "What difference does it make to the world—to anyone—what I do? But there are many people who care what you do."

"I know what's best for me. Many men come to my father. Men from everywhere. I've never seen one who looked like you. I've come to you to learn the one thing I want to know more than anything in the world. And I know many things."

"You do?"

"My tutor is clever, and I'm not lazy. But what I don't know—and what you're going to teach me—is what it feels like to have a man inside me. What do I care if it is wise? Not wise? Don't you want me?"

"Yes, I want you. And if I take you? Well, then—the Crown property—" He gave a light shrug, smiling.

Arabella laughed. "That's nothing. I know what to do. A distraught husband will believe anything. A cry of pain—a little blood from a pricked finger." She touched his chest again, standing very near. "Now—please. I know what I want. Just do it—whatever you're going to do. If that's not what you intended, then why are you here?"

"I told you I'd be here."

"Don't—for the love of God—make me wait."

To her surprise, then chagrin, he laughed. She looked away, embarrasssed. No one laughed at the Princess Arabella.

Quickly she looked back, to catch his expression—hard, intent, determined. He took her hand. "Come along."

They walked together, slowly, passing beneath low boughs into a clearing where the wagon stood. The horses were grazing nearby, and the handsome dog stood at the foot of the few steps leading to the opened doorway of the wagon.

The gypsy gestured Arabella ahead and as she started up the steps, all at once hesitant and uncertain, she paused and looked down, speaking to the dog in a friendly confidential tone. "Hello, you elegant creature. What's your name?"

"His name is Caliph. But he understands only Romany. And it's best not to touch him, or gesture toward him."

"I see. And is he always silent?"

"Except when there's danger."

All at once, aware that she must move very quickly or lose courage, she ran up the steps and stood looking into the wagon. "Oh, how beautiful. All gold and shining—silk carpets, tapestries, colors, colors everywhere—magic." She turned, as he closed the door and the lock snapped, softly repeating, "Yes. Magic."

She kicked off her low black leather boots and, barefoot, looked to him for what would happen next.

Her dress was yellow velvet, embroidered with black roses and leopards. The sleeves were tight and laced to the elbows. The top was tightly fitted, cut in a straight line across her shoulders, laced from neckline to below her waist. The flared skirt trailed upon the floor and, all together, she was more or less imprisoned in it. "I can't get out of this alone."

He stepped out of his sandals, kicking them aside, then tossed away his shirt.

Arabella extended her arms, palms upward. They exchanged smiles, and he set about deftly unlacing the sleeves, then the laces of the dress, concentrating with a rapt intention that delighted her. "So independent—and so helpless."

"That's because—" She stopped, for she had come near to reminding him of her rank. "Because of the way I live."

He drew the dress slowly from her shoulders, peeling the sleeves down her arms, spreading the laces to push the dress low on her hips. It fell upon the floor and she stood naked,

13

showing him the Arabella who had been hidden beneath all
that royal finery.

She faced him unselfconsciously, arms at her sides. He
looked at her silently for several moments and then his
palms lightly touched her breasts, while he shook his head.
"My God," he repeated softly. "My God."

Arabella remained motionless, but was all at once ner-
vously apprehensive. It was about to happen, whatever it
was; the great mystery, her body, was about to be opened.

The bed was behind her, against the wall, set on a frame
two or three inches from the floor, piled with Persian carpets and, over them, three feather beds, covered with white
silk sheets.

Slowly she backed away from him toward it as he untied
the cord that held his trousers and stepped out of them.
Arabella sat on the edge of the bed, looking at him, intimidated by his size, and reminded herself that he was a man,
not a thirteen-year-old page.

Eager to begin, she lay back, spread her legs, folding her
arms behind her head, and as he knelt before her, placed her
feet against his shoulders. By now her vision was blurred,
her skin was turning damp, and her heart's heavy beat made
her breasts shake. It was difficult to breathe. And still he
had not touched her.

All at once, frantic to end the unreasoning fear, she seized
his shoulders. "Quick! Do it now!" Looking down she saw
him place himself against her. His fingers carefully parted
her lips, opening them wide as he began moving into her.
She gave a despairing cry of impatience.

"I don't want to hurt you—" He moved a little farther.

"I don't care—what difference does it make." She began
to sob, for the night hours had driven her toward a nervous
hysteria, a response as unfamiliar as the feeling of him
moving slowly into her.

He pushed himself a little deeper and she felt that first
warning pain she had felt with the pages.

"If it begins to hurt," he said, looking into her eyes,

"stop me. There are other things to do—" He pushed a little farther. "There—"

The red bulb was inside her. He was moving slowly, insistently, while he spread the lips wider, watching, then looking up quickly into her face, to be sure she had no pain. Her eyes were closed, her arms flung outward, her legs wide apart.

"It didn't hurt—and now it's over. Come deeper—as far as you can. Move fast—faster—oh, good Jesus—yes—it is glorious—"

His mouth covered hers with a kiss, deep and exploring, a seeming afterthought for both of them. He began to move more rapidly.

"It can't be long," he told her apologetically. "When do you want it?"

"Not yet—oh—" She gave a sound of despair, for he was moving so swiftly that in another moment she would lose him.

"If I have to stop, I'll come back. Oh, God—"

Pulsing and throbbing, the muscles in her belly seemed to stretch and spread, releasing her from some unrealized bondage. She lay quiet, her arms circling him. He did not leave her and minutes passed, minutes of small motions, as if he might begin again. She seized his hair, trying to look into his face.

When at last he raised his head and looked at her, his eyes narrowed in surprise. Arabella's face was wet because for several minutes she had been crying, crying from a relief, a giving of herself, crying tears of neither sorrow nor joy, but of a recognized finality.

He moved slowly, and she moved with him, until his fingers began to explore her. Then he moved away so swiftly that although she tried to hold him, his tongue was already inside her, drawing new pleasures, which gave more reassurance than challenge.

"Turn over—I won't hurt you—I'll put it in the same place."

She turned, kneeling, and as his fingers continued to press at her, the throbbing release was there with a rush. She felt him begin to enter her slowly, as if he were not quite ready. All at once he was there, so deep that she cried aloud. He paused.

"Don't stop—whatever I say. Do everything to me—"

He manipulated her so that now she was astride him, bending over him while he drove into her with a steady rhythm, longer and deeper than before. It was true, as she had heard, that after the first great rush and loss, desire came back stronger and more fiercely—an increasing madness.

His fingers crushed her nipples, and with his hands about her waist he moved her forcefully upon him. She heard distracted cries of pleasure and hopelessness, the pleasure for its own sake, the hopelessness of knowing that it must end, and she felt some vague surprise that the voice was hers.

When they lay side by side, he was silent and calm, breathing deeply, his eyes closed. Presently she turned from looking at him and closed her eyes, since she had slept little the night before.

She awoke to find him dressed, setting out bread and cheese and raisins for their breakfast, and at that she sat up with a start, pushing the hair from her face. "I've been asleep," she said, accusing herself of having missed something he might otherwise have given her or done to her. "For how long?"

"Half an hour, perhaps. Are you hungry?"

She lay down, smiling a little, looking at him with troubled adoration.

"Maybe. I have to meet my maids at noon. Do you know how late it is?"

He stepped to the doorway. "Not yet noon." He smiled. How easily he had captured her.

She approached and embraced him, and standing in back of him reached into his trousers and brought forth the miraculous object, shining, an obelisk of flesh, tipped with purple-red. She sank to the floor and lay on her back. He knelt, entering her slowly and moving upon her slowly, before withdrawing to put his mouth between the lips and to fill her with his tongue. In a moment he was straddling her and she sucked him eagerly. But when it seemed about to happen, the warm stream pouring into her mouth, he moved away again and thrust into her with increasingly swift strokes until she felt that beginning pulse, that beat of him inside her, that surging charge which left her muscles trembling with something deeper than fatigue.

When he moved away to lie beside her, one hand on her breast, she was surprised to discover that once again she was crying, softly this time, with a sense of profound despair.

"Does this ever end?"

His hands stroked her body. "Never. As long as life continues."

She closed her eyes, shaking her head slowly, wonderingly. "Can you do it again? Once more."

"You want very much, for one so recently a virgin—literally speaking." He was smiling, caressing her breasts, and as she touched him she felt the hardness begin.

"I want more than I could ever have guessed. More than I imagined possible—this morning, when I was riding here. But whatever I expected, and I can't even remember what that was—it was nothing, nothing at all like this—" Her hands passed across his head, over his chest, beneath his arms, down his belly, and fastened upon the thick hair surrounding his slowly hardening flesh.

He lifted her buttocks, moving into her deeply, thrusting at a steadily increasing speed, until, after some time she could not guess at, he gave a soft sound of pleasure and despair, and lay still.

Presently he moved apart from her, raising himself up on one elbow, giving her a serious questioning look. Apparently she had surprised him, or he had surprised himself.

She touched the side of his face. "Now the world is mine."

"Yes?" he asked cautiously.

She sat up. "Oh, God, I must go. They've been arriving

for days. There's a feast tonight in the Great Hall." She shook her head. "I'll never be able to stay awake."

He stepped naked to the doorway. "Your friends are there—some distance away."

"I must go, I must go," she murmured, as if to convince herself. "They will wonder what we've been doing for so long. They're all virgins—I think. Except Maria. I will have so many lies to tell."

"Your mother, the Queen?"

"Oh, it's easy to lie to my mother. She has too many lies of her own to keep track of anyone else's." She lifted a strand of curling black hair. "Take me, for example."

"You?"

"I'm the only one in my family, for three generations, who is not blond and blue-eyed." She smiled. "What do you think of that?"

"What does your father think of it?"

"The timing wasn't easy to establish. He left for the Holy Land and I was born ten months later—perhaps a little less. They say I resemble him. He loves me, and I suppose he prefers to believe it." She looked away. " 'Beware of love' —that's what she said, the old gypsy woman."

"She was right. Remember it."

She looked up in quick surprise, then knelt before him, taking him into her mouth. He stood before her, legs spread, and when she lay back he was quickly inside her. When he moved away, Arabella gave a protesting sigh.

"I can never have all of you I need or want. Tomorrow? Here?"

"Tomorrow," he reminded her, "is the day of the tournament."

"I must see you."

He was silent for several moments, looking away. "I'll be there." He smiled a little, as if at some unexpected secret plan.

"You promise?" It seemed quite simple. She wanted him. He would be there.

"I promise."

◈ CHAPTER THREE ◈

Seated in the Queen's pavilion, Arabella had watched anxiously for the arrival of some knight who might be the gypsy in disguise. She had believed him when he said he would be there. But even before she had reached the castle, its surrounding fields by then almost impenetrable with men and animals, tents, pennants flying from the staffs of every duchy or fiefdom in the land, men lying drunk in the afternoon sun, she had realized that he had said it to silence her. For the task itself was impossible.

No knight might enter the lists in single combat who did not appear in recognizable armor astride a horse caparisoned with his master's colors, his name entered long before, to be called out after the flourish of trumpets, announcing him and his opponent.

No. He would not come.

She began to grow listless, uneasy, wishing she could find a way to escape from this brilliant early summer day with its colors and confusion, its clashing of weapons as two armored men tilted at each other, lances clanging against shields.

There had been a hush when the crier announced that the Duke of Guise had been detained, his horse had fallen, he had struck his head upon a rock. He was recovering and would soon make his appearance.

Arabella was not surprised to see her father throw back his head and laugh heartily. "The bloody fool! A Duke who cannot hold his seat!" He signaled for the next pair of combatants.

Arabella smiled at the king's hearty condemnation of Guise, his friend and rival. Falling from a horse was one crime the King would not condone. No other deeds were criminal, in the King's judgment, except of course disloyalty to himself, real or imagined.

Murder was a tool of government, often a strategic necessity. Theft, provided it be on a large enough scale—the King's ancestors three generations before had stolen nothing less than a kingdom—was a legitimate means to power. But to fall from a horse was an ignominy impossible to forgive.

Arabella was as scornful of such clumsiness as the King. She had never fallen, even as a young child. Her brothers had, but not Arabella, for she valued the King's admiration as much as his love.

And then, when there were only two more hand-to-hand combats before the knights took the field in general melee, when the slaughter might well begin in earnest, killing men whom His Majesty would have preferred alive for his future use, the trumpets blared and the crier announced the next contenders. The Duke of Guise galloped forward in silver mail and a green-plumed helmet, visor covering his face, his horse caparisoned in green and silver brocade. At another flourish of the trumpets, he charged his opponent with a ferocity and swiftness that caused the nobles and ladies to cry out, shouting applause.

It was the work of no more than three minutes, and the Duke, who had plainly made a quick recovery, tumbled his adversary from his horse, and graciously let him keep his life.

Guise's horse galloped with swift purposefulness before the pavilions and Arabella leaned forward, for she knew the Duke of Guise, and while it was his horse and his armor, it was not his style of riding, nor his style of combat.

As he passed her, the eye visor was raised slightly, and a pair of eyes flashed at her for a triumphant instant, shining blue eyes, not the Duke's, which were brown. The gypsy had come, after all. And then he was cantering across the field of tournament, out the gates at the far end, and the final pair of single hand-to-hand combatants were being announced.

Inadvertently Arabella had risen from her seat and might have made some move to leave the pavilion, but for the quick grasp of her wrist by Maria, whispering, "Sit down, before someone takes notice of you. Compose yourself, Your Highness."

Arabella returned at once to her role as princess, gazing with impersonal coolness upon the two men below, ferociously engaged.

"Your Royal Highness—" A soft voice spoke beside her, and she glanced up to see a young squire, wearing the livery of the Duke of Guise. "His Grace regrets the delay and has asked me to deliver his apologies." He slipped a paper beneath her hands, which lay folded on her lap. He bowed.

"Thank His Grace. I was not offended."

The young squire moved away and Arabella, wondering where she could keep the paper until she could find a place to read it, felt it taken from beneath her palms by Maria. "It will be safer with me, for the time." It disappeared into the top of Maria's gown.

After some eternity of further noise and bloodshed, trumpeting and screaming of horses, men trampled, the tournament was closed by a signal from her father.

Arabella and Maria made their way out quickly, finding a deserted hallway. Maria surrendered the slip of paper.

I must go far away. By midnight I will be near the village of Fourchon. There is a forest giving upon the fields of a farmer named Garron. I advise you not to try to come. It is hazardous. And when the Duke returns it will be more hazardous still.

Arabella read it over, memorizing it, and tore it into scraps, which she deposited in Maria's hand. "Burn them."

She was able to leave the feasting early, dismissed by her father, for the men were drunk and most of the ladies were leaving. As much carnage could be accomplished at the feasts of celebration as at a day's tournament.

"These are the men my father and all the others need for their perpetual wars," Arabella whispered scornfully to Maria, as they made their way to her chamber. "Now, you must help me."

"Whatever Your Royal Highness wishes. But he has warned you. It is hazardous. A woman riding alone at night, through forests with who knows what wild animals—or men? He was telling you goodbye."

Arabella gave her a furious glance. "Oh, no, he wasn't. He will never tell me goodbye. Now, don't stand there talking like a fool. It will take me how long to reach Fourchon?" She was stripping off the black silk tights and stepped into the heeled black slippers again. There was no time to change the cloth-of-gold gown with its embroidery of the King's black roses and black leopards.

At a little after nine Arabella and Maria, covered by black cloaks drawn across their faces, passed out of the castle through almost empty corridors, neither approached nor spoken to by the few men or women, most of them servants, whom they passed.

Maria had been able to discover, very quickly, the one sober man among them—a young knight who had been waiting for her to come to him. Declaring that he was honored to serve Her Royal Highness in any capacity, he had gone to bring his horse and the one Arabella chose, her favorite, Solomon, to a quiet place near the moat. The drawbridge had been left down for the celebration.

Neither Arabella nor Maria entered the stable. Arabella would ride bareback, since it would arouse less curiosity if the knight took Solomon for a brief canter around the encampment without his saddle.

Astride the horse, Arabella leaned down and kissed Maria's cheek. She felt tears on her face and stroked it, saying,

"God bless you, Maria. You have been closer to me than my sisters. I will always love you. Remember me."

Maria was kissing her hands, crying too bitterly for speech, until Arabella gently withdrew her hand. "God be with Your Royal Highness."

Arabella and the knight crossed the drawbridge softly, circling far outside the encampment. If watchmen were about they were too drunk to take notice of two cloaked riders, or incurious. There were no outsiders likely to be about on this occasion.

Soon they began to gallop, and when they had gone beyond the sound of the camp Arabella pulled Solomon to a stop and turned to look at the castle, brightly illuminated.

She made no farewell gesture, but turned quickly back. "How long will it take?"

"About four and a half or five hours, I think, most of it through dense forest, little populated. I think it best we travel in silence."

"You lead."

They were slowed from time to time by the difficulty of finding even the narrowest pathway, occasionally detouring into open country, passing farmers' houses where the dogs barked, but did not follow them, being chained for the night.

Arabella had stopped thinking. She concentrated upon the precariousness of the ride, Solomon's frequent shying at tree roots and stumps, the small streams to be forded, and hoped only that she would not be thrown.

At last, when she had begun to believe they would never arrive, he said softly. "I think we are in the neighborhood."

"He must find us. Can you whistle very loud? Let's stop and wait."

They stopped and he put his fingers to his mouth, blowing a piercing sound. They waited. There was no reply, and he whistled again. Far away, came a faint answer.

"Wait here," Arabella said. "We can't find him, but he will find us. Perhaps you should start back now."

"With Your Highness's permission, I will wait until you are safe."

Another whistle was heard, nearer, and evidently he was traveling on horseback, for presently they heard the crashing of his horse through the underbrush. The forest was black and the night moonless.

"Give me another signal," he called.

The knight whistled again, and in a few minutes, horse and rider were near them, barely visible. Arabella turned. "Go now. I know his voice." She gave him her hand. "Thank you." His horse began to blunder back into the forest.

"Arabella?"

"Here I am." She slipped down from Solomon's back, and he alighted beside her, but did not touch her. "How in God's name did you get there? And in Guise's armor, riding his horse?"

He laughed softly, as at a bitter joke. "I'll tell you later. We have serious things to talk about."

"I'm here—and we're going to talk?"

"I had no expectation of seeing you after the tournament. It was absurd for me to make that promise—I kept it because of our peculiar sense of honor. And then—when I saw your beautiful face, your eyes, almost tragic—I had to give you the choice of meeting once more, if you wanted it. Guise's squire, who thought I was his master, brought you the note." There was another soft laugh. These events were not pleasing to him. She heard resentment in his voice, and when she touched him, he moved away. "Shall we start back? It will soon be growing light."

"Start back? I didn't come so far for only this."

She stepped quickly forward and put her arms about him, her mouth to his, but after a brief kiss, he moved her gently aside. "Sit down. You must be tired."

"I am never tired."

But when he sat, she hesitated a moment and then sat facing him.

24

"I can take you far enough to give you safe passage, depending on the light and the crowds when we get there." She could not see him clearly but his voice was hard, practical. "We must start now."

"No." After a moment, she added, "I want to be with you. I will be with you."

"You don't know what you're choosing. You can go back easily now—the feasts will last another two or three days. And if you're questioned—you went for an early ride. That's your custom anyway."

"And you? Where will you be? When will I see you?"

"You won't."

"In a few months?" She reflected on that. "I could never wait that long."

"I have an enemy, you must remember. The Duke of Guise is not likely to forget what a fool he was made—even if only four other people know of it, and none of them talks. When I leave here, I'm going south, to the sea. That's where I grew up. That's my land. And your father will give you a husband of the proper rank. You can be pleased by another man as I have pleased you."

"Hah!"

"When you know the difference between lust and love, you will understand the old woman's warning."

"Why can't I have both?"

"You have both now. You love me, I'm afraid."

"Yes."

"And your love, if you insist upon it, may bring you to harm—perhaps disaster. That's why you must go back before they begin to search."

"I want you. I need you. I must have you." She could think of nothing else, and she repeated it.

"Love is jealous, and jealousy closes the world. Love is possessive, intolerant."

"How do you know?"

"There's a way to find out."

"How?"

"I can bring you another man. And watch you with him."

"Surely you would kill him."

"I might. Or I might enjoy seeing how you behaved with him. What if your pleasure were as great as it is with me?"

"Don't bring anyone to me. Only this—" Her hand reached toward him, and again he gently put it aside.

He was silent a long moment. "My life has depended so little on others, I can't believe it would cause me anything but excitement to see you spread out for another man—to see him push himself into you—to hear those sighs—"

"Maybe I hate you, after all. I am going back—you'll never see me again."

"Good. Shall we start now?"

"Is that why you said that?"

"No. I said it because I have to know. You must not risk your life only because I give you pleasure. Pleasure is the easiest thing there is to come by. Easier, far, than a good dinner."

She laughed softly. "Bring him, then. I'm not so horrified as I pretend. Modesty and reticence are no more valued in the castles than they are in the barnyards."

"You don't believe I'll do it. But I will. It's something I must know."

"About me—or about you?"

"About me. I know about you."

"Yes?" Her voice slid upward, skeptically. "What do you know about me?"

"You would enjoy it—at least enough."

Arabella became aware that she was smiling faintly, that even as he talked she grew vaguely warm at the prospect. Then it passed. "Do what you want. I will obey you."

"Don't obey me, Arabella. If you stay with me, you'll have sorrows enough without that. It's when the sacrifices begin, and they will, that you start to learn the difference between the uncomplicated pleasures of lust and the demands and obligations of love."

"Sacrifices?" she asked warily.

He was silent a moment. "To begin—if you come with me, we must get rid of Solomon.

She was on her feet. "I forbid it! He belongs to me. You cannot—"

"Hush—sit down." She hesitated, but then again sat cross-legged before him. "If you are going to stay with me—as you say you are—there will be sacrifices. But before I meekly give up my life to Guise's men, or your father's, I will take what precautions I can. Getting rid of Solomon is the first."

"Do you mean to kill him?"

"Of course not. Even if he were not yours. Kill a magnificent creature like that? I know a man who will buy him for a very good sum, and who will treasure him. I won't give Solomon's name. As for his pedigree, his appearance speaks for that. I'll say I stole him. The only thing more dangerous than having him with us—a honeypot for every thief or bandit in the neighborhood—would be for you to be seen outside the wagon during daylight. When it's dark, you can sit beside me. Otherwise you must remain inside, until we're much farther south. You're accustomed to freedom. Does this sound agreeable to you?"

"No."

"I can take you back safely now. But if you wait another several hours, it won't be possible."

"If I come with you, is there to be only danger and pain and death? Where is what we had yesterday?"

He leaned against the tree and she knelt, fitting herself upon him with a sigh of relieved gratification, which seemed to have come after prolonged abstinence. Their pleasure was greater, the avidity keener, with a fine edge of ruthlessness to it, an abandonment to sensuality which continued so long she began to hope it would never end. They remained locked together, moving at that remorseless pace as if they had been joined into one being.

"Yes," he said softly, as he was leaving her. "It's very strong—very deep." There was thoughtfulness in his voice,

27

and sorrow. "And if you come with me, as you say you want to, these early sensations will seem ephemeral. Each time there'll be new pleasures, more intense. Finally almost intolerable."

She had not moved, though it did not seem likely he would enter her again. "It's almost intolerable now. I suppose you tell me this to be sure I will leave you?"

"I tell you because I want you at least as much as you want me. More."

"You couldn't."

"I do. Because I know what you refuse to believe. If you stay with me, one or both of us will die." He took a deep breath. "No. We have no time for that again. We have at least an hour's ride to my camp. Come—" He stood and reached down, and in another moment she was astride Solomon. The gypsy's horse went ahead, and they rode in silence.

❂ CHAPTER FOUR ❂

As they entered the wagon and he lighted a candle, Arabella kicked away her shoes and pulled off her dress and tossed it aside.

"It's about four o'clock," he said. "I can make it to the town where the man who I think will be Solomon's purchaser lives in about three-quarters of an hour. If negotiations go well, I'll be back in less than two hours."

She was staring at him in disbelief. He meant to do this thing to her. Take Solomon away. Sell him to a stranger. He had put his gold earrings on a table and was tying a black scarf around his head, knotting it behind one ear so that his blond curls were covered, although they were in a countryside of blond and blue-eyed people.

"Do you want to see him once more?"

"No! Take him, since you're going to take him!"

She turned her back and heard him cross the floor. But then he returned and she felt his hand pass gently across her shoulder, turning her slowly to face him. His mouth touched her wet face.

"There's no choice. We can be traced through the gossip of people who've seen him with us."

"Leave, then." Her eyes grew larger with anger. "Did you give me one of those love potions?"

He was looking at her with hard distrust. "It's not too late. I can still get you to where you'll be able to find your way back. But by late afternoon some of the men will be leaving. They will have been told to keep alert for a gypsy wagon answering to this description. Decide now, Arabella. Is that what you want?''

She threw herself on the bed. "No! You know it's not what I want!''

"Caliph will be with you. If you hear sounds, unless Caliph barks, it will be me. He can tear a man apart in two minutes—providing he's not in full armor." There was a slight smile as he talked, though the anger remained in his eyes. He was plainly wondering how he came to be in this predicament. "Keep the windows covered with the leather shades." He kicked open one of the two great chests nailed to the floor at the rear of the wagon and took out a large red cashmere shawl, which he spread over her. "They're filled with loot from every country the Crusaders have passed through. You can't go on wearing that royal rig." He nodded briefly. "Amuse yourself. Whatever you find is yours. Goodbye." He blew out the candle.

"Goodbye," she replied sullenly as the lock snapped. She resisted the impulse to get up and watch him leave, and to see Solomon one last time. She drew the shawl close and fell to thinking of him with resentment and something which resembled hatred.

He's going to sell Solomon. He said he must sell the wagon, since he has been in the neighborhood for three months. He will trade Damon and Pythias for new horses when we get farther on. The only animal he hasn't mentioned getting rid of is Caliph.

Next—will he sell me? Is that why he kept me? Not because he wants me—but because my father would give anything but his head to have me back?

She fell asleep so swiftly, in the midst of her suspicions, that she awoke with a start to find him standing beside the bed, another young man, by no means so beautiful, beside him, both of them gazing thoughtfully down at her. He had removed the shawl.

"Is she not everything I told you?" The gypsy's face was impassive, with a set grimness.

The young man gave a soft helpless sigh. "She's more beautiful than I could have imagined."

Arabella was awake abruptly. But she made no attempt to retrieve the shawl, or to cover herself, and found she was enjoying their admiration and the young man's pleading look of desire.

"Did he sell me to you—along with—"

The gypsy, standing just behind the young man, probably squire to the man who had bought Solomon, shook his head warningly.

"Only if you agree," said the squire, and his voice had an uncertain quaver. "No, I have not paid for this privilege of—looking at you."

"Who do you think I am?"

"A very beautiful woman. The most beautiful, I should imagine, in the world."

She glanced quickly at the gypsy, his arms folded across his chest, his face impassive, less grim now, waiting for what she would do with an indifference which seemed to her quite majestic. Still, it might be possible to hurt him. This was the test he had described, the test which was to satisfy his curiosity about his own feelings, convinced as he was that he knew hers.

He did not believe he was capable of jealousy?

"I ask you to do nothing. Send him away if you like," the gypsy told her.

She looked at the young man and was somewhat surprised by the slow stirring warmth low in her belly. "Let me see you."

He untied the strings which held together the frontpiece of his tight hose, and there quickly emerged, alertly eager, that male blossom of flesh and blood.

She leaned back, glancing once more at the gypsy, his face without expression, and parted her legs. The squire lay

31

upon her and she raised her thighs, putting one hand upon him, guiding him. There was a quick pleasure, but then, as he began to move, she turned her head away, not wanting him to kiss her, not wanting to see the gypsy's face. His movements were quick and experienced, but she had intimidated him—she and, no doubt, the presence of a jealous lover, for in a few more movements he gave a gasp of joyous surprise, a sound of bitter disappointment, and was still. Arabella moved from beneath him.

The gypsy spoke to her sharply. "Go back of the curtain. There's clean water and fresh herbs and soap and vinegar. Quick!"

She jumped up and ran behind the curtain to follow his instructions. She was still aware of a warmth, but a warmth which would not last long. The young man was being ushered from the wagon, and she heard their voices outside, very low, then the sound of one horse's hoofbeats galloping away.

"I brought food," the gypsy said. "Roast capon, bread and cheese and nuts. I'm going to reconnoiter the roads west. I think we can travel by daylight today, there was little traffic this morning."

His voice sounded impersonal to her. She sat in a tubful of water, cleansing herself inside and out, leaving no trace of the stranger.

The door slammed, the lock snapped, and he was no longer in sight. When she emerged, drying herself with a linen towel, she discovered, all at once, that she was savagely hungry, and began to eat. The young squire had left her no lasting sensations. It might as well not have happened.

He'll never do that again. He wanted to kill him. I saw it in his eyes. Now he knows he's capable of jealousy, a murdering jealousy, and of course he thinks he's lost something. A part of his independence is gone, and he will never get it back.

She smiled, cutting a slice from the capon breast with a sharp knife, savoring it with supreme pleasure.

She noticed the gold earrings and slipped them into her ears, going to the mirror on the wall behind the curtain, and turned her head from side to side, smiling. She opened one of the chests, but the riches lying there, everything neatly folded, seemed inexhaustible. A great treasure trove to explore another day. Five lutes, she was pleased to notice. Three were stacked in a corner and two were hanging on the back wall—lutes of remarkably fine quality.

She shook her head and clicked her tongue, smiling wickedly. "What a thief he is. Everything, everything—"

While he transferred the contents of the wagon to a new one, she remained in a small corner closet, where she sat with arms clasped about her knees, moving an arm or leg restlessly from time to time to keep from groaning with the pain of stiffness in her muscles. The closet had contained his store of dried herbs and medicines, which he had removed to give her a hiding place. He took care that no curious children or adults came near to see what was going on by keeping Caliph on guard.

She listened to the racket of the gypsy encampment, where they had arrived two days before, hearing the laughter of children, the incessant barking of dogs less well trained than Caliph, the outbursts of sudden song, wild and beautiful, and voices speaking in Romany. She could hear Robert talking in that same mysterious, softly gliding language.

From time to time he closed a door between the two wagons and let her move about, but paid no attention to her. He was occupied with tearing down the cloth-of-gold which had been swagged over the ceiling, packing the medicines, and preparing the new and bigger wagon he had bought from one of the gypsies. It was painted black and yellow and green. The man had wanted this one in return, but Robert had refused to sell it.

Whenever she told him she could tolerate another hour or two in her closet prison, she crept in and heard the lock snap, sending a shudder across her shoulders.

She began to understand what he had meant when he said his life had depended so little upon others that he could not imagine caring seriously what another human being did. And yet everything in that free life was changing because of her.

She brooded in the dark closet, she grew angry, she cried silently, and wished she had not come with him, and now and then decided to escape. It would be so easy—jump out of the wagon at night when they were traveling—for there had been no daytime travel after the first two days. With the knights and lords returning from the tournament, the roads streamed traffic. She could run away from him easily. She could find a farmhouse or someone who would return her to where she had come from. He would not try to stop her. He would, she suspected, be very much relieved to have her go of her own free will.

But when he allowed her a few minutes' freedom to stretch her muscles—even though he did not look at her, and although his face was grim, his eyes narrowed whether with concentration upon his various problems or with the same rage she felt against him—then, the sight of his beauty, and the memories of what he had given her these past two weeks, changed her rage to desire, and her regret to gratitude.

Enclosed once more in the cubicle, she reminded herself that he had warned her of everything, including the possible consequences of their lovemaking.

"Remember—pleasure has its own forfeiture. At least for women."

"Oh, yes," she agreed, for any such possibility seemed too remote to consider while they were lying side by side and the sensations of their just-experienced pleasure still flowed throughout her body, making their blood one shared lifestream.

"But you have potions for that, too."

"I have potions. They are effective. But they cause much pain. I've seen it happen, and it's very ugly. At least, of course, you don't die from it."

"But to keep it from happening?"

"I'll do what I can to protect you—and some women are lucky."

"I hope I'm one of them. But even if I'm not—I wouldn't give up what you make me feel."

He had warned her of many hazards when they had talked in the forest. In fairness, she could not blame him for her predicament. But Arabella had not been taught to value fairness to anyone but herself. Nor justice, to anyone but Arabella.

And she sensed something of this in the gypsy.

She decided, in her prison—as she heard his footsteps moving back and forth between the two wagons, and occasionally the footsteps and voice of another man as they were transporting the two big chests and the wooden tubs—that although he declared himself a gypsy, spoke their language, and told her of various of their skills, he did not plan as a gypsy would plan.

When the other man was gone and she was again set free, the wagon was empty but for a long roll of Persian carpets on the floor, piled one upon the other.

"All this planning—" she said. "Enough for a war."

"And that's what I'm planning for." He did not look at her, but searched the interior of the wagon.

"I've heard my father use such reasoning. You think as a prince thinks—not as a gypsy thinks."

"It is, nevertheless, the way we think." He was prowling about, searching for anything which might have been overlooked.

"We. Ours. No, you're not a gypsy."

"If I'm not—then I don't know who I am."

He gave a kick at the carpets, unrolling them across the floor. "Lie down. I'm going to carry you into the other wagon. Let your muscles relax—there are curious onlookers out there. A gypsy camp is like any other place."

Quickly, but carefully, he rolled the carpets around her so that they extended beyond her head and feet. She felt him lift her, place her face downward across his shoulder, and walk into the next wagon where he locked both doors and then carefully deposited her upon the bed, unrolling the carpets as she looked at him with a happy mischievous smile, as if they had accomplished a fine stratagem of deception.

"I didn't hurt you?"

"No. This is our new home?"

"It will be, when I have time to put it together. And now—" He threw a white silk sheet over the piled feather bed. "I'm going to sleep for three hours. Then we'll set out."

"Sleep?"

His clothes were off and he threw himself onto the bed with the abandon of luxurious exhaustion. She lay beside him, but although he surrounded her with his arms, quite obviously it was only to comfort her for the pain and silence she had endured throughout the day. "I've slept less than twelve hours in the last three days. Without sleep, I won't be able to travel tonight." He kissed her mouth, closed his eyes, and was deeply asleep.

She lay for some time, longing to wake him, but intimidated. And once again her reflections turned bitter.

He doesn't care for me. He thinks only of planning his escape from my father and Guise, who are probably thinking of other things and have all but forgotten us. Suppose we stayed here? The gypsies would find out there's a woman with him, and sooner or later they would see me. If men did come inquiring, would they sell our secret? He thinks they would.

He awoke suddenly, moved across her without touching her, and was dressed in a few moments, while she looked at him with incredulous disappointment. He pushed back the carved Egyptian wooden shutters and moved aside the leather curtains. The sun had set, it was growing dark.

"It's time," he said, motioning for her to conceal herself. He went outside to bring in more provisions, food they could eat without having to make a fire. She heard him talking to Caliph in Romany. No doubt he had some deep reason for keeping that comparatively secret tongue for their private use.

She could hear him enter and leave several times, setting down heavy objects—the tin tubful of fresh water for their bathing, which fitted into a heavy wooden tub nailed to the floor; fresh drinking water in a gold ewer, which also had its nailed-down wooden container, and then he said, "We'll leave now, but you must stay out of sight until we're many miles from the camp. We may be followed."

"You don't trust your own people?" She smiled ironically.

"I don't trust anyone. With one necessary exception. We must try to trust each other—and hope that if it becomes necessary, we can. I trust gypsies as much as anyone, and of course they know I've been adopted into the tribe—"

"Oh, you do admit that you've been—"

"Arabella, we have no time for personal histories. I know yours well enough, and I can tell you mine in fifteen minutes. Now, remember to stay out of sight. The gypsies are a nation without allegiance to any other. But they, like everyone else, are fond of money. We're rather famous for it." He smiled. "And if your father's men or Guise's should happen on this encampment—" He shrugged. "My people might talk to them. If they do, I hope we'll be far away. Anyway, there are more fools than wise in the world."

"Suppose my father's men find Solomon and the squire?"

"I've stuffed his ears so full of lies, his purse so full of money, I expect his loyalty, whether from conscience or cowardice. I promised I'd come back and kill him. Now, I'm going out." He bent to draw the shawl over her head and for a moment looked directly into her eyes, his face growing less implacable than it had been for some time.

"Just once—" she whispered. "Just for a little while—"

"There's no such thing as just a little while between us. I can't tell you this is serious for both of us, because you refuse to believe me. It's dark enough to travel."

In a few minutes the wagons began to move slowly, and she heard low voices speaking to him, his answers in Romany. Farewells, good journey, she guessed.

The wagon bounced and rattled. Arabella lay pitying herself for having come with him only for the glorified sensations he had given her—which he now refused to give. He seemed fanatically intent upon escaping some imaginary captors sent by her father and Guise.

The wagon rattled on for what seemed hours. When she dared peek through a slit between the leather curtains, the night was black, moonless, and he was traveling without a light. She tried the door, but he had locked that, and she lay down again to wait.

If anyone had tried to take her captive she would have fought until she freed herself or was killed. Yet this predicament was one upon which she had insisted. It was too dark to move around, and at last she fell asleep.

She awoke to find him lighting a candle on the small table where they took their meals. Without turning, he said warningly, "Stay there. I'm going to set the wagon afire. It's been seen by too many people in the countryside around your father's castle. When we're away from the flames, you can come up front if you want"—he glanced at her with a slight smile—"and help me stay awake."

He left the burning candle, taking another with him and a pitch torch. That afternoon he had put her black-and-gold gown and black shoes and hooded cloak in the other wagon.

The wagons began to jostle backward and forward, the horses' hoofs trampling heavily, and she could hear them snorting. Sliding aside the leather curtain she saw a burst of flame from the old wagon and the next moment the horses were at full gallop. Arabella watched as the old wagon flamed wildly upon the night. She turned away, surprised to find tears in her eyes, for something lost that she could not identify.

As she looked out from time to time, the flames grew

dimmer. Finally the wagon halted, his key turned, and they faced each other questioningly.

"There go your roses and leopards."

"Let them go."

Then, slowly, the resentment she had been feeling turned to pity, and she felt disgust at her willfulness, which had placed him in this predicament. Yet, he had chosen it, too. He had sent the note to her by Guise's page. He had brought her with him through the forest.

They stood facing each other across the table, eating slowly, slices of capon, bread, cheese, and as they ate they watched each other as if they had never met before.

This Arabella, in her costume dredged from one of the chests—a gold tissue Persian skirt baring her belly and the upper part of her buttocks, a red silk blouse opened to the waist, a yellow embroidered vest, and around her neck a strand of gold from which depended an emerald the size of a walnut lying between her breasts—was someone quite different from the princess bound and laced into velvet dresses.

She moved nearer, hesitantly. He seized one of the carpets and went through the door, signaling her to follow him. "Sit beside me, if you can endure it. It's not comfortable."

As if she had been granted some unusual favor, Arabella followed, smiling at him. In the light shed from the torches on either side of the wagon, she climbed upon the seat where he had folded the carpet. With a quick slap at the reins they were off, Caliph running silently beside them.

"Forgive me," he said after a few minutes. His voice held the warmth and caress which had charmed her in the beginning. "I can't look at you. There's a steep embankment. And I can't make love to you—not until it begins to grow light and I've found a place for us to spend the day."

"I'll wait," Arabella promised, with all good intentions.

Nevertheless, after several minutes her hand rested lightly upon his thigh, then reached toward the inner part of his leg, then a little farther to explore the folded opening in his trousers, and at last she held him, warm and hard. She turned to him eagerly.

He gave a low sigh, and the horses slackened their pace to a halt while she eased herself down upon him, moving slowly as his hands clasped her buttocks. Her fists began to pound his back, releasing the frustrations of hours of longing and angry resentment.

Somehow he drew away from her and, as she started to protest, seized her wrist and pushed her ahead of him into the wagon, undressing both of them during the few steps between the doorway and the bed. There, as she lay back, he seized her ankles and spread her legs so high that when he entered her they were clasped about his shoulders. He drove deep inside her. As he had warned, the pleasure was intensifying with each encounter and it was not so easy to make love for only a while. They wanted much more than a brief throb of final release from each other, ending in a fury of sensation. They were striving after some massive form of mutual conquest.

She began at last to feel some strange distance from herself and remembered being told about the gypsy art of ravishing a woman into unconsciousness. She was aware that he was saying something in Romany as he continued the deep thrusts, the slow withdrawals and swift plunges. She could not hear him plainly over the sound of ringing inside her head, a steady remorseless chiming she had heard only twice before: once after a wild gallop on Solomon; the other time when, playing a childhood game, she had run straight into a tree and regained consciousness with that same ringing in her head, the same clammy dampness spreading over her body.

"Shall I stop?"

"No, no—for the love of God, don't—"

He did not move her about this time or change position. He changed only the depth, the momentum and rhythm of his thrusting. At last she gave a prolonged outcry, not in pain or in pleasure, not in protest, but an uncontrollable wild sound of triumph. Slowly her body seemed to dissolve into his as he became quiet—finally motionless, heavy upon her.

But he was quickly alert, moving away, muttering distractedly, "Jesus Christ, where the hell are we? Stay here. We can't trust each other."

The door slammed, the wagon began to move again, and Arabella lay quiet, crossing her legs, as if she could keep him inside her, forgetting his instructions about the soap and herbs. Throughout her belly the slow heavy throbbing persisted, even as she fell asleep, aware of a soft smile of gratitude. Another mystery solved, the exact nature of which she did not understand.

❧ CHAPTER FIVE ❧

He warned her that if she was going to ride beside him at night, there must be no more such episodes. They had lost almost two hours of traveling time. Whether or not Arabella would believe it, there was no safety for them until they were beyond the boundaries of her father's domain, and those of Guise's, which adjoined it.

Once they left the main highway they traveled trails which were at times almost impassable, never clearly marked. She could not imagine how he was able to recognize them. At three or four in the morning he would find a secluded place near running water where they could hide until it was dark enough to set out again.

On these deserted byways they saw a few farm people, or an occasional group of pilgrims—to be avoided since they were given to pillage and rape on their progress toward salvation in the Holy Land. And since peace was prevalent throughout the land, they encountered no soldiers.

"I think the King would have married me to Guise two years ago," she told him. "Except that he wanted to marry me to a nation, not a duchy."

He described to her how he had arrived at the tournament in Guise's armor, wearing his colors, mounted upon his horse.

"It was chance. I had made that absurd promise, and so I set out at two in the morning, on foot, leaving Caliph to watch the horses and wagon. I had with me three knives, a length of rope, and a black hood to cover my face. Many men were traveling, en route to the tournament, but they were in groups and there was no way to select my target. It was not until early morning that I happened upon poor Guise."

"Poor Guise. He's not a good man."

"Even a bad man resents being made a fool. He had met a farm girl and sent his men ahead, keeping only his battle horse, the horse bearing his armor, and two squires. I gagged one squire and roped him to a tree, and sent the other to announce his master's temporary absence. He was glad to get away, knowing Guise would kill him if he told the truth, then or later. Guise was too occupied with the girl to notice anything else. That was how it happened he struck his head on a rock, except that the rock was in my hand."

"Oh, Guise, Guise!" Arabella gave a cry of delighted laughter.

"I roped Guise and the girl together, and the squire helped me into the armor and onto the horse. Neither was a good fit." He was smiling, pleased in spite of the consequences. "I tied the squire by the neck to the tree trunk, but left him conscious. I would need him when I got back."

"But how dangerous for you. The man-to-man combat was almost over—and you rode by my pavilion and sent the message."

"How would you know I had come? I found another of Guise's squires to take the message to you. Then I went back and set the squire free to help me out of the armor. Perhaps I should have discarded it, but if Guise didn't appear I decided they'd start searching for me all the sooner. The first squire had seen my eyes and knew my height. Guise and I looked at each other a moment, as the squire rolled him over, dousing him with cold water. You think he's likely to forget that? And, of course, your maids have told about the gypsy and your visit to him. They know who they're looking for."

"Not Maria," protested Arabella. "She loves me."

"But are you sure the others love you? And women cannot keep quiet when just to tell one person a secret can give them self-importance. They're looking for us—your father and Guise. Your father never intended your life to be spent with a gypsy. When it seems we've put a reasonably safe distance between us and them, I'll get another horse for you and you can ride a few hours each night. But during the day, for some time, you must remain out of sight. I'm sorry."

Each morning, when he had found a place for them to remain concealed, he reconnoitered the neighborhood, making inquiries, bringing fresh water and food.

His living arrangements puzzled her, and when they had been traveling three or four days, Arabella asked, "Who takes care of you?"

"Takes care of me?"

"Cooks. Does your laundry. Keeps all this in order." She gestured at the elaborate furnishings of the wagon.

He smiled. "In the past I cooked my own food. Now, because we mustn't send smoke signals, I buy it from a farm woman, or in a town. The farm women wash the sheets and my clothing, for pay."

"Of one kind or another?"

"For money. Of course."

He continued with his story some time later, how he, blond and blue-eyed and tall, came to be living with the gypsies, that small-statured, swarthy, and, Arabella thought, ugly tribe.

"I know only as much as my stepfather, I suppose I might call him, told me, when I was eight or ten. A young woman had brought me, at about the age of two, to the encampment. She said she would pay handsomely if they would take the child and treat him kindly. This superstition that the gypsies steal children is just that. They have children of their own. But the husbands of fine ladies spend so much time at war or traveling to the Holy Land, that many children are born who must be put out of sight, when the men return. Some are killed. Whoever my mother was, a lady or a serving girl, she was more compassionate. Perhaps she loved me. Perhaps she had loved the man who was my father. She gave my name as Robert, nothing else. And when the Elder, who had two older sons and a younger daughter, agreed to take me, she gave me up. Not without much hysterical crying, I was told. But whether she was a lady or a serving girl, she surrendered me to a life that's given me more pleasure than any other I could have had. Whatever few words of her language I may have known, I forgot, and for the next ten years I spoke Romany. They're a wise people, the gypsies. They have a rich lore learned from their origins or travels in India, which the Europeans would do well to learn. But the gypsies guard their secrets jealously. If my stepparents hadn't loved me, I'd have learned less than I did."

"She was no serving girl or maid-in-waiting, your mother," said Arabella, thinking that now the puzzle had been solved. "If she paid the Elder a large sum of money, she wasn't a serving girl, because a serving girl wouldn't have been trusted with money. She was a member of the nobility, and your father no doubt a noble or member of a royal family traveling to the Holy Land. We have three such children living with us. They're treated as one of us—because they are. My father or mother know who their parents are."

"Think that if it amuses you, Arabella. Whoever I am—other than myself—doesn't interest me."

He could split a man's skull between the eyes throwing a knife at ten paces, and demonstrated it by making a bull's-eye on a tree. "If the target is moving, aim for the throat." He nodded. "Almost nothing else I learned is more valuable. The lances and broadswords, all that cumbersome equipment of the European men puts them at a disadvantage—unless, of course, they are many together."

The tribe had taught him other lessons of value: how to train a horse; how to train a dog. Which herbs and plants were beneficial and which were poisonous. Potions to cause sleep; potions to cause abortions. Potions to cause love, and potions to cause hate.

"These last two work on the imagination, although the gypsies don't think so. There are potions to drive a woman mad with desire, but this is dangerous, and ugly. I've seen it done, and I would never use it."

"Why should you?"

"The women tell fortunes, as you know, and they are clever about guessing what a woman wants to hear. It's always women who want their fortunes told, since they have so little control over their lives."

"And what did they teach you about women?"

"They think that European men are graceless, clumsy lovers. I was taught to make love for three or four hours."

"Three or four hours?" she asked cautiously.

"Five?"

After a moment of thinking that over, she glanced sideways and found him smiling a little. Whether he was teasing her she was not sure—that idea would take some time to absorb.

When he went to the farms to get food, or to take laundry to be washed—at an hour when the men would be out in the fields and a farm woman or serving girl would be alone in the house—she had sometimes wondered if he took them. But she did not ask.

He had given her the choice of accepting or rejecting the young squire. She had acquiesced out of curiosity and not because the gypsy wanted to know what his response would be. She wanted no other man now and could not imagine ever taking one. Yet if he was faithful now and in the future, it would not be because she had asked for it.

They continued south by devious ways. He evidently knew the region as if he had the map drawn on the palm of his hand. But, because of the byways they were obliged to take, progress was slow.

When the gypsy returned from his daily morning search of the neighborhood, bringing food and fresh water, he slept for three or four hours, and then was out again on his constant search for news.

Day by day, he re-created a replica of the wagon he had set on fire—Persian silk carpets and tapestries covering floors and walls, the ceiling swathed with cloth-of-gold. Several gold brocaded cushions with iridescent threads of crimson, yellow, green, bright blue were tossed upon the bed and in the corners. And at all times the air was heavy with a blend of many fragrances—perfumes, aromatic oils, fresh and dried herbs sprinkled on the floor around the bathing tub.

When she was alone Arabella spent time experimenting with the contents of a cabinet filled with ointments and lotions. She found henna to redden the palms of her hands, the soles of her feet, her nipples and areolas. Black kohl to outline her eyes. She searched the chests and found transparent silk skirts or trousers, blouses and vests, long gold coats and flat backless slippers with turned-up toes.

She asked no questions about how he had contrived to steal so much, for she was careful not to say anything which might annoy him, distract him from the possibility of lovemaking. For now it seemed she thought of little else. She felt a painful desire for him even when she had been recently, profoundly gratified.

The gratification only served to create a new need, and this continuous need produced an undercurrent of terror, a foreboding.

Something evil must come of this. I need him too much. And he needs me as much, but not more.

Yet she was still perversely eager to know something of what had gone to compose this man who seemed a species of idol, too beautiful and mysterious for her comprehension.

"When did you first make love to a woman?" she inquired conversationally, and heard him give a low laugh. They were traveling at night, the best time to ask questions, since he was too preoccupied to make love.

"You ask questions you don't want answered."

"It was so long ago. I don't care what happened before you knew me."

"No?" He sounded skeptical. "I was twelve."

"And you could—"

"I could fuck a woman, if that's what you mean."

"One of the gypsy girls?"

"No. They didn't appeal to me, I'm sorry to say, and evidently my stepfather knew it. She was a farm girl. My stepfather told me I must begin to learn what a woman was, and went along to be sure I made a good beginning."

Arabella laughed. "He went along?"

"It was better for him to show me what he knew than for me to spend the next several months or years blundering along like a European."

"You hate the European men. Yet you're one of them."

"Coincidentally. And I don't hate them. I despise them. They know so very little about anything of importance."

"The farm girl—where did you take her?"

"In the fields. She was pretty—reasonably. And clean— we bathed in the stream. Was I curious about what a woman looked like? No, I'd known that for years."

"They were kind to you, the gypsies. They must have been, because you command yourself. And yet you left them."

"I didn't leave by an act of choice. It was what my stepfather called an act of destiny."

"A woman."

He laughed softly. "Yes."

"Who was she?"

"She was a lady, a Countess. There's no need for you to know more, and the less you know the less you will have to feed your jealousy. You have a good deal of fierceness in you, Arabella. It's in your eyes sometimes, and I feel it when we're making love. You want everything with a violent intensity, greater than I've met before. There, I'm sorry. I shouldn't have said it."

"Why not? I know it. But I must know something more, since I know she existed in your life, this Countess. Tell me. I won't be jealous. I promise."

He gave her an amused glance. "No? Very well. She came to our encampment one day with her ladies-in-waiting."

"How familiar." Arabella's voice had turned mocking. The farm girl made no difference. The Countess did. "And—"

"I was a few months beyond twelve. She looked at me, with curiosity, I supposed, as the only blond in the camp. She had her fortune told. She talked to my stepfather about me, and she returned the next day. My stepfather said it was better that I go with her. The gypsy women would never please me—they weren't beautiful in my eyes. This lady would make me her page, her squire in a year or two. One day, a knight."

"You went gladly."

"I refused at first. I loved them. But she came back, again and again. The women of the nobility have their own power, as you know."

"She was beautiful?"

"Yes." He hesitated. "Very."

"Don't tell me anything more about her."

She was able to resist questioning him for the next two nights, when all at once she inquired, softly and innocently, "What did the Countess do when she got you to her husband's premises? Once she had you outfitted in her husband's colors, that is."

He laughed a little. "She sent for me and asked if I knew what she wanted. I said that I did. A year later, I knew much better. Two years later, better yet."

"How often did she want you? Did you sleep with her at night?"

"Are you sure you want to know?"

"Yes. Idle curiosity."

"Three or four times a day. Now and then she liked to watch me with one of her ladies-in-waiting. But then she fell in love with me and grew jealous. Yes, I slept in her bed."

"Oh!" Arabella was shocked by her jealousy. "The nobility are all alike! And as you stayed with her—she saw that you were taught other things, too."

"My obligations required twelve or fourteen hours a day. She put me under a tutor who taught me to speak as they did in that region. He taught me to read and write in their language. He taught me the rudiments, at least, of Latin and mathematics and the ancient myths. I was given lessons in deportment suitable to an aristocrat. I learned a different style of riding. I learned to joust and participated in the tournaments, which proved useful not long ago. I was being groomed to replace her husband. Each morning when she heard mass, she prayed that he would die in Jerusalem."

Arabella was silent for several minutes. Then she said, slowly and decisively, "I hope she is dead so that she can't remember all that you did with her."

"Sometimes, Arabella, you are barbarous."

"You'd have become barbarous yourself—if you'd stayed with her. Our own wishes are all that concern us. The rest of the world is not important."

The questions continued from time to time, directed toward some unknown end which would permit her to put his past life away and think no more about it ever.

He had stayed with the Countess until he was sixteen and word came that her husband was returning there in a few weeks. The lady was pregnant.

"And so you have a child—a son or daughter."

"She was planning to abort it when she sent me away."

"She didn't grieve to lose you?"

"There was no choice. We hadn't been secretive. Even if we had—as you've said, a castle is not a very private place to live. These—my stock-in-trade, as I call it—were her farewell gifts. I took them because—well, I could use them. And they meant nothing to her. The remnants of ancestral excursions during Crusades over the past two hundred years.

They were stored away—forgotten. No one would ever look for them. Caliph was about a year old. She had given me him as a puppy, and she insisted I take him with me."

"How old was she?" Arabella was hoping for some indecent age—perhaps thirty-two.

"When I met her—fifteen."

"Oh. Well, please don't talk about her anymore." There was a reflective pause. "Four years. It would take us a long time to do everything you did with her."

"There are no repetitions in love. Didn't the young squire I brought to you prove that? It was one of the reasons I brought him."

She was silent. All at once she demanded imperiously, that old imperiousness, lost these past weeks, when her need of him had made her unnaturally passive: "Did you love her?"

"Love her? Twelve to sixteen? Love?"

"Not for men, perhaps. For women. But she gave you pleasure."

"And I gave her pleasure."

"Don't, I beg of you, talk about it."

"I won't. But I suppose this much was necessary. Just one thing more—I have never seen her again or gone in the vicinity of her husband's domain. Until you began to ask about her, I had nearly forgotten her."

He glanced at the night sky, the stars dim, the moon invisible. "There. You see—it's time to begin looking for shelter. It's going to rain—in a day or two—and rain hard. We must find a place to shelter the wagon and the animals. If it lasts long, as it sometimes does in this part of the country, they would be in danger of getting sick."

By the next day, when he had found that necessary shelter, the air was beginning to feel different, even to her. She was grateful for the prospect of a prolonged storm and the shelter of the great barn. He paid the farmer very well to give it over to his privacy for as long as they needed it. He explained, with logic and geographical references, that he was in the employ of a merchant and charged with carrying a shipment of woolen cloth—which was not likely to rouse the farmer's cupidity—from Marseilles to Calais.

He lied so easily, almost professionally. Arabella was amused to think he knew as much about lying as she did.

⊠ CHAPTER SIX ⊠

arned to keep hidden, Arabella heard the gypsy and the farmer walking about the barn. The gypsy talked in soothing and persuasive tones. They climbed to the hayloft and explored it. Arabella knew that he wanted to make sure no one was hidden up there. They discussed means of getting fresh water, cooked food, and having the laundry done. He insisted upon privacy. The journey had been arduous and he needed sleep.

No, he would not require the services of the farmer's sons to feed or curry the horses or the dog. In fact, the gypsy suggested, it would be advisable for no one to approach the dog even with the best intentions, for the dog had been trained to take no stranger's intentions as well meant. And he had his own locks for the doors.

Once all this was understood, the farmer was assured that more money would be forthcoming in generous quantities, depending upon the gypsy's needs and the length of the storm. He was ushered, with a display of cordiality, from the premises and invited not to return.

"When I need something, I'll get it myself, or go to the house and ask for it."

Arabella heard the locks snap shut, and all at once her heart was beating faster. This was why she had come with him, to be alone for some unpredictable period of time. He could have her as he would. And she in turn would have all she wanted of him, which she was convinced was beyond the realm of possibility, but not beyond the possibility of making the trial.

She was looking at herself in the mirror on the back wall of the wagon, sorry that the mirror bought at the gypsy encampment to replace the small one which had been adequate for him still showed her Arabella only as far as her waist.

She had decorated herself with henna and kohl and was wearing a skirt made by tying a gold-embroidered scarf low on her belly. The emerald pendant she had not removed since the day she put it on hung between her breasts. She was brushing her hair, a task which required almost two hours a day, now that she had no one to do it for her.

The chests, which she excavated day by day, were filled with pleasures and surprises provided by those connoisseurs of Eastern luxury, the Crusading ancestors of the Countess and her husband.

Arabella wondered whether to add something, an embroidered vest, a floor-length gold coat, when the door opened. She saw him watching her with a slight smile, and turned slowly.

"I'm going to feed the animals and curry them, bring fresh water and set out the tub before the rain begins. You mustn't leave the wagon—the barn has more holes than a cheese. Can you stay here as long as it lasts?"

He moved toward her and, as happened each time she felt the imminence of another encounter, her heart beat faster, her breathing slowed, as if she might soon suffocate, and she looked at him without a smile, her eyes larger, questioning.

He did not touch her, and so, having made that announcement, she supposed he intended to go about his several chores. But his hand had slowly drawn apart the folds of his Turkish trousers, and there was that proud display, blue veins throbbing, reddened bulb hard and glistening, and as at a signal he had not given, she dropped to one knee and took him into her mouth, while his fingers reached into her hair and held fast. She looked up to see him watching her with a glittering intensity of concentration. This was what he wanted this time.

He began to move, slowly, while she took him as deep as she could, as if no other way of making love could be imagined or desired. He continued to hold her hair, and from time to time drew her head back, forcing her to look up at him. His concentration seemed almost reverential, until all at once his eyes closed, she heard a soft low sound of pleasure, and as he spurted into her mouth she drank him eagerly. The flow came, jet after jet, and ended in slow eddies.

He released her hair, stroking her head, as she sank back to sit upon the floor, curiously depleted by this brief but nearly savage encounter which was, she knew, no more than an omen. He brushed his hand across her breasts, secreted himself within his trousers, and was gone.

Arabella sat still, her heart slowing gradually, hearing his activity outside, talking to Caliph in Romany, unharnessing the horses and leading them to their stalls, unlocking one of the doors to set out the tub to catch fresh water, and then she heard the rain begin, delicately, and felt for a despairing moment that it would not be so long a storm, after all. There came a great crack of thunder and through the slits in the barn wall she saw flashes of sheet lightning.

Slowly she stood up, surprisingly tired. Always before, he had completed the act of love inside her, and this had left her uncertain, a little shaken. Yet she was gratified in some curious new way.

She looked around as the door opened and he was standing just inside, but he approached swiftly. "What do you want?"

"Whatever you want. Did I give you pleasure?"

"Of course. My God!" He smiled suddenly. "Let me know if there's ever anything I can do for you—climb a mountain, kill a man—" There was a joyous exultance on his face she had not seen for some time.

The lassitude was gone, and she was as eager to suck him again as she had ever been to have him inside her. She knelt, bringing him out of the trouser opening, and this time he did not hold her hair or touch her but stood with legs wide apart. He began to move, slowly. The urgency had been satisfied, and he must be coaxed to flower. This time the task was hers. He could not so readily give her that final fountain of himself.

At last he bent slightly, holding her breasts, then grasped her nipples between his thumbs and forefingers, crushing them until she gave a protesting murmur and began to bite him gently.

He moved faster, still crushing her nipples, but when she thought she would cry out, miraculously the pain was gone, and once more he gushed into her mouth. Slowly he softened, and at last she let him go.

Surprising them both, she gave a wail of despairing loss and threw herself upon the floor, pounding it with her fists.

"Arabella—" He knelt beside her, taking her into his arms. Her eyes were closed and her head fell back, as if she might have fainted. "Arabella—"

He held her closer, gently, but there was no alarm in his voice. No doubt he understood that a woman might cry as readily from a great joy as a small sorrow.

She gave a bitter little laugh, eyes still closed. "I want you, one way or another, all the time—"

He carried her to the bed, kissed her lips lightly, and, saying he would return soon, was gone. Arabella lay quiet, bewildered by the intensity of reaction to what they had only begun.

This time he was gone longer than before. She got up and pushed the leather shade to one side. He was currying Damon while Caliph slept nearby. She lay down again, still too bewildered to take up the lute, comb her hair, or think of anything to pass the time.

She heard him enter the wagon at last.

At last, she knew, might have been after an hour or after

a few minutes, for she had lost all sense of time. She heard water splashing in the tub and got up quickly, finding him scrubbing off the smells of Damon and Pythias. He smiled a smile as free and whole as if there had been no dark flashes of madness between them. She approached, looking at him, and found that he floated upon the water, quiet, perhaps at this moment beyond arousal.

He beckoned slightly, she bent, and with a twist of his fingers he untied the scarf which fell away as two fingers slipped into her. He put his mouth to her breast, guiding her hands downward to touch him, and she stepped into the tub, lowering herself upon him.

He was not ready for her, and pushed her gently backward, exposing her so that his fingers might caress her. That deft twist of his knuckle brought a soft cry of surprise and its accompanying shudder, and he took her astride him in the water.

Suddenly he stood, still holding her, then knelt upon the floor, and with a few deep violent surges came to full engorgement. Another few moments and the pulsing throbs ran between them.

Arabella thought it unlikely she would move again. She felt him drying her with a soft cloth, turning her to dry her back, and she looked up to see him standing, straddling her hips, smiling. "You like it better that way?"

"I like it better any way. But this is—different. So often—so soon—"

"I want to empty myself into you, first."

"First?"

"Before we begin to make serious love."

"Serious?" She gave him a skeptical smile.

"If it's to last, as you say you want, three hours, four hours, longer, it's much more serious. For me that requires concentration, and the sacrifice of some minor pleasures. For you—some sacrifices, too. You must be quiet, perhaps for quite a long while. Can you be quiet, Arabella, and let me do what I want to you?"

Her heart began to beat precariously at this suggestion of prolonged lovemaking. One hour, two hours, they had done that. But there had been no sacrifices of quick pleasures, only occasional warnings to her—not so quick, not so insistent.

"So many hours," she said doubtfully. "How does it feel?"

He shook his head, smiling, as if he supposed her to be playing a kind of game. "I can't tell you how it will feel to you. I can't even be sure how I'll feel if it lasts as long as I hope it will."

She was looking at him with wondering fascination. To have that beautiful magical object, almost a separate being, inside her for three or four hours—longer—

He smiled with a trace of irony. "The gypsies say that if it can be done—it comes near to sublimity. No one, they say, thinks of anything but experiencing it again."

This time she took him into her mouth with little hope of bringing forth another fountain of that fluid his body so quickly produced. He wanted the pleasure of her, in whatever form it came.

He stood motionless and her mouth moved upon him, but he did not touch her, only waited for what would happen. Arabella felt no sense of time, her excitement increasing steadily. There was a faint stir and she sucked more greedily, longing to bring pleasure for him without his having to satisfy her with the force of his body.

Slowly he hardened, grew fuller and larger, and at last began to move with deliberate slowness, seeming to wait passively for his fulfillment; it seemed he had finally become satiated. Perhaps nothing more was possible between them now.

Still, when she began to move away, he pressed her head against him, and once more he was moving, at that same leisurely pace, as if he meant this to continue indefinitely, the two of them brought to an intensity as great as they had ever felt. Arabella moved more slowly, and slowly ran her hands along his legs, examining him, admiring his legs, long and splendidly formed, not heavy of thigh or calf, as beautiful as everything about him.

She looked up with painful intensity at the beauty of his body, looked into his face, searched his eyes, finding there the questioning, demanding, seriousness, deeper and more solemn than any expression she had seen before.

They continued, slowly rocking forward and backward. Slowly the tension mounted, slowly he grew harder, thrust deeper, and all at once, with none of the usual portents, she felt him pouring down her throat. Then he grew quiet, softened, and she let him go.

They were silent, Arabella still kneeling on the floor, he still standing before her. Finally he asked, "Are you tired?"

She sighed. "I feel as if I have been—drugged." She looked up quickly. "Have I?"

He gave a low laugh, without humor. "When? You've had nothing to eat or drink for hours." He stroked his hands across her breasts, and she caught one hand and held it, then eased it down to rest between her legs. Again they were quiet, motionless, as he squatted down before her. The feeling of his hands, a kind of protectiveness conveyed, was enough at that moment.

"You're tired. Shall we sleep?"

There was the reassuring sound of the rain splashing upon the roof. Finally, they had that great luxury which they seemed to have been pursuing since the night in the forest: time.

She got up, moving away from him reluctantly, yet not as reluctantly as usual. Those recent sessions, intense and quickly repeated, had demanded more from her in some way she did not understand—more than what she had always thought of as their real lovemaking. She wanted to be away from his touch but she was afraid that with his quick intuition, he would know that.

At one of the windows she moved the leather curtain slightly and peered out into the semidarkness of the barn.

"Is it morning or night?" She was silent a moment. "Did we sleep? I feel—as I've never felt before."

The wagon was warm, too warm, but because the barn was full of holes, and the heaviest rain would not keep the farmer or his inquisitive children from trying to see what was going on in that mysterious visitor's wagon, they could not open the door. Perhaps it was only the warmth which made her feel a slow fatigue moving along her arms and legs. Her body felt curiously swollen, full and profoundly replenished.

The horses stamped and dozed in their cells. Caliph lay in what appeared a sound sleep.

Arabella searched for something to say which might distract them from this profound concentration upon each other. It had begun to seem ominous, almost a threat, a demand for something she could not or would not give.

"I've never seen Caliph with a bitch. Is he celibate?" She gave the gypsy a slight smile, pretending that her concern about Caliph was real.

"Caliph prefers women."

She continued looking out the window. "Who taught him that?"

"I did. Have you never seen it? A dog and a woman?"

"I've seen it. I've told you—you see everything, growing up in a castle. One of the Queen's ladies-in-waiting had such a dog." She turned, smiling. "Where do you find Caliph's women?"

"Farm girls. Money, sometimes. Sometimes, they offer. The pleasure, some women say, is greater than a man can give—with none of the risks. It's to my advantage he doesn't run after every bitch in heat we pass."

Arabella turned, noticed one of the lutes lying upon the stool beside her, and, as if she had found a defensive implement, picked it up and began slowly plucking the strings, listening carefully. She sang, softly, two or three lines of a song one of the troubadours had sung at night in the Great Hall. He watched her, no longer smiling, quickly aware of the change, and willing to wait until she came to him.

CHAPTER SEVEN

I s it day—or night? I still don't know." She continued plucking at the lute, an instrument she had studied from the age of four or five, and played with a proud skill. But that was not why she played it now.

"It's midafternoon. I spent much of the morning taking care of the animals, as you remember—"

"It's what happened when you weren't taking care of them that I remember."

He stood with arms folded, leaning against the wall, and was evidently no more eager than she to begin that promised period of prolonged lovemaking, three hours, four hours, five hours. Longer, if she wanted it enough to be quiet when he told her to be quiet. If, he had said, she could control her usual avidity for that bursting flood of feeling which when it came, almost unexpectedly, was a storm of surprise overtaking them both.

"Are you hungry?" He nodded toward the table, the dishes covered with a clean white damask cloth. "I bought the food on my last trip to the farmhouse. It's fresh."

But while he talked of food, he was looking at her carefully, studying her breasts, the tinted nipples, her flat belly and round hips, the triangle of curling black hair. And as he looked at her, her apprehension increased. She glanced around the wagon, as if there might be a place to hide, and continued holding the lute, pretending to concentrate on the sounds she made.

"I'm not hungry. Are you?"

"Yes."

He passed her, took a leg of capon, broke it free and began to eat, then offered her a bite. She hesitated before putting her mouth to it. Presently they were eating, teeth almost touching, as they bit into the meat.

Rapturously intent upon the food, her eyes closed. When his hand touched her, she moved her feet apart and his fingers slipped into her slowly. Her hand took hold of him, carefully, gently.

With his free hand he broke off another capon leg and they attacked that between them, their attention now divided between the gratification of hunger and the responses they were evoking in each other. The capon leg was set aside, and with arms about each other they moved slowly, it seemed almost reluctantly, toward the bed with its smoothed silk sheets. A fate had been sealed between them, its conclusion known or perhaps guessed at by him, but not by her.

Arabella lay down, arms behind her head, and looked at him as he knelt, knees on either side of her hips. Her smile was questioning, tentative, almost frightened. "What are you going to do with me?"

"Whatever you want. Whenever you want."

Her legs parted slowly. "I've heard that if a man and woman—"

"Yes?"

"That if a man and woman want each other too much— for too long—their prayers may be granted. They may never be able to part again."

"To part?"

"To get apart," she whispered. "They may be—by desire— locked together forever—and—one day die that way—"

"Arabella, Arabella—the things they teach in those castles—"

"You've been in castles. But don't tell me about it," she added quickly. "Don't tell me if you were ever with the

Countess for three or four or five hours." She glared at him, unsmiling, stricken with tormenting jealousy of that woman he had not seen for four years, and had nearly forgotten.

"Were you?"

He looked at her steadily and seriously, saying nothing.

"You must have been." All at once she moved quickly from beneath him and stood up.

He turned to sit on the edge of the bed, leaning forward in that posture he sometimes took when he was thinking, legs wide apart, elbows on his knees, staring at the carpet.

"What difference does it make?" he asked finally.

She was staring at him with her eyes bright and unforgiving, as if that earlier time had all at once changed the balance between them. For not only did she hate him for whatever had happened between him and that other woman, but she felt terror for reasons she could not guess.

There was a long silence, until he said, "I don't know what's troubling you. Or, I should say, I do know what's troubling you. Put out of your mind this project of prolonged lovemaking. It has frightened you. Just now, you hate me."

She smiled slowly, feeling some small triumph of cruelty, and then looked directly into his eyes. Her face softened, her smile saddened, as it would have if they accomplished it, had it over and done with, that eternal lovemaking, all the hours, perished—and they perhaps with it. That was how it seemed to her, in some fiercely held superstitious way she could not define—there was no other possible outcome of such total abandonment.

"Yes. It has frightened me. And perhaps I do hate you."

She looked away and around at the red and gold and green interior of the wagon, with its shining silks and tapestries, its soft light, growing softer as the day darkened, darkened, while they waited—for her fear to diminish, disappear, or possibly keep them apart, after all.

"Why should you not be frightened? I can't be sure what I'll do—after three or four hours inside you."

"You might decide to kill me—to have it over, once and for all? Never to have to do that to me again. Would it relieve you? Have we made each other sick in some way? Sometimes—it seems to me that we have. There is—nothing else. Nothing else I want."

"Arabella—" He was silent a long moment, for Arabella would not look at him. "Arabella—"

She still refused to look at him, and abruptly, to her surprise, he lay back upon the bed, knees slightly parted and flexed, arms behind his head, and was asleep immediately. He was not pretending to sleep, he was sleeping, for she knew how his chest rose and fell, how his lids moved or were still, how his mouth parted slightly.

She stood and looked at him, finding that now he was no longer aware of her, thinking of her, desiring her, she was almost unbearably moved by his beauty, the blond hair curling over his head, curling lightly upon his chest and arms, clustered thickly in his groin. She gazed at him for a long while.

Then, taking care not to wake him, feeling that his sleep was something precious which she must guard, for he was on watch so many hours of the day and night—not entirely willing to trust their safety even to Caliph—she lay beside him, not touching him, and closed her eyes and slept.

When she awoke the wagon was dark, although a candle was burning, and he was gone.

"Where are you?" She got up quickly, went to the window and moved the curtain.

He was there, his cloak streaming water. He had been in the rain, bringing water for the horses, for Caliph, for them, and the horses were eating, while Caliph stayed close by him. Now and then the gypsy paused to run his hand across Caliph's sleek handsome head.

Her fear of him was gone. Disappeared while they slept. She wanted him with a desperation never experienced before; not on that first day—how long ago? He had told her four weeks and a half, although it seemed an uncountable eternity of days and nights.

Although she scoffed at him for fearing her father's and Guise's men, she knew that they must be following her.

Her father would never give her up, however long the search. And after what had happened to Guise, the blow on his head in the midst of his caper with the farm girl, the stranger entering the tournament on his horse wearing his armor, toppling his opponent—neither would Guise.

She knew that Maria would lie for her, but her other maids would have the opportunity to give vent to their years of covert hostility, of wishing to be the Princess Arabella themselves.

She went to lie down, and did not move when he opened the door. She heard his clothes flung upon the floor, the splashing of water, and closed her eyes, waiting.

She heard him cross the floor and felt him sit beside her. Looking up, she raised her arms to fold them about his shoulders. He lowered himself gently upon her and was motionless for several minutes, touching her body with the full length of his own, supporting himself with his arms, looking into her eyes as they questioned each other. Her legs parted and she drew him downward upon her.

"Please—it is what I want. Everything you want—"

He entered her slowly, so slowly that her head bent backward, straining with the anxiety of waiting for him to fill her, for the movements to begin, those movements which brought her steadily increasing pleasure until, finally, the pleasure became unendurable and resolved like a giant flower spreading open in her belly, stretching apart nerves and muscles; a pleasure never quite remembered, surprising her each time.

All at once the fear returned. "I will die of this one day, for one reason or another—"

He moved suddenly, several swift strokes, perhaps to silence her. His head lay beside hers, the curling blond hair against her face, as they moved in some perfectly established rhythm, some magical truce established, whereby they discovered a new harmony of motion and joy, not striving, as they usually did, for the greatest intensity of sensation at every moment, but content to let the moments build one upon the other, the pleasures building slowly as their rhythm slowly increased, slowly diminished, as if he silently ordered her to follow him, not force too much from him too quickly, but take whatever came with keen appreciation for each nuance of sensation. Her legs locked high upon his back and the slow steady rhythmic rocking continued for an uncountable time.

All at once he moved swiftly, more swiftly. Her legs unlocked, her arms flung apart, her neck arched backward, and she gave a cry of joyous alarm and freedom. She began pounding his back with her fists as he moved faster. "Now, oh, please, now—do it now—no longer—" She felt some desperate need to have that eternity of lovemaking concluded all at once, while she was still aware of who she was, what they were doing to each other.

He was silent, and even as she pleaded with him, as if understanding what prompted that pleading for quick release, his movements grew slower, her arms fell at her sides, her legs spread wider, and he had lulled her into acceptance of the slower rhythm, the slow steady pulsing beat which threaded through their arteries, seeming to join them irreparably. She was aware of some low soft sound of distressful moaning, coming from a distance, although it sang in her own voice, and at the same time became aware that he was swearing under his breath, in Romany.

All at once he raised himself above her, withdrawing until he had almost left her, placed his hands upon her shoulders, and bore down forcefully. Then, with a sudden swift motion, he was deep inside, jolting her body, causing her to protest at the sudden pain, which subsided before the cry had ended, resolving in a low sound of gratitude.

Again he withdrew, and again plunged into her, and she

found that she was sobbing joyously, clasping her hands around his back, bringing her palms together in the attitude of prayer. He continued the slow withdrawals, the deep sudden powerful thrusts, again and again, and all at once stopped, deep within her, and lay still, stroking her hair, gently wiping the tears from her face.

She lay motionless and silent, thinking that perhaps if she were to try to move she would discover that it had happened: They were locked together, they could never be torn apart, not by will, not by strength, not by desperation, not by other human hands at whatever dim future time they might be discovered.

He continued to lie motionless, but still hard inside her, arms around her, his mouth moving with tender and, she thought, remorseful kisses.

Perhaps he knows he has killed me. Perhaps he knows it and feels some sorrow. I warned him it might happen if he did this—if he did to me what I've begged him for.

The throbbing continued throughout her belly, while her muscles rhythmically opened and closed around him. He began to move again, slowly withdrawing almost to the point of leaving her, returning slowly, burrowing deeply. While her back arched and her hands clenched at his shoulders, he moved more and more slowly, that same gentle remorseless pace. She grew increasingly anxious, began to pound his back with her fists, to move restlessly beneath him, still trying to force that yearned-for and dreaded conclusion of this act.

All at once, without leaving her, he flung her astride him so that as she sat facing him he was deeper inside her, his hands holding her breasts, forefingers and thumbs crushing her nipples.

With his hands under her arms he brought her high, then pulled her down upon him with intense force, so that her head snapped backward. He repeated the movement again and again, lifting her high, bringing her down forcefully. Then once again he was motionless, holding her hard, look-

67

ing straight at her for the first time since they had begun this wild journey. His eyes shone, glittering in the unsteady light of the dying candle—more than four hours had gone by, for that was the candle's length of life.

"Arabella—" It was not followed by a question, only her name, spoken as in a prayer, a curse, a benediction, a farewell, a greeting. "Arabella—"

The candle flickered out, and as if that had been a signal she was all at once flung beneath him without any separation having occurred, he pounding into her, and then he was quiet, his body motionless, while his hands moved over her breasts, and there was again the despairing low sound of her name, "Arabella—"

They lay quiet, and for the first time, she felt no need to move or to feel his movements. He drew her legs together so that he lay higher upon her. He was hard, filling her more completely it seemed than ever before. Had this prolonged pleasure caused him to grow inside her, become a part of her body? She felt that he could never leave her. She had him with her forever—fulfillment of the wish which had run beneath all her spasmodic fears of dying in his arms. She was imprisoned by her own need. Nothing could ever put them apart.

The dark was absolute, and the darkness had sealed them faster. She felt him throb, but the throbbing was not accompanied by motion and brought no diminution of hardness. His hands moved slowly, tenderly, down her body. He raised himself slightly above her, moved back and forth slowly, thrusting deep each time, and when she began to spread her legs, hoping to engulf him further, he pressed them together, his hands closing around her breasts, holding them gently, gradually pressing the nipples more firmly, until the pain brought a soft sound of protest. The pressure continued, and at last she sighed, the pain passing into profound gratification.

Very slowly, so slowly she was not for some time aware of it, he increased the distance of his withdrawal, increased the speed of his return, and when at last he swung her legs high, raised himself upon his knees and brought her legs to his shoulders, he was pounding into her with a ferocity and speed which made her cry aloud, holding out both hands to ward him off.

The movements continued, more and more swiftly, and when she felt him at the moment of leaving her, once again her legs were fast around him and they lay quiet, soothed, mollified.

Yet, she discovered, it had not happened. He was hard, hard and slowly moving.

And the sensations were no less keen, no less acute, no less gratifying. What he had accomplished during those hours seemed some kind of unholy miracle, for she could no longer imagine an Arabella unoccupied by him, empty, unfilled by that hard part of him which, now, almost before she realized it was happening, slipped slowly backward, and left her alone, although very quickly, as if the unexpected deprivation might prove too sudden to be tolerable, his hand covered her and two fingers slipped inside, soothing her with gentle movements, and as his knuckles twisted deftly she gave a quick cry of pleasure and dismay. His mouth covered hers, and one hand moved across her breasts, while the other continued to stroke and soothe her.

Her arms held him close. "Come back. You're as hard as before. Robert. Please don't leave me—"

⊙ CHAPTER EIGHT ⊙

But he did. With one more kiss he had left the bed and was looking through the window. There was a streak of daylight.

"Is that how it ends? Is that how you leave me?"

He pulled the curtain to and lit a candle. He was smiling, but looked tired, and Arabella discovered that she was exhausted. She watched him getting into his clothes, as the stalk of hard flesh slowly subsided, unfulfilled.

"That's how I leave you," he agreed. "The rain will stop by midday. I've got to see to the animals—reconnoiter the roads." He came and looked down at her, touching the side of her face. "Sleep. I'll be back."

And as she drew the sheet to her shoulders she fell asleep, awaking with the terrifying conviction that she was alone, not only alone in the wagon, in that great barn—but in all the world.

She was sure she would not be able to move, but all at once she sat up and began to stretch. She stretched her arms and legs, pointed her toes, spread her fingers.

There was fresh food on the table, a roast capon, farm cheese and rough dark bread. She wrapped the shawl about herself, feeling chilled, and began to eat.

Pythias was not in his stall, though Damon stood in his, restlessly stamping, and there was Caliph, treading his ceaseless round.

She went to the mirror, apprehensive that some diminished, prematurely aged Arabella would look back at her. She saw Arabella as she had seen her last, and yet quite another Arabella altogether, never likely to be reconstructed into her former self.

She bathed slowly, dried herself slowly and dressed slowly, tying a green silk scarf about her hips, slipping on a red silk Moroccan vest, and saw, as she admired the emerald pendant between her breasts, the purple shadows left by his hands.

The door opened and she turned quickly, feeling herself trembling, as if she were about to encounter a stranger, his needs and intentions unknown to her—someone possibly dangerous—and wondered if she could endure another contact with him, another entrance of that hard and beautiful throbbing organ, withholding its gratification throughout its inquisitive ruthless questioning of her flesh.

He smiled, as frankly as if they had been for an early-morning ride in the sun, not needing to ask her how she had slept, how she fared, if she was tired.

"The storm is over—only a light rain. Later today, I'll take another try at the roads. They're still impassable."

He took off the rain-soaked cloak, removed the muddy boots and tossed them aside, peeled off the shirt, the clinging wet trousers, and she saw with relief that he was normally relaxed. He stepped into the tub and began to scrub himself, standing, as he usually did.

"We'll set out as soon as possible. We've been here too long."

"How long?" She approached, drawn toward him by an impulse beyond her control. Just a little nearer, not near enough—only to look at him more carefully. "Do you know?"

She was looking seriously into his face, and still he smiled at her, with nothing there to remind her of the hours—how many, how many?—which had passed with them caught together in a vise which would never let them go. Yet he had broken out of it at the moment he wanted to, it seemed, easily, unregretful.

"Thirty hours. The farmer is suspicious. He's turned away two other wagons and several horsemen seeking shelter." He stepped out of the tub and dried himself quickly, picked up a clean, faded striped shirt and slipped it on, glancing at her in slight surprise as she took one more step and her hand closed around him. It surprised her, too, being so far from what she had been thinking.

"We may be traveling tomorrow?" she asked.

They looked at each other questioningly, and Arabella felt a rising warmth, when only a few minutes before she had been wondering if she could endure another invasion; as she stroked him he was hard and swollen, the dark red tip glistening with tightness.

He sat on the stool beside the table and she settled upon him slowly, astonished anew by the sweetness and fulfillment spreading throughout her body. "When will you finish this?" she asked, as the movement increased in swiftness and her anxiety grew for that accustomed burst of fulfillment and temporary finality.

His hands took hold of her waist, bringing her up and then down with a forcible thrust. "Now, if that's what you want. Or do you want this—whenever you want it?"

"You can do that?"

"I can now. Perhaps for some time."

She shook her head, eyes closed. "I thought I could never want you again. And now—I can't remember what happened between us before last night."

"Take what you want now. When you've had enough—we will have each other again—whenever you want—"

"Whenever you want?"

He laughed. "Don't we want the same thing, at the same time—"

"Then why must we travel? One more night here—"

"To try to live a little longer. To get out of your father's domain. And Guise's."

He pulled her shoulders downward and brought himself into her so deeply that she caught her breath, then gave a soft moan as her head fell forward so that her face was against his. Still he held her, forcing her shoulders steadily downward, slowly penetrating more deeply.

After some time he spoke softly. "Do you want me to let you go? Is it too painful—to be pleasurable?"

"No—no—I change as you hold me. Don't pay attention to what I say or do. Do everything you want—whatever you want—"

The penetration had reached its greatest depth, the most acute pain and most profound pleasure, and they remained motionless—Arabella's eyes closed hard, the gypsy with his mouth against her face, holding her there, silent. He held her astride his legs for what might have been minutes or hours—all at once she began to pound at his chest and shoulders.

"Let me go—let me go—" She was caught by a sudden terror.

The pressure eased, the pain lessened, and so did the accompanying weird wild pleasure. He released her, but when she was free she did not leave him but began instead to push with all her strength downward upon him.

The pressure began again, and he shifted his weight slightly, so that when he pressed upon her shoulders he was deeper than before, still motionless, while she clenched her teeth to endure the flashing pleasures and sharp pains which ran throughout her belly. With the tightening and relaxing of his buttocks, he moved so slightly that the pain and plea-sure, simultaneous, intensified and slightly decreased, inten-sified again and slightly decreased.

Her hands pushed against his chest, her face contorted, and as he released her she opened her eyes to find him staring at her, but not directly into her face; it was the

73

devout concentration of a blind man, his face muscles taut with the intent awareness upon everything he was feeling.

What can it be? she wondered, marveling at this man whose expression showed him transported far from her, while still he held her upon him.

He looked at her quickly, alert once again—and his hands settled on her breasts. Slowly, without any intentional volition by either of them, the depth of his penetration lessened, and after a very long time, they faced each other as they had at the beginning.

He drew a deep shuddering breath, and her arms folded about his neck, drawing his head against her breasts. She began to move, lowering herself with hard sudden thrusts, as if she could bring him to the same depth, once again experience that tormenting pleasure.

He seized her waist, speaking quietly, holding her motionless. "Be still. Don't move. Unless you want it to end now."

"It must end sometime—"

"Not now. Not yet. Believe me—" He moved her slowly upward until he was free of her. "Not now—" Her hands closed over him longingly, but he moved away. "You'll want something more—sooner than you think. He smiled. "So will I."

She said sadly, as if at some betrayal, "You're getting dressed."

He laughed. "Yes. I must tend the animals—and have another try at the roads. If they're passable, we'll start during the night. I'm wondering how much more to give this farmer—and if it will buy his silence, whatever it is."

"It won't."

She might have fallen asleep where she sat, but he picked her up, holding her as tenderly as if the almost motionless violence of the past hour or two had never occurred, carried her to the bed, and laid her gently down.

When she awoke it was dark, and she was aware of a shaking all around her. The wagon was moving, perhaps had been moving for some time. They had left the farmer's barn, and there was no sound of rain. He had decided it was dangerous for them to remain any longer. They must find some new place to hide, until the roads were dry.

When next she emerged from that sleep of exhaustion, the wagon was still and she became aware that although the curtains were shut, it was daylight. He lay sleeping beside her.

The gypsy had his own sleeping habits. A few hours of sleep. A few hours of activity. This might or might not have been usual for him, for since she had been with him he had been continuously preoccupied with getting farther from the possible range of her father's or Guise's spies or searchers.

Perhaps, she had told herself, one day, when they were safe—

But she was not able to go much beyond perhaps—for she was no longer more sure than he that there was any possibility of safety in the future for them.

Impulsively she reached out, meaning to stroke him, to reassure him of her nearness, but withdrew her hand. They had traveled ten or twelve hours after she had slept, and as she felt him move slightly, then settle into deep quietude again, she was once more asleep.

It seemed they awoke at the same moment, and looked at each other with inquiring surprise. Then quickly he stepped across her and stood looking down at her.

"Where are we now?"

"We've had to travel back, unfortunately. I didn't trust the farmer not to follow us, and I was right. But a word or two from Caliph sent him on his way. We'll stay here a few hours, at least." His face became serious. "I didn't hurt you?"

"No." She lay on her belly to watch him dress. "Where are you going?"

"I'm going to see how secure we are from anyone who might be on the roads this morning. And I'm going to look for food. We haven't eaten for at least twenty hours—didn't you know that?"

"I didn't know anything, after you moved me away from you."

He ran his hand over her hair and as she sat up he drew her to the edge of the bed, knelt, slipped quickly inside her, moving quickly, but after several strokes, swift, intense, gratifying as any prolonged journey they had made, left her, but remained beside her, studying her face. "I told you that if I could do it, you'd never think of anything else. And apparently, neither will I." He was silent a moment, smiling reflectively. "The gypsies think that if it's possible to find the riddle of the universe, it can only be found by a man and woman, joined in such a contract. It can only be found in quiet, in peace, in oblivion of the self." She was watching him in silence, awed by this talk of universal riddles, and as if to reassure her, his hand passed across her head and along the side of her face. "One of my stepfather's friends swore he had understood it, for less than a moment."

Arabella hesitated, not sure she wanted to know the answer to the riddle of the universe. Then: "What was it?"

Robert laughed. "He had forgotten."

"Good. No one should learn it, ever."

He went to the door. "Don't move the curtains. If Caliph barks, don't look out. I'll be back when I can."

◉ CHAPTER NINE ◉

For a few moments she lay still, then got up to bathe, wash her hair, smooth the bed, and decorate Arabella.

But looking into the mirror she found her expression bewildered and troubled. This unholy alliance which had formed between them these past weeks, reaching what must be its greatest possible intensity in the nearly immobile ravishment of last night, had acquired such power it seemed they would inevitably become the same entity, no longer two distinct personalities.

When the pleasures suffered, seized, enjoyed, craved, when the waiting for him seemed unbearable, or feeling him inside her reached sensations she thought she could endure no longer, she began to tell herself: After all, sooner or later we die. And even that prospect brought only resignation, near to fatal indifference.

She bathed and began to wash her hair, all at once singing a song she had learned from one of the troubadours not long before she had gone away, and with the song a tranquil joy replaced near-despair.

When at last her hair was dried and the tangles undone, the henna and kohl applied, she found a gold-embroidered scarf which she draped across one shoulder, swathed around her hips, and knotted to one side.

The door opened and she turned, quickly alert.

"We're safe enough for a few hours. The roads are drying,

and we can start south." He threw a parcel upon the table. "Food. Are you starving?"

As he stood in the tub, soaping himself, she brought him a slice of capon breast.

No foreboding thoughts of separate or simultaneous oblivion, no qualms of unholy alliance, no fears of loss of identity could change the response when she looked at him. She brought him a goblet half filled with wine and water, for he drank little, not as her father did or other men she had known; one more advantage he had over European men.

He stepped out of the tub, dried himself quickly, and with one surprising maneuver was bending over her and, as she knelt slowly to the floor, moved into her deeply, carefully, for in this position he penetrated too deep for her to endure it longer than a few moments. But now, ignoring this, he spread her legs, penetrating farther, bending her forward until her head was between her elbows, and continued slowly spreading her knees apart, opening her body wider.

His hands closed over her breasts as he began to move. He drew back, until the red bulb touched her body's opening. His hands moved to her belly, spreading across it, his fingers pressing inward, as if he sought to feel himself entering her, to learn what he was doing to her.

In this position, where they could not watch each other's faces for clues, there came new need for every possible pain and pleasure. He entered and drew back, pausing, then entering slowly, suddenly plunging so that she caught her breath, but made no sound of protest, while still his fingers probed her belly more deeply.

He moved swiftly, plunging and waiting, as if to take all pleasures from this full possession, withdrawing and returning more swiftly each time. At last he left her slowly, raised her gently to her feet, held her against him, but refused to let her touch him, even when they went to lie upon the bed.

When she awoke he had left on another reconnoitering

trip, for as she had seen they were in a ravine, and the green trees rose so thickly, arching above the wagon, that the branches almost obscured the sky. The sun was lower, and she guessed it was near four in the afternoon.

She stood, running her hands over her body, dropped to the floor, made a cradle of her arms for her head, and began to cry.

The tears were slow, and the sounds quiet at first. But soon she was sobbing with a conviction that this time he had abandoned her forever, gone to find his safety alone, since he would never find it while she was with him.

Her hands went to her breasts, and once again she felt what she had become aware of during the past few days. Her breasts were tender, painful when she pressed them. Although she had assured herself that it was his roughness, there was that other emerging fear, suspicion, disbelief.

She should have begun to bleed more than two weeks ago. For it had been five weeks since that first morning visit to the gypsy's wagon, when he had shown her the precautionary paraphernalia. But then in the sudden discovery of pleasures new to her, new in some different way to him, they had forgotten.

He had said nothing. He had not noticed? Unlikely. He noticed everything, remembered everything. More likely, he thought that she was young, not yet regularly established, and was hoping that presently the bleeding would begin.

If it did not?

She shook her head in vigorous denial, although she could not stop crying.

She was crying bitterly, disappointed as only the Princess Arabella could be disappointed, when some favor promised was not fulfilled. Yet she did not honestly believe she could be pregnant. Something would happen, any day, any moment. For pregnancy, in their circumstances, was an unimaginable disaster.

She looked up as the key turned, beginning to dry her eyes with the sheet, a guilty childish gesture which made him pause in the doorway, then smile inquiringly.

She gave him a strange little smile, quite unlike herself, thinking that if it were true, he would hate her. After all the other dangers she had brought him—their flight toward some unknown port of safety, when quite possibly there was no such port—she was terrified of offering him yet one more hazard.

For they had talked of possible routes of escape, and rejected them: not North Africa or the Holy Land. That would require that he sell not only his possessions, but also the wagon and horses, for there wasn't a ship which could accommodate them. Anyway, to sell his possessions discreetly would require a year or longer, while to sell them to one buyer would make him a certain target. He would be killed.

"And," he had said, "a woman like you does not travel far with only one man and no place of concealment. Crossing the borders into Catalonia or Lombardy, if it could be done, would put us at the mercy of countrysides swarming with brigands. I can think of no other land where we have even a minimal chance—"

"No. There isn't one." They had not discussed it again.

Now, seeing her strange smile, he knelt beside her, touching her chin, gently urging her to look at him. "Arabella— you've never cried like this. You wish you hadn't left them, don't you?" His hands held her face, his eyes brooding over her. She looked at him, asking herself how this could be the man who not long before had seemed determined to split her body apart, tear everything inside her loose with his violence. "I shouldn't have let you come," he said softly.

Her face turned wise and skeptical. "And how would you have prevented it?"

"By taking you back."

She pushed aside his hands and stood up, looking down as he sat on the floor, arms clasped around his knees. "I do what I want to, Robert. And I wanted to come with you. If I was crying—well, women cry from time to time—" Then she laughed with real gaiety, once more convinced that the elasped two weeks and a half meant nothing. The pain in her breasts was to be welcomed, for it provoked a continuous awareness of him and had surely been caused by him and not by changes taking place in her body.

She looked at him seriously. "When can I leave this wagon—just for a few minutes? I've lived almost as much of my life outdoors as you have. Can't we go out—for only a little while?"

All at once, sensing that this need had become a matter of desperation, he was on his feet, took a burnoose from a hook and wrapped it about her, bringing its hood over her hair, and they ran down the steps.

Arabella drew in a deep breath of air, heavily scented by summer flowers, for they were now much farther south, and she bent to caress the deep moist grass, stroking Caliph's head as they passed him, giving Damon and Pythias each a smart clap on their rumps by way of delighted greeting and gratitude for this sudden freedom she had only partly expected.

As they walked they talked earnestly of the wet grass, the flowers, the air, the sky, the difference between this countryside and the one through which they had passed. They were at last coming near to the land he had known most of his life.

She turned to him suddenly, surprising herself, and her eyes were bright and pleading. "Now. Right now. Will you?"

He began to answer, but since her expression had the same desperate earnestness, he lowered her to the grass. She sighed deeply as he entered her. All at once they were moving at a swiftly increasing pace. This time she was determined to force from him that final culmination, after days of denial, too many by now, for both of them—or so she thought.

But he held her buttocks, stopping her from moving. "I don't want this to end here—and it could happen easily. We'll go back—"

He drew away from her, passing his hands across her breasts, looking at them as he did so, touching them carefully, as if the touch were an examination. He could see the slight changes—or could he? He saw something else. Why would he not have seen that the blue veins were a deeper color, the full breasts slightly fuller, the nipples redder, even without the henna?

Walking back they again talked seriously and urgently of the beautiful countryside they had reached. Whatever he had noticed, if he had, he plainly preferred not to discuss it yet. If they began to speculate about every possible misfortune— and they could think of many—then they had indeed made a fatal decision: Not only their lives would be at hazard, but confidence in their individual and mutual resolve was forfeit as well.

Inside the wagon she threw the cloak aside and turned to him. Their mouths came together, for often during these past days they had forgotten to kiss, an intrusion upon keener sensations. He knelt beside her as she lay on the bed, and bent her legs almost to her shoulders, slowly moving inward.

"Let me hurt you a little, Arabella. I must—it distracts me—"

As their need and pleasures had increased during the past days, they had both grown more violent. Now he was watching her changing expression as he eased her steadily backward, slowly moving deeper. Pain and bewilderment showed in her eyes, though she made no protest and he held her fast, remaining motionless a long while, until her body had accepted him, the pain disappeared. There was only the sense of having become once again whole and complete.

"It's been so long—" she whispered, as he pressed deeper,

slowly, steadily. "Do it—if you want to. It must be hard for you. Oh, Jesus—"

"I don't want to. I don't want to until I can't stop it from happening. And I can still stop it."

With that, he moved away so slowly she caught hold of his shoulders. "Soon—soon—"

He had left her but still knelt beside her, silent, watching her carefully, at last smiling a little. Then, surprising her, he said: "You were the favorite child—not only for what your father thought you could bring him, but because you have much of him in you. The fierceness I feel when your muscles take hold of me—the teeth marks you leave on my shoulders—the welts from your nails on my back." He was not condemning, he was still smiling, reflectively.

Nevertheless she looked away guiltily. "I don't know I'm doing it—"

Each time she saw the marks she had left on his shoulders, the streaks where her nails had raked his back, she took a solemn oath it would never happen again. And each time he had driven her to that delirium where she felt forced beyond boundaries of mind and body—it would happen again.

Now she looked so forlornly penitent that he laughed softly. "I don't know it's happening," he told her, "until much later."

"I would never mark this beautiful skin—" Her palms passed slowly across his shoulders. "I would never cause you the littlest pain."

He laughed again. "Oh, yes you would. And so would I—from time to time—cause you pain. Sometimes, I think, more than a little. Your eyes beg me." His face grew serious, and he put himself against her, as her legs closed slowly around his back. "If we were rational every moment—" He pressed slowly deeper and deeper.

"I don't think when you're inside me—there—oh, God—think—now?"

She fell silent as he made a sudden thrust, but did not relinquish her hold as once again he tilted her body backward, forced himself deeper, farther, while her nails dug into his flesh. But when she felt him begin to move away she seized his shoulders, trying to keep him with her. He withdrew slowly, and presently she had lost him.

◙ CHAPTER TEN ◙

There's a gypsy encampment not many hours from here. I want to reach it before daybreak."

She sat beside him as he drove, wide awake after sleeping four or five hours.

As well as predicting the weather, could he also predict gypsy encampments which were not permanent settlements to be remembered from earlier travels through the area?

"Who told you about it?"

"The farmer, though he didn't know what he was telling me, a farm woman I bought food from yesterday, and a boy I passed crossing the fields." She heard a slight smile in his voice. "Never ask a direct question. The wrong people may hear of it later. Ask several people unrelated questions and piece them together."

"Will we stay long?"

"Not more than a day. I must sell Damon and Pythias—they've been seen too near the King's domain, and I prefer to trade with my own people—their horses are good, but not too good. Damon and Pythias are somewhat too handsome. People admire them."

"And my horse? We'll get him, too?" She had waited so long, now she was almost afraid to ask.

"What would a man traveling alone want with a third horse? I trust my people, as I've said, as much as I trust anyone. But that would leave something to wonder about when we're gone—if someone happens by with questions and money. We'll find your horse a little farther on. Soon. I promise."

Although she had been sent inside some time before, they arrived at the camp as the sky was beginning to lighten. She heard the sounds remembered from their last encampment—outbursts of song, the barking of dogs as the wagon drove along the outskirts, Robert's greeting in Romany to men and women, and their gay responses.

Presently he brought in a pot of hot stew.

She sat across the table and they looked at each other for a long moment in silence. Both seemed ready to speak, to begin talking about the one subject they had avoided—and then decided to avoid it a little longer.

They dipped into the pot with their fingers, eating slowly, juicy pieces of beef, succulent and gratifying after the cold capons which had been their fare. As they ate they watched each other carefully, almost warily.

Unexpectedly he reached out, parted the unfastened vest, and his hand enclosed one breast.

She felt her heart begin to beat apprehensively. The silence continued, and she decided he had noticed no change, that it was a caress, a prelude to making love before he went to conduct the transactions for Damon and Pythias.

"We've been together," he said slowly, "for five weeks."

She took in a quick shallow breath, dipped into the pot for another piece of meat, then set it on the plate. "Yes." Now he was going to question her. Why not before?

"And there's been no bleeding."

She looked down, as if ashamed at some fault she had committed. "No."

"When was the last time, Arabella?"

Arabella kept a careful accounting of her cycle, a practice her mother had assured her she must perform and never lose track of until sometime, sometime, in the unimaginable future, when she would not need to continue.

Suddenly his hand closed forcefully and she gave a surprised cry of pain.

"I've hurt you."

"Only a little." She fell silent again, but then spoke quickly. "The last time was April twenty-fifth to the twenty-ninth."

"We met on the ninth of May. You came to me the next morning. I've caused you pain again—it must have happened that first day."

"I think so." She looked away, still feeling that the fault, as it seemed to be, was hers. A pregnant woman was a greater hazard than their circumstances could tolerate.

He smiled a little, but the smile was serious, and his hand grew tender as he caressed one breast and then the other. "It may have happened the next night in the forest—no later. Whenever it happened, it seems to have happened. But you're young. Perhaps it will—"

She stared at him defiantly. "Ever since I was twelve years and two months old, it's been exact—"

"I thought about it—but I thought—"

"You thought the same thing I did."

He got up, looking down at her seriously. "Don't move the curtains. No one must know I'm not alone. This will take a few hours."

"If it's true—will you be angry? You said that you have a potion—"

He made a grimace. "I do. But I don't want to give it to you. Oh, Arabella—I should have left you each time." He stroked the side of her face.

"But that's when I need you most," she protested. "How could you think of doing such a thing to either of us? Give me the potion—I'm not a coward." All at once she looked at him with that same tragic expression which had struck him when he rode past the pavilion. "Might I die?"

"My God, my God." His arms went about her, holding her as if she were a child. "Is this what you've been thinking? No, Arabella. You will not die. It is painful—it is ugly—and it's too early. Something may happen. Say your rosary. Pray a little." He smiled tenderly. "That's the best advice I can give."

"Pray a little," she repeated bitterly. "Perhaps when I begin to ride again—"

"Perhaps."

Left alone, Arabella stood gazing at the silk Persian carpet, and at her bare feet, the toes colored with henna. She went to the mirror, studying her breasts for whatever evidence there might be of something growing inside her. She placed both hands upon her belly, flat and hard, and told herself the bleeding would begin—soon. Later today. Tomorrow.

That had happened once to Maria, at the exact time when she was in deep despair of having to call in a midwife. All at once, as if by magic—

That's the way it will be with me. I know it.

But to her surprise, she did not believe this. She noticed that her face had turned moody and realized that she was deeply resentful of him. He should not have let me come with him.

She looked at herself sullenly and felt something she guessed might be hatred of this man. She had heard of women who had died of the potion.

But neither had she believed his warning, when he had urged her to return to her father saying, "You don't know what you're choosing."

All she had thought of choosing was the gypsy, and what he would do to her when she went to his encampment, sending her maids-of-honor to ride the countryside for five hours, more or less.

What could she have been expecting of those five hours? A great deal, he had told her, for a virgin—even one who was a virgin only literally speaking.

I want you. I need you. I must have you.

She had repeated it helplessly. He sat, his back against the tree, talking softly in the darkness so dense they could not see each other. He refused to touch her, or let her touch him.

It's when the sacrifices begin that you start to learn the difference between the uncomplicated pleasures of lust and the obligations of love.

And as a first lesson, he had sold Solomon.

You're accustomed to freedom, he had reminded her. And if she went with him, until they were a great distance from her father's domain and that of Guise, she must remain out of sight during the day.

Will you like that?

No.

But she had not known how little she would like it.

She placed her hands over her breasts, pressing until she felt a twinge of pain, and turned away.

He can send me back with one of the gypsies. My mother will find someone to get rid of this—whatever it is that's inside me. My father will forgive me, I think.

She was not so sure of that, for in the past the King had had nothing to forgive her. He might instead decide to imprison her.

She sat on the bed, chin on her fist, full of righteous fury at this betrayal of her body.

Presently she went to the table and took a slice of cold meat, placed it in her mouth, then removed it. It was no longer appetizing. In fact, it was disgusting. Another bad sign. She glanced about the wagon, and the beauty of its golden cloth, its Oriental carpets and tapestries, its brilliant colors which had so beguiled her, now made her angry.

He must send her back. She smiled a little to think of how shocked he would be when she told him. Or perhaps he would be relieved to have had the decision made for him.

When several hours had passed and he had not returned, while all about the wagon a riot and din continued, she wavered between rage and self-pity, blaming him for having taken her freedom, her very self, the Arabella who had ruled her world, and making her a prisoner of his absurd fears.

Deeply sunk in contemplation, she gave a start of surprise when he entered, glanced at her swiftly, evidently reading her thoughts, and shut the door.

"I have the horses—both piebalds. I can arrange to have three of the men take you back, starting tonight. They won't harm you, because they know I'll be waiting when they come back—and they must come back to get the money. This is your best chance, Arabella. If you stay with me—if you wait to see what is going to happen—don't. Because I can tell you, you will have to take that bitter potion, and it is bitter. I can't help you endure the pain. And I can't promise it won't happen again. Hate me, if hate's any help to you. Now—go behind the curtain. I'm bringing fresh water and supplies. Someone will be with me."

She followed his instructions, astonished that he had spoken first, that he had no recriminations for her lack of love for him at the first clue of serious sacrifice. Stunned with anger and surprise at this unexpected hardness, she heard the door open, his footsteps, then those of another man, their voices in Romany, the setting down of the heavy tubs, and again the door closed.

"Come out." He spoke peremptorily. "There've been inquiries here, three weeks ago. Two men on horseback, looking for a blond gypsy traveling in a red and green and blue wagon." He smiled slightly. "You're surprised? The wagon is being painted again—dark blue, this time. At nightfall you can set out. I'm going to sleep. It's been a long day."

She stood silent, wondering at this man she had thought she knew. He was prepared to part with her and seemed relieved to have the opportunity. They were being sought, and for her to leave now was the only good hope he had of saving his life.

His clothes were off, and she watched him, marveling at

the beauty of his body, his face and the shape of his head. He gave her a quick challenging glance as he lay down, legs apart and slightly bent at the knees, sprawled in luxurious abandon across the bed. Then he fell asleep.

She stood a long while, looking at him, hearing his breathing deepen, and told herself that after tonight she would not see him again. It was not only the best hope for both of them, it was the only hope.

He might have been a statue lying there, arms loosely folded behind his head, his wide chest with its light covering of golden curls, the muscles of his belly and groin, the male organ, large and beautiful, even in this quiescent state, surrounded with blond curls, and Arabella could not imagine what it would be to awaken tomorrow, far from him, unable to go back, knowing that she would never see him again.

She removed her clothes, taking care not to disturb him, and found a place to lie which, so long as she stayed awake, permitted her to be near him without falling off the bed. She awoke with a start, to find herself on the floor. He was leaning over her; then getting swiftly to his feet, he took her hands and drew her up to face him. She looked at him with that familiar adoring wonderment.

"No," he said decisively, rejecting the appeal on her face. "No. That is what you are going to do, Arabella."

"What am I going to do?" She was smiling slightly, no longer intimidated.

"Go back. That's where you belong—not with me. They're looking for us, and they've lost no time. We could meet them any day, or night."

She twisted away. "Not long ago, I hated you. Yes, real hatred. I was going to leave you."

"You are going to leave me."

She turned slowly, placing her back against him. They remained motionless and silent, until at last his hands lightly touched her breasts. All at once he carried her to the bed, lay full upon her, and as her legs clasped around his waist he moved more and more quickly, covering her mouth with one hand as she began a soft unconscious sound of pleasure. All at once he was still.

He's not going to send me away. And I'm not going to leave him. Not now, not ever.

He began to move inside her again, slowly, carefully. Then he left her without a word, got dressed and went out.

Arabella continued to lie with eyes closed, but thought no more of hatred or resentment, of returning to her other life.

What had come of all this lovemaking, if she was pregnant, did not concern her. Whether or not they were being followed, what might happen one day in the near or far future, was of no importance. The warmth, the closeness, there was the one reality.

He returned soon and as she gazed up at him from her dreamlike reverie he leaned over her, looking seriously into her eyes. She lifted her arms to him and he settled into her, sliding in and out slowly. Yet despite the slowness, the tension increased and she began moving beneath him restlessly, pleading for that final release of energy. Very slowly, he grew quiet. "Not yet. Once more. Come—let's have something to eat."

❧ CHAPTER ELEVEN ❧

He seemed eager to leave the gypsy encampment. Perhaps he was not convinced that his people were more reliable than any other. Suppose it had not been three weeks since the inquiries, but three days? Or suppose the searchers were in the neighborhood, and might be notified?

They traveled from dark until the first light, and most of that time Arabella sat beside him. Her earlier hostility had given her a need to be near him, as if the anger had worked its sinister magic, even after she had renounced her vow to leave him.

"Don't talk about it," she had told him. "I won't leave you." She glanced at him swiftly. "Do you want me to?"

He was concentrated upon the driving and said nothing. When she gave a light admonitory slap on his arm, he shook his head curtly. "No, I don't want to lose you. But I don't think our chances are good. You must believe that, Arabella, or we can have no understanding. You would be safer with almost anyone than you are with me. Even if their intention is only to take you away—accidents can happen when men fight."

"I know," she said, as if having considered this possibility for the first time. She had always ridiculed the notion that they could not outmaneuver her father and Guise and all the searchers they might send. Or weary them of their search.

Her father was no more likely to weary of the search than

he was likely to weary of power or life itself. He and her mother had held high hopes for what she would add to their holdings, and had discussed this in her presence during the past three years.

"She will be worth more to us than all her brothers," her father had observed, and Arabella had smiled wisely in agreement, for although she did not crave the responsibilities of power, she had taken for granted its exercise, and by the age of twelve was as addicted to authority as her parents.

"It's true," she told the gypsy. "They won't stop searching. But you mustn't imagine that if my father should find me—he will be kind to me."

She was silent, remembering her father's rages—which came infrequently, but were terrifying in their intensity and abandon. He had never turned against her or her mother or sisters—now she was no longer safe from being victimized by his fury.

"He might kill me, if he found me now, with your child inside me. If there is a child. Is there?" Experimentally she put her hand to one breast, then the other, pressing.

Of course there is.

"I think so."

"When will you know?" She laughed. "I ask as if you can answer every question. But I believe you can. You take counsel with the supernatural. I know you do. How else did you become what you are?"

He said nothing and they were silent. It was beginning to grow light. He sent her inside, where she undressed and fell into a deep sleep with some last hope that before he went to sleep he would wake her.

He did not, and when she awoke in midmorning she found him standing beside her, dressed as a squire: hose which fitted his legs and buttocks like his skin, one leg green, one yellow; a short mail-lined doublet, striped green and yellow. The livery of the Countess's husband, for he had shown it to her once, when her curiosity demanded to know what he had looked like when he had been with her.

This was the day he was going to a nearby town where he had news of a fair, to buy the promised replacement for Solomon. They were far enough south, far enough from her father's domain and that of Guise, that they might risk her riding beside the wagon at night. Risk or not, she could no longer remain immobilized.

"I'll be gone for some time. There is food."

She sat up quickly, with a sudden suspicion. "You're coming back? You're not leaving me?"

"I'm coming back. You aren't very trusting, are you?" He smiled. "Neither am I. You might decide to take Ptolemy and leave me."

And once he was gone, once she could no longer see him and Odysseus through the window at the back, she began to consider that possibility, which had not occurred to her before.

She sat on the bed, holding one breast in each hand, trying yet again to determine if the tenderness was real or imaginary, or only the result of his occasional roughness.

Consulting her oracle the mirror, she was convinced she had become more beautiful these past weeks.

She turned away and stepped into the tubful of fresh water.

Let her beware of love. So the old gypsy woman had warned, and so she had meant to do. So her parents had meant her to do: Love was a hindrance to their plans, a doorway opening upon disaster.

But the Arabella she had not suspected might exist, gave herself over to him, and lost whoever she had been in the process. Arabella was scarcely able to believe that this remarkable being was, in effect, her property; this creature of warm flesh and passion, who looked at her sometimes with unforgiving belief that she should exist, a continuous prompting to his body's needs, often satiated, waiting impatiently for the time to come around again when he would be inside her. No easier to satisfy than she was.

Her life had been her own, provided she heeded that one

admonition: She must be prepared to give her husband an intact hymen.

"If you are foolish, Arabella," her mother had advised her, not long before her twelfth birthday, "for I know how you amuse yourself with the pages, there is only one remedy. You know what it is."

Maria, who had more experience of life, had told her what was done to princesses no longer virginal, to make them acceptable on their wedding nights: Stitches were taken by a midwife in that delicate flesh, and the description had made Arabella moan softly with prophetic pain.

Yet when she had seen the gypsy squatting beside the campfire, this man who had a kind of nobility which the nobility who surrounded her did not have, and when he had looked at her directly, as if he had been expecting her, she had known that she must have him.

It was late afternoon when she heard the sound of horses' hoofs, although no sound came from Caliph, who invariably greeted his master in dignified silence. She looked out the window to see the gypsy swing down from Odysseus and turn his attention to a sorrel stallion, stroking his neck, slapping his sides affectionately, and all at once Arabella forgot her troubles and ran to the door, knocking hard.

"Let me out—I must see him—"

The door opened, but before she could rush by, he caught her shoulders. "It's still light. Put on a cloak, cover your hair." She snatched the cloak from a hook and they went to inspect him, studying him in silence for several minutes, strolling around him, missing no detail.

"He's not Solomon," the gypsy said at last.

"I wasn't expecting Solomon." She spoke gently, for there was pain in his eyes.

"But another such animal would be as dangerous to us as your Solomon was."

"He's very fine."

She knew horses, no doubt as well as the gypsy did. And perhaps that was all she knew as well as the gypsy did.

The sorrel stallion cocked an observant eye upon her as he stood tramping up and down, seemingly somewhat apprehensive of his new masters and surroundings.

"Is he of good disposition?"

"Very. That's one reason I got him. We haven't time for you to break him."

"Oh, but I could do it," Arabella assured him gaily.

"I'm sure you could. But all you need do is to make him yours."

He had explained to her the gypsy way of making a horse obedient to one master and one master only, and from time to time, glancing out the window, she had seen him carefully, gently, slowly caressing his own animals, while they stood, at once alert and passive, as his hands passed over their bodies, much as if he were caressing a woman, leaving them, it seemed, relieved of whatever anxieties might have provoked them, and filled with a new energetic eagerness.

"Why the European men have not adopted this treatment for their animals is one more of their abominable mysteries," the gypsy had told her.

She was stroking the stallion's neck. "What is his name?"

"Saracen. He's three years old. He's accustomed to the name. I think it's best not to change it."

"Saracen," she whispered. "Saracen. You and I are going for a long ride." She turned. "Now?"

"It's too early."

"We're isolated."

"I passed three men, just beyond the river. Later, when we travel. Go inside now, Arabella." She gave him a resentful glance, but went, and he followed her.

"Who owned him? Someone who was kind to him? Who knew how to ride?"

"He's been well used. I rode him for several kilometers."

He was washing his hands and face, bending over the tub,

and she stood watching him. When he turned, drying himself, she approached him slowly.

They looked at each other, not touching, as if measuring what each meant to the other, how much each was worth the risks taken so far, the risks yet to be taken.

Without having touched her, he went out to tend the animals.

Aware of an empty sickness, as if he had told her she was no longer necessary to him, Arabella looked through the window. Although she stood there for some time, she got no answering glance.

It had been almost a night and a day since he had made love to her, but for those few minutes before they left the encampment.

Now, watching him currying the three horses, she thought: He hates me. And why not? I may kill him. My being with him could cause him to be killled—today, tomorrow—next year—

My life has depended so little upon others.

Was that still true? No. Now he depended, if not upon her love for him, then upon his love for her—which might have become more important than any dangers he could meet.

Yes.

The gypsy, she knew, had forsaken most of his life's philosophy by now, and had no chance of ever getting it back.

At last he approached the wagon, but she did not turn as the door opened and he set the tub of fresh water in place. Whatever was to happen next, must come from him.

She continued studying Saracen, unable to resist finding the deficiencies when compared to the incomparable Solomon. Her father had valued the bloodlines of his animals almost as highly as he valued his family's; and he had taught her much of what she knew.

She heard the sounds of the gypsy undressing, the water moving in the tub, but still she continued to look at Saracen—

waiting for Robert to speak, and the waiting seemed interminable. It had grown dark but she lighted no candle. Then the sounds of cloth moved briskly over his wet body, and then his footsteps.

He stood behind her, not touching her. At last his hand moved across her breasts, beneath the opened vest, drawing her against him, and as he sat on the low leather stool beside the table, he brought her down upon him, very slowly, as she sat facing away from him. Her head bent forward, and she sighed as that stalk of pleasure penetrated deeper and deeper, slowly, while he pressed her belly, raised her slightly and brought her down again, forcibly.

She gave a soft cry, relief, delight, some slight pain, when all at once she felt him spurting inside her for the first time since he had made his vow of abstinence, for their mutual pleasure. There were words, spoken softly in Romany, which sounded as if they came through closed teeth.

Her fears dissipated, the jealousies and vengeful thoughts vanquished.

"Oh, thank God—it was beginning to hurt me as much as it must have hurt you," she whispered.

The pulsing throbs ran through her body as he continued to hold her closer against him, her breasts and belly crushed by his hands, as if he would absorb her, break through that barrier of flesh and bone which kept them from becoming one flowing stream of life.

For some time he made no further movement, and very slowly the pulsing subsided.

And this was the way the world ended, she thought—that world of six days and nights, which must at last have become for him an unendurable torment. Yet, through it, they had achieved a more profound closeness than they had come near before.

For several minutes they remained motionless. After those first few words in Romany, he was silent, pressing her body against him, one hand holding her breasts, the other probing deep in her belly. There seemed now nothing to fear from the world, or from her body's probable treachery. Only this deep motionless penetration, which grew steadily deeper as he pressed her downward and backward against him.

He could not so easily, so quickly, let go of the accumulated tension and anxiety and desire, and Arabella waited, her body accommodating itself to the depth he had reached.

With his hands about her waist, he lifted her and turned her to face him in the dark. They could not see each other, but had reached a level of primitive communication where light would have been a form of separation.

The movements began, slowly, and then came the throbbing, accompanied this time by no words, an almost breathless silence on both their parts. The throbbing continued long, diminished, and at last stopped.

He disengaged them, moved her the few steps between the low stool and the bed, and with a sweeping stroke of his hand across her back, signaled her to kneel face downward on the bed, and the penetration began, as slowly as if he were reluctant to complete any movement, prolonging each sensation until it had become an unendurable apprehension for them both.

All at once he moved swiftly, with a fury which startled her, although she accepted it passively, expecting that soon she would lose consciousness. Once more she felt him throbbing, still moving, deeply inward, outward to stroke her, then again swiftly, deeply inside.

She heard her voice sobbing, rising up the scale and sliding downward, as her fists beat upon the bed, while he moved into her and then suddenly out, hesitating there each time.

"Don't leave me. For Jesus Christ's sake—don't leave me—"

Still he hesitated, as if waiting for some uncontrollable moment, then all at once plunged into her with such force that she was thrown forward. He caught her arms, holding her in position for him, driving into her again and again, and once more she felt the throbbing, less intense though still prolonged, while she was vaguely aware that her voice had diminished to a quiet mournful crying which continued forlornly as he pulsed inside her.

She was lying on her belly with his weight upon her, unsupported by his arms, a welcome weight she felt she would gladly have borne forever. But he was leaving her, not of his own volition, and as he moved away she turned over, circling his back with her arms and kissed him.

"Come back to me—"

He made a soft cautioning sound. "I will, I will. It isn't over yet. Lie still—"

His mouth moved slowly over her body, and when she would have touched him, he held her hands, still controlling this encounter. Swiftly, unexpectedly, he spread her legs wide, rose upon his knees, and drove so deep at one swift plunge that she put forth both hands to ward him off.

Once again her body resolved itself to welcome him, and she caught hold of his shoulders while the thrusts pounded deep and swift. As suddenly as it had begun all movement came to an end in a series of pulsations, and he lay motionless.

Presently he moved away, giving her a final caress with his hand, saying softly, "Arabella—Arabella—" He kissed her mouth lightly. "I can give you nothing more now." In another moment he was asleep.

She was to go out now and acquaint herself with Saracen.

The night was dark with a thin moon, but the animal would remember her voice. The gypsy had told her to stroke him gently, talking to him continuously, soothingly, and to stroke him with both hands, neglecting no smallest part of him.

Arabella threw on a black cloak, and although her legs throbbed and it seemed her body was pulsing with fatigue, she was sure that in a few minutes she would recover her energy and enthusiasm.

She had two hours, more or less, to make friends with her new mount before it was time for them to begin traveling. She approached Saracen where he stood tethered at a distance from Odysseus and Ptolemy. She talked to him reassuringly, as she had been accustomed to talk to Solomon. Slowly she began stroking him, her hands passing across his muzzle and head. He made a slight uneasy movement, but as she continued talking, continued stroking his head and neck, he grew quiet.

Yet as she stroked him she was longing to lie beside Robert, sleeping. And it occurred to her as she went on talking, stroking, that for the past several days she had fallen asleep more often and for longer periods than usual. She reminded herself that was another token. One more sign had appeared.

◙ CHAPTER TWELVE ◙

Saracen was not saddled, for Arabella wanted to ride bareback, and she placed one foot in the stirrup and was astride him as easily as if she had dismounted from Solomon only a moment before.

"Don't get far ahead of me. If you must ride fast, ride only a few lengths ahead of the wagon, no farther."

They set out. The feeling of this animal beneath her, surprisingly obedient for the first time she had ridden him, moving at the pressure of her knees, the gentle guidance of the bridle in his mouth, was the exhilaration she had been longing for.

The earlier feeling of depletion was gone in the excitement of bringing Saracen under her power with her voice and hands. She felt she had mastered him.

She rode ahead of the wagon, hearing the hoofbeats of the two horses pounding along behind her, drawing up whenever she heard his warning voice—never calling her name. "Slow down."

She felt a crazy desire to ride as she had ridden in the past, kicking Solomon in the ribs and giving him his head, galloping until both of them were exhausted. But that, she had been warned, for the gypsy had predicted this desire, would be her last ride.

And then, too soon, she heard the wagon stop and his voice called to her. "It's time."

She came cantering back. "A little while longer?"

He didn't respond. She dismounted without his help, handing him Saracen's rein as she climbed up to sit beside him. The wagon started off, Saracen trotting beside them, Caliph running between Odysseus and Ptolemy.

"You enjoyed him?" he asked, as she took his hand, folded it and kissed the backs of his fingers, for she knew it troubled him still that she had had to surrender Solomon.

"Oh, yes! Can I ride again tomorrow night? Every night?"

He was silent for a few minutes. "Your breasts—did you feel discomfort?"

Inadvertently she placed one hand beneath the cloak, feeling at a slight pressure the soreness. "Yes," she said reluctantly. "A little."

"Why don't you sleep?"

"I'm not sleepy. I want to be with you."

But in a few minutes her head fell against his shoulder and she was asleep. She awoke when the wagon stopped, to find herself lying in bed, the cloak thrown aside, her shirt off. He was stripping away the tight Indian trousers.

"Go to sleep. I'll find a place for us to spend the day before the sun comes up." He stroked her forehead as he might a child's and drew the sheet to her shoulders, then kissed her gently, taking care not to waken her fully. "Sleep." Obediently, she did.

When she awoke the wagon had stopped, it was daylight, the leather curtain was partly closed, and he was lying beside her. She looked at him, longing to touch him, to wake him, but reminded herself that since yesterday morning he had spent most of the day on horseback or making love to her, and had slept no more than four hours.

She fell asleep again and, next time she awoke, he was gone. Searching for food, she guessed, since they had eaten little the past day and a half.

Arabella sat up, then quickly lay back, puzzled. What was it? Some feeling of queasiness, some intimation of a sick feeling in her belly, rising quickly toward her throat.

I'm not going to start vomiting, am I?

After a while, she again began to get up, slowly and cautiously, and was relieved to find the queasiness gone—only hunger pains.

She bathed and combed her hair, brushed her teeth, and stepped into the tub, where she still sat when he came back.

"I found a farm not far away. I bought a quarter of roast lamb—"

She smiled at him as he set the supplies on the table. "Come here. Come here please."

He turned swiftly, glanced at her, and as at some magic signal stripped off his shirt and trousers, kicked aside the boots, stepped into the tub and sat as she stood above him. Then slowly she lowered herself upon him, exhaling deeply as she felt herself once again full and completed. He moved out of her, paused, and then he was back, and again there came the sense of renewal and completion, the sense that only when he was inside her was she whole.

They looked at each other, motionless, their expressions serious, concerned. "There are times," she said, "when I feel as if we have become the same person."

"I know. I feel it, too."

Four mornings later, when she awoke alone, she began to get up and then, suddenly overwhelmed by the conviction that this time she would vomit and there was no way to stop it, she got out of bed and knelt beside the chamber pot, retching, spewing out very little food, but unable to stop the retching.

That was where he found her a few minutes later and she gave a long wail of protest. "Oh, please—don't look at me. I'm ugly—"

He did not go away. He took a clean cloth and wiped her face, filled a porcelain basin with fresh water and gave her salt to brush her teeth. He helped her to stand, somewhat unsteadily and took her carefully into his arms. Soon she was sitting across the small table, eating languidly, assuring him that what had happened—she avoided using the word—

sometimes happened when she was hungry. She smiled and ate more than she wanted.

All at once she put down the slice of lamb. "Robert, what are we going to do?" Her voice and face were apologetic.

"We'll try not to think about it until another six weeks have passed. That will be, as nearly as we know, three months and a day or two."

"And that's when you must—or I must—"

"Yes."

She looked at him, her eyes searching for some indication of resentment, repugnance, perhaps hatred. She saw only his face as it always looked to her; his eyes watched her with tenderness and sorrow—for he knew better than she what she must endure.

"Will you still want me?"

He laughed softly, shaking his head. "Never think of that. You know I will."

The vomiting occurred every morning when she awoke, usually after he had left. Although at first she hated herself, her feelings turned to anger; she blamed him for having caused not only this vileness, but worse experiences to come. And yet each day in an hour or two, her normal vitality returned, and with it her unquestioning adoration.

Several days later the sickness stopped.

"Maybe it's over?" she asked wistfully, for the resentment was never there when he was present.

These physical results of their lovemaking caused him no disgust, as they did her. He accepted them as he accepted any occurrence of nature. And to her surprise their responsiveness to each other had become even keener, the need almost continuous.

"Some women never vomit," he had said. "Some spend most of nine months throwing up."

There were occasional attacks of jealousy.

So much information, casually dispensed, seemed intended to accustom her to thinking of what would happen one day as being only a normal procedure, not the hideous experience he had earlier described.

Where did he learn all this?

And then, quite miraculously, she found that it no longer troubled her that other women had peopled his life. He loved her, and he had not loved them, and she marveled that this simple truth should have been so difficult for her to accept when there it had been, plain and incontrovertible, since the day he had ridden in to the tournament grounds astride Guise's horse.

If I had not been so afraid of someday somehow losing him, she told herself, I would have known all this a long time ago.

Each night she stroked Saracen, slowly winning him, so that he came to trust her. She was able to control him with scarcely any guidance from her knees or the reins she held lightly. A few soft words and he ran at her will, sometimes too fast, too far, so that the gypsy repeated his warning.

"The roads are deserted," she objected.

"They may, or they may not be. Not every traveler makes himself known. Those who travel at night are going somewhere in haste, or on errands they prefer not to have discovered."

"Like us."

Arabella, turning Saracen in small circles to keep him near the wagon, laughed softly. She rode for several hours each night, her muscles beginning to sing with energy, after the first few days of stiffness.

They would reach the sea—an event to which she looked forward with eager anticipation—and they would be safe. Forever.

She had no very good concept of what she meant when she talked to herself about their future. Yet she believed devoutly that they would never be parted, their lives would be careless and joyful, devoted to each other and to those pleasures which, as he had predicted, grew more necessary, more frequently indulged, more needful to her body, to her sense of spiritual completion. She had regained the feeling that no harm would come to either of them.

"I am so happy," she told him one morning, as he came to bed shortly before dawn. Her arms embraced his shoulders as he lowered himself upon her. "Suppose you had sent me back that night in the forest. All those warnings—"

"All those warnings were real."

Lovemaking silenced them both, but for the inadvertent sounds she made, more out of sorrow or pain than joy, or the occasional muttered words he spoke in Romany.

She remembered the warnings—not when he was with her, but when she was alone, bathing, selecting her skirts or pantaloons and jeweled vests, combing her hair, painting her eyes and the palms of her hands, or seated beside a window, plucking the lute and singing the songs he was teaching her, quite different from those she had learned in the north; this was melancholy music, the product of a people with a long troubled history.

And she remembered the tone of resentment in his voice as they sat in the darkness of the forest: It was a promise I kept because of our peculiar sense of honor.

The gypsies' peculiar sense of honor—his people, as he continued to insist.

You don't know what you're choosing, he had warned her, while she assured herself that she knew quite well.

She was choosing him. She was choosing what Arabella, not her parents, wanted.

When I leave here, I'm going south, to the sea. That's where I grew up. That's my land. And your father will give you a husband of the proper rank—

A husband of the proper rank would not know, and would never learn, anything of what he knows about me, and has known, since that first morning.

That first morning had been seven weeks ago.

"If it had been going to happen," she said, "it would be over by now."

"Probably. But we must wait."

Arabella preferred to wait—anything to postpone what scared her more than she wanted to admit. Certainly more than she wanted him to know.

She pretended that the pains, the blood, the strong potion which, he warned her, would make her think she was losing not only the growing baby, but everything inside her, could be endured by Arabella as well as by anyone else.

"You won't leave me when I take it? You'll stay with me?"

He gave her a glance of incredulous wonder. "Leave you? Jesus Christ—leave you?" He shook his head, as if she baffled him.

She preferred to lose those anxieties in their pleasures, while they waited out the next few weeks, until there could be no further hope of a spontaneous disposal of the small creature inside her. For she could not imagine that scrap of living tissue, alien, a stranger to them, product of lust and love, prolonged passion—product, no doubt, of that first morning, when they had both forgotten all he had told her of soap and herbs and vinegar.

Each night when she rode Saracen, putting him through as many strenuous paces as could be encompassed in the short run of roadway permitted her, she returned with the hope that the solution would be there, a spreading stain of blood on the saddlecloth.

Finally she told herself she must stop expecting it.

The gypsy would give her the medicine when he was convinced, by examining her inside with the pressure of his fingers, the other hand pressing low on her belly, that it was time. Her advancing pregnancy would in effect imprison them, condemn them to inescapable danger should they be discovered by her father's or Guise's men.

Each night the experience of riding Saracen grew more intoxicating—but as the sense of freedom increased, so increased her impatience with his precautionary advice.

She longed to set her heels forcefully against Saracen's ribs, to pound him into his fastest speed, to see how far and how hard they could run together. That was the only way to ride a horse.

"Just once?" she asked plaintively, when she had been summoned back from having run too far ahead of the wagon on a dark night. "Just this one time and never again?"

"There's no such thing for you, Arabella." There was a low laughter in his voice, but he was serious. "Suppose you outrun Caliph—and Saracen can do that for a while. He's a better animal than I realized. Stay near enough to the wagon so that if a stranger appears, Caliph will be with you until I can get there."

She set off again, quite gaily, as if no warning had been issued, giving Saracen a defiant kick in the ribs. But they had scarcely begun running when she heard his voice in Romany. When she pretended not to hear that, kicking Saracen again, there came a sharp piercing whistle, and she glanced around to see Caliph racing after them up the moonlit road.

For a few moments she rode on, but then slowed, reluctantly, bringing Saracen to a halt as Caliph reached them and stood watching them, waiting for his master to arrive.

Breathing in the warm air, fragrant of flowers and orange and lemon trees, which floated around her seemingly palpable, Arabella stared straight ahead down that path of moonlight so glitteringly beckoning.

She was happy, with that sense of freedom and arrogance riding always gave her—and she was angry. She refused to turn or look at Robert when the wagon stopped beside them, and then she became aware that he stood beside her.

They remained that way for a minute or two without speaking, without moving, Arabella looking straight ahead, all at once aware that she was the Princess Arabella, a thought which had scarcely occurred to her since that first morning when she had kept her promised rendezvous with that man of glowing golden warmth, whose beauty had left her wide awake most of the night.

He took firm hold of Saracen's mane. "Arabella, do you think I'm trying to control you? Is that why you ride a little farther ahead and a little faster each night?"

She refused to look at him. "I ride that way because it gives me pleasure. Great pleasure. There's no one on the road. We've been traveling for hours."

He turned abruptly, going back to the wagon. "You know better than that. Stay near the wagon, or don't ride at all."

Arabella was silent, watching as he jumped up on the seat, slapped the reins, and the great wagon came toward her, rumbling and bounding along the rocky roadbed. As he drew alongside and would have passed her, Arabella spoke clearly, quoting to him his words that night in the forest: "Don't obey me, Arabella. If you stay with me, you'll have sorrows enough without that." He had passed her, and she called after him. "Did you mean that, or not?"

He did not glance around, and she came cantering up beside him. He was silent for some time, while she waited for his answer.

"I meant it, of course. Do you think I want to insist that you obey me? But in this, you must."

He still had not looked at her and now Arabella leaned far over Saracen's side, extending her hand in a peace offering. "I won't do it again. I promise."

They rode side by side for several minutes, until he said, "I would give anything—everything—to see you ride as you did that first morning when—" He paused, as if it had become painful to talk about this. "That first morning when you and your maids-of-honor came to my camp. You were free and joyous."

"I still am," she said softly. "Not so free. But more

111

joyous. I was joyous then because I didn't know how not to be. I'm joyous now because—"

She gave him a quick wave, afraid she would begin to cry, and rode a short distance up the road, turned Saracen in one of his agile pirouettes, cantered back and around the wagon, waving to him as she went by, and her laugh sounded in the night with a joyous melody. She wanted to reassure them both.

⊚ CHAPTER THIRTEEN ⊚

S ome two weeks later, when the road was well lighted
by the moon and the stars spread across the sky,
without plan, she kicked Saracen's ribs, kicked again,
harder, and began to ride as fast as he could carry her,
scarcely hearing the gypsy's warning shout.

She could hear the hoofbeats of Ptolemy and Odysseus
pounding steadily faster, dragging the cumbersome wagon,
far behind. And still she kicked her heels into Saracen's ribs,
leaning flat upon his back, clutching his mane. She rode
with only a saddlecloth and stirrups, talking urgently into
Saracen's ear. The sense of full freedom came to her with a
surge of uncontainable joy.

Then came the gypsy's shrill whistle, and the first answering bark she had ever heard from Caliph. But she did not
glance around, for Saracen's speed was great enough, and her
bareback seat precarious enough, that concentration was
needed to keep him running beneath her without stumbling.

The hoofbeats of the two horses stopped suddenly, and at
that, alarmed, she slowed Saracen to look back, where she
could dimly see that Robert had unharnessed one of the
horses and was astride him. Caliph was approaching with
alarming swiftness.

She kicked Saracen again, lying hard upon his back, talking in his ear, urging him to do his best—or worst. They
were some distance ahead of the gypsy and Arabella foresaw
a splendid race between them, which she must surely win,

not only because she had started far ahead, but because neither Odysseus nor Ptolemy had been bought for speed, rather for endurance.

From somewhere to her right, a horseman emerged at full gallop from the side of the road. Perhaps he had been traveling toward her for some time, and turning about she had not seen him.

"Stop! Halt! In the King's name!" An old trick, she knew, of robbers or others bent upon mischief.

He came so swiftly that Arabella, terrified by the suddenness of this apparition, continued a few moments riding straight toward him before she leaned far to the left of Saracen, kicking him, directing him to turn swiftly. She clung to his mane as they passed the stranger.

The horseman was close behind. "Halt! In the King's name!"

He seized the edge of her burnoose, but she snatched it back so forcibly that it tore loose from his grasp. As he came abreast of her, she flung it over him.

Vaguely, for fear and excitement had reduced her vision to a blur, she saw the gypsy approaching, and the next moment he had passed her, yelling: "Go back to the wagon!"

Caliph had streaked by him and as Arabella turned Saracen in his tracks, forcing him upon his hind legs as he wheeled, she was near enough to the gypsy and the strange horseman to hear the snap of the tendon as Caliph bit through the horse's ankle and his rider toppled onto the roadway, the horse screaming in pain, the rider struggling to fight off Caliph.

The gypsy leaped down from Odysseus and approached the horseman, but Caliph had reached him first and lunged at his throat. The man, with a great yell, began to spurt blood.

Struggling to breathe, Arabella sat astride Saracen and saw the gypsy, a knife in his hand, bend over the horseman, then straighten, having found the job done for him. He wheeled about.

"Go back to the wagon." Arabella slid down from Saracen's back and approached in a blind fear, sure that there was more protection at his side than away from him. "Go back—he may not be alone." She did not move, and the next moment felt the flat of his hand on her face, a blow which made her stagger. He gave her shoulder a rough shake. "Get away from here!"

He turned to the horseman, coughing as he drowned in his own blood, then the gypsy glanced at Arabella once more. She ran toward the wagon, not forgetting to lead Saracen with her.

When she turned again, she saw the gypsy was kneeling and with one swift clear motion he passed the knife across the horse's throat, sending an unholy scream of animal surprise and agony into the air.

"Oh!" Her outcry was inadvertent, for she knew the horse must die, since he would never walk again.

The gypsy snatched the burnoose from the dead man and came toward her, moving swiftly, menacingly. She abandoned Saracen and ran to the safety of the wagon, jumping up as the gypsy reached her, and saw him beginning to put Odysseus into harness again, grasping at Saracen's loose rein and fastening him so that he might trot beside them.

He glanced at her, but as he started to spring upon the wagon Arabella gave a protesting scream, and ran into the wagon, slammed the door, and heard the lock snap.

She pounded at the door. "Let me out!" Her fear turned to rage. She felt he had imprisoned her and had some sinister purpose in doing so.

"I'm turning off the road," he shouted. "We'll have to take our chances. Hold fast!"

The wagon jolted back and forth as he got it into position. It started down a rough steep incline. She lurched forward, flung from one side of the wagon to the other. When the wagon seemed about to fall upon its side, she found the safety of the nailed-down bed and clung to it.

"God damn him."

She was sobbing with fear, with fury that he had struck her, and with terror at what might have happened, might still happen, if the horseman was traveling with companions. She clutched the side of the bed sobbing, until they came to the bottom of the incline. There the wagon began to move slowly, noisily, up a stony streambed, the water splashing about the wheels.

With difficulty, she gained her footing, although she could see nothing, and made her way to the door. "Let me out!" She pounded with both fists.

He gave no answer.

After some time, she sank to her knees, then threw herself upon the floor, crying helplessly. There seemed no possible end to this weird episode, but the death of one or both of them.

She fell asleep, or so it seemed, becoming aware that the wagon was traveling more swiftly now, still in darkness. She could no longer hear the water splashing and knew they had left the creek bed.

She crept across the floor toward the back of the wagon, a fixed resolve in her mind.

In one of the chests lay a box, a finely ornamented box of cypress which contained, laid out as carefully as any display of jewels, a selection of sheathed knives brought back by some crusader, steel blades, in perfect cutting condition, too sharp to venture touching, the gypsy had warned her. They were meant to kill, slip through a man's throat or into his ribs almost before he could realize what was happening.

She opened the lid and cautiously extracted one of the knives, discarding the sheath and wrapping the blade carefully in whatever thick cloth she found. She closed the chest and made her way back to the bed, where she slipped the knife under the bed, its handle facing outward, piercing the carpet with its tip to keep it from sliding away. There it was, where she could seize it the moment he opened the door.

Filled with thoughts of vengeance, hatred, lurid images of plunging that knife into his throat, she fell fast asleep, the increasingly deep sleep which of late she fell into without warning.

She lay there flat on her belly, not moving for several hours. When she awoke it was daylight. One leather curtain had been slipped back a few inches.

It was moments before she realized that the gypsy was there still fully clothed, kneeling beside the bed, and in his hand was the knife, its hilt extended toward her, offering it for her to take and, if she chose, to use.

Arabella lifted her hand in protest, as if he were menacing her with the blade, and turned away. His eyes looked at her steadily, but his face showed no indication of what he was thinking or feeling, neither love nor hate, sorrow or pity, only an implacable straight stare, without question or challenge.

"Put it away," she pleaded softly. She began to cry, keeping her face turned from him, guilty and ashamed, as griefstruck as if she had in fact done him some injury, fulfilling the vow she had made before falling into that gulf of sleep.

She heard him cross the floor, open the trunk, and when she raised her head, he was standing beside the bed again. She sat up suddenly, but his expression read as a warning not to touch him, to make no overtures of peace, and her hands fell, gripping the sides of the bed as she looked up at him.

"No one has ever done that to me," she whispered, but still there was no response in that impassive merciless face. "No one has ever touched me in anger."

She noticed that his trousers and shirt were stained with dried blood, from the horse, from the rider, both of them how far away? They must have driven all night and into the morning.

117

"It wasn't anger," he answered quietly. "It was terror. He might not have been alone."

"He was alone."

"We didn't know that. We don't know it now. He may have been an outrider or an advance courier." Now there was a slight grim smile, a new expression to her, and she closed her eyes and shook her head in childish protest that he should look at her in that way.

"Have you seen anyone else?"

"I left the main road, surely you remember, and traveled some distance up the riverbed, leaving no tracks to follow. And I traveled into the morning to put as much distance as possible between us. Arabella?"

She looked up eagerly. "Yes?" He was silent a moment. She reached out and seized one hand in both of hers. "You forgive me?"

He gave a brief bitter laugh, reminding her of the laugh she had heard in the forest, when he had warned her of the consequences of coming with him. "A few hours ago you meant to kill me. Suppose I had come in here just after you had taken the knife—while you were hysterical. Would you have killed me, Arabella?"

She let go his hand and bowed her head, crying softly and steadily, tears which now seemed to be foolish and useless even for apology or grief. She had meant to kill him, or had thought she did.

"I don't know," she whispered. "You wouldn't have let me, anyway."

"I might have. If you had hated me so much—Yes, I might have."

Arabella threw herself upon the bed, her sobs louder, her voice rising to a wail, her breath coming in hard sobs, until she began to grow sick upon her grief and despair and remorse. "Forgive me, forgive me, forgive me—"

She heard him move across the floor, but she was still sobbing beyond control. Perhaps he would leave her, take the animals and leave her locked inside the wagon, to starve or be found by whoever would find her.

He had taken off the bloodstained garments, replacing them with clean trousers, a shirt, and sandals. "It's mid-morning, late. The horses can forage here, but Caliph has had nothing to eat for more than a day. Neither have I. I'll be back soon." She felt him touch the back of her head, stroke it lightly.

Once more sure that he had forgiven her, she looked up at him, and finding that he was smiling faintly, although his eyes still watched her with that cold expressionless stare, she seized his hand and brought it between her breasts. "Have you forgiven me?"

He laughed softly.

"Yes?" She moved his hand across one breast, and he did not withdraw it, but neither did he caress her. "You have?"

"I'll leave fresh water."

He withdrew his hand slowly, looking at her for a long moment, and was gone.

The door opened and she heard the usual sounds as the big tub was emptied and refilled with water from a nearby stream. The door slammed and the lock snapped shut.

As she peered out the window she saw him moving through nearby trees, and very soon he was gone, out of sight.

He will never come back. He has left me forever.

The conviction was absolute, the despair so keen that she turned physically and emotionally numb. She pulled the leather curtain shut and returned to sit on the bed.

His bloodstained clothes, her own, and the burnoose he had torn away from the dead rider, lay in a heap—tossed aside the night before.

Dazedly, she went to look in the mirror, approaching it warily. The light was dim and she could not see very plainly what Arabella looked like today—someone quite different from the last time she had encountered herself there, before some devil of temptation—and it could have been the work of no lesser evil—had prompted her to break into that wild ride, demented with defiance and joy.

She pushed aside the leather curtain to let in a noonday sun and moved close to the mirror, dreading what she would find.

She discovered the same Arabella she had seen the night before, and remembered what he had said, more than once, when she had gone to examine the after effects of some unusually prolonged and violent lovemaking.

"That's one of the many beauties of youth. Nothing can change how you look."

Of course he loves me.

She looked at her breasts, and as she cupped her hands beneath them was surprised to find them now even fuller than when last she had held them in that way, several days before. She stared with a fascinated admiration and awe at what her body was becoming, without any urging, nothing but time to work its changes.

Quickly she drew the curtain closed and stepped into the tub.

She had the design of dressing to distract him from what had happened the night before, if such a thing could be possible. She was convinced that he had decided to punish her by never making love to her again. Perhaps he could not make love to a woman who had planned, however insanely, to kill him.

She found a long loose dress, made of white silk lightly embroidered with gold thread, and when she slipped it over her head she found that it fell in loose folds to the floor, and the neckline left her breasts uncovered.

Her work with the henna and kohl completed, she grew fearful again. The mirror was no longer reassurance. He would forgive her. He would never forgive her.

She gazed out the window. At least two hours had gone by. The three horses lay at ease or asleep, while Caliph sat some distance from the wagon, gazing steadily in the direction where his master had disappeared.

She began to pluck at one of the lutes, attending carefully to the sounds. After a while Caliph stood alertly. The next moment the gypsy stepped out of the heavy growth of trees, bearing with him a sack from which he poured for Caliph the most succulent feast Caliph had seen for some time, bones and pieces of raw meat, which he fell upon with eager relish.

Arabella was newly alarmed and once again her heart beat apprehensively as the gypsy came quickly toward the wagon, paused in the doorway as he saw her, and smiled. It was not his usual smile, but a smile of sorts, all the same. He kicked the door shut and bore to the table a kettle which he opened, sending forth an aroma of stewed meat and herbs and vegetables which caused Arabella to clap her hands.

"Oh! I'm so hungry! And so glad you're back."

She approached him slowly, but found that she was not able to make an overture. She felt she must wait for him to speak or touch her.

He did neither, only quickly brought out two gold bowls and spoons, ladled stew into them, and gestured to her to sit and eat, seating himself opposite her.

"I found a farmhouse nearby. The area seems unlikely for travelers, and there's been no one through here for several weeks, if I can believe what I'm told. We'll stay a day or two in case the unlucky horseman had followers or companions."

Arabella, eating hungrily, which did not happen often nowadays, smiled at him winningly, placatingly. "How good it is."

She felt quite innocent of any wrongdoing, whether in sending Saracen into his mad gallop, or in placing the knife beneath the bed. She had forgiven herself. Now it was his turn. She did not willfully hurt people, for she preferred to be loved, but neither did she think that whatever she did could be very wrong if she did it.

They ate in silence, but since she knew he did not sulk, or waste himself in grudges, and his face no longer bore that formidable expression of impassive judgment, she decided that he was scarcely thinking of her at that moment, avoiding looking at her not out of anger but because he was planning what was to be done next, and then next again.

He did not think of today and tomorrow, but of weeks and months—perhaps even years—ahead. This, too, was a mystery. But then her life had been planned by the routine of the court: the tournaments, the hunts, the tutors, the horseback riding, the dancing in the Great Hall, her play with the pages.

They finished the meal and he took the bowls, washed them, and replaced them in the cabinet where they were kept with two or three dozen others of similar design.

Presently he peeled off his shirt and trousers and stood in the tub, scrubbing himself. Arabella watched him for a few moments with yearning admiration, as if this were a performance she had never seen before, but something in his manner of preoccupation continued to intimidate her.

She looked away, then glanced quickly around to find his eyes upon her. They exchanged a quick smile, with something like the look of two conspirators who knew each other's secrets, every last one, and knew each other better than either had ever known another human being.

Reassured by that quick glimpse of the Robert she had always expected to find, Arabella sat on the bed, drew her knees to her chin, folded her arms about them, and fell to thinking of what would happen first. After the promise implicit in that smile, she must still wait for him to approach her. He was quickly dressed.

Yes. I must wait. He has something more to say to me.

So he did, for presently she heard a sound of clinking metal poured on top of one of the chests, and his voice spoke quietly. "Come here, Arabella. I want you to see something."

She went to him. His back was toward her as he bent

over the chest, looking at what she saw was a considerable number of gold coins, one hundred or more. He spread them thoughtfully with his fingers. A leather pouch lay beside them.

"Where did they come from?" she whispered.

"The horseman was carrying them. I thought to search him. Look." He picked one up and placed it in her outstretched palm.

Arabella looked at it curiously, then examining it more closely, her heart began to beat as if she had been physically threatened. She looked at it for several more moments, and at last, still staring at it, whispered, "Guise. Yes." The profile of the Duke of Guise was embossed upon the coin. "Guise. How strange."

He placed another coin beside the first, and this time she gave a low gasp. "The King."

She wanted to give them back, throw them away, pretend she had never seen them, but she continued to gaze at them, with a look of awe as she examined the portrait of that man who was her father. As she looked at the coin, he became some sinister intruder into her life, coming to her from the distance to remind her of her obligations and the risks those obligations once flouted presented to herself and to the gypsy. "The King," she said. "Yes. I—can't believe it. Are they all—"

"They are all of Guise or the King."

◙ CHAPTER FOURTEEN ◙

She closed her eyes briefly, then looked up at him, extending her open palm, preferring that he take them from her, rather than let her toss them with the others on the chest. He picked up Guise's coin, and as he was about to take the other she closed her hand and held the King's coin, gazing down at her fist as if something there had mesmerized her.

That man, whose profile on the coin looked to her nothing at all like the man she thought of as her father, was a man who had from time to time appeared to her: a stranger, a dangerous alien; a man of ominous authority and power—and she was shocked into sudden recognition that this stranger, the King, might have her killed or permit her to be killed.

She opened her fist, speaking just above a whisper, "Ten weeks—I'm no longer of any use to him. There aren't enough lies in the world to explain ten weeks."

She looked at the gypsy and found his face impassive, relentless as the expression which had confronted her when he offered her the knife hilt. "He's known for a long time that I went with you of my own choice. He can't use me now to drive a good bargain, not any bargain at all—and he thinks I've made him look a fool, not only to his own people. He may hate me. My mother may hate me." She nodded. "We are together, you and I. Yes." She turned her head, not wanting him to see the tears which came, then seemed to disappear before they had fallen. All at once she gave him a bold, brilliant smile.

She returned the coin and he tossed it upon the others, swept the whole into the leather pouch, and flung it into a corner.

After a few moments she asked, "What will you do with them?"

"I'll use them for what they were intended—to buy information."

"Where?" She gestured contemptuously. "These—farmers—"

"Of course not. When we get to the seacoast towns, I know them—like this—" He spread his right hand, showing her the delineation of his destiny upon his palm's surface. "A man with money can always buy information. The question is how much truth he has bought with it." He was smiling a little, watching her carefully, as if taking the measure of this wild young being for whom he had assumed responsibility. "If you know where to look—and I do—everything is for sale along the sea. A man's head—a whore without arms or legs—"

She gave a protesting cry. "Don't tell me anything more. I'm beginning to be afraid of the world."

"You must be afraid enough to be less brave. I can't protect you as your father could. Here—in this world—you are a danger to yourself and to anyone who is with you. You're a temptation to men who can love—and to those who can only hate."

"I will never do again—what I did last night."

"Even if you don't, that solves nothing. They're looking for us, and they'll continue to look. There's no place where we can be sure of not being found. We've considered the possibilities. Any one of them would be a greater risk than what we're doing." He shook his head slowly. "Our last clear chance was that night in the forest."

"You knew all this. But you let me come."

"I wanted you. And I lied to myself. I thought I knew the

country better than anyone they could send. I thought I could outmaneuver them. I thought—I thought many things." His hands were moving gently upon her shoulders and back, scarcely touching her. "Here we are."

He continued caressing her, lightly and slowly, without either of them responding with the anxiety or urgency which had seemed inevitable once the first contact was made.

This was a caress which required that she do nothing at all, remain as she was, leaning her forehead lightly against his chest, arms at her sides, quiescent.

She closed her eyes, allowing those touches upon her back to lull her steadily to a quietude he had never before been able to induce, perhaps because he had never wanted to. The sensations, gentle but profound, stirred her deeply, as if her belly and breasts had become full of him.

Here I am. Arabella. But I am someone different, too.

The difference was her fear that they might not live to that vague forever she invoked. Forever, she had been forced to realize by the appearance of the horseman, with his cache of gold coins, might be a few days, a few weeks, with luck perhaps a few months.

Very softly he said, "You don't know what it means to die."

"I've seen people dying ever since I can remember."

"Have you ever seen someone you loved die?"

"I saw my two sisters die." She laughed softly, without amusement. "That's a lie. I didn't love them."

"I should have found a way to send you back."

"How? When I wouldn't go?" She was silent a moment. "And if we are killed—what difference will it make? We won't know it. After the first few seconds—or minutes—of fear—" They were silent, and then she continued. "I've seen death so many many times. The men brought back from battle—or the tournaments—I've heard their screams, their prayers, I've seen them lying in the Great Hall waiting for the surgeons. I've seen—" She shook her head slowly. "It is nothing. A veil disappears. It is there—that veil between the living and the dead—and then it is not there. That's all. We won't even know we aren't together anymore." She gave him a quick angry glance and turned, so that her back was against him, and for several minutes they stood silent and motionless.

Then his hands passed lightly across the tips of her nipples, cupping her breasts, but he made no effort to draw her closer. She had closed her eyes as he touched her and kept them closed, waiting, speaking finally almost as if she were in a trance.

"I hope that if the King sends any of my brothers—it will be Raoul. I can talk to him. I can make him understand."

"Are you imagining they will come only to congratulate me for having taken good care of you?"

She refused to give up those flashes of hope, conviction, that the end would prove this to have been a game, a dangerous game, but still a game, which would be won by Robert and Arabella.

"Raoul and I have a pact. We've never talked about it. But we have one. We were the only two who knew each other. Not my sisters. Not my other brothers. Only Raoul and me." She nodded. "Yes. We did. We do."

She caught her breath, surprised by the flare of desire as his thumbs once again caressed her nipples. "We couldn't be any closer if you were inside me." She made a soft sound. "You are inside me." Her pregnancy had given her the mystical sense that he was a part of her.

He moved to strip off the trousers and flung aside the shirt, but as her hands clasped him, he placed them at either side of his legs.

"Can you be patient, Arabella? Can you trust me to give you pleasure even if it comes more slowly than you think you want? Can you feel whatever I do to you, without doing anything at all to me?"

"Yes—" She closed her eyes, moving her head to lie against his shoulder.

She felt they had been melded together in some aftermath of the night's terror, the morning's hysteria, and there was no leap of expectation which had always announced the imminence of lovemaking. There was a sense of resignation to whatever might happen, to her, to him, to them, if one day they were found. With this resignation came a release from the doubts and misgivings, which she recognized as having been with her since their meeting in the forest— that need for quick pleasure, pleasure shading in and out of pain, pleasure never slaked, merciless in its will to subdue them both.

The soothing movements of his hands, gentle movements, not sudden alarms or demands, continued for a seemingly interminable period of time.

She supposed he had cast her under some spell of gypsy magic, or his own magic, from which she suspected she had not been free since the morning she and her maids-of-honor had gone cantering up to where he squatted on his heels near a campfire.

That first sight of him as he glanced up, directly at her, had held the promise, or threat, of everything that had happened later. They had looked at each other, then quickly looked away. Again and again, as she and her maids ambled on horseback about his encampment, she had encountered his eyes, watchful, alert, aware of her slight answering smile.

Nothing more than that. And we had looked the future straight in the face without recognizing its warning.

Signal of danger though the horseman may have been, with his cache of royal coins, she could not imagine a time when she could not stand as she did now, Robert's body against her back, his hands moving over her slowly, his fingers leaving a tracery of sensation, a slow rising intensity of expectation. His hands closed upon her breasts, crushing them. The pressure increased, and he pressed her nipples with a sudden angry need to cause her pain, perhaps to ease his own.

His hands pushed the loose silk garment from her shoulders and it fell to the floor.

He bent her body forward, still pressing against her, and while he held her breasts with one widespread hand, two fingers entered her and began a slow exploration, movements which seemed unfamiliar, until without warning there flowed through her belly the warm throb of completed pleasure.

This, she guessed, was the beginning of another period of prolonged lovemaking, perhaps as long as the last time.

Quickly he was inside her. He moved once or twice, and the pulsing began as he held her against him, now so forcefully that she felt a vague fear. He could kill her easily, if he had not forgiven her.

He won't kill me, but I may die of this anyway.

He carried her to the bed and she lay on her belly, where he entered her swiftly, moving with such force that she gave a quick outcry. His hands held her breasts, as if he would test their increased weight, their sensitivity, their capacity for sensual pleasure or sharp stabs of pain, and she felt him beginning to grow again inside her.

He did not move for several minutes, but continued to caress her breasts, gently, tenderly, then quickly crushed them.

He raised himself above her, braced at arms' length upon his hands, and as she caught at his wrist with her teeth, biting hard, he moved more rapidly, several quick piercing strokes, and once again she felt a long series of pulsing jets.

As if waking from a spell of unconsciousness, she looked at his wrist and saw the mark of her teeth, the seeping blood. Daintily, she licked away the blood, liking the faint salty taste of it.

He had not left her, and all at once Arabella felt a need for him as great as if he had not touched her. Her buttocks slowly raised and lowered, and her mouth ran along his forearm, her lips brushing the light covering of curling hairs.

His hands went to her belly, pressing hard, as he had done recently, as if trying to determine if anything growing there might be felt. Suddenly he withdrew to her body's rim and plunged deep. One hand went beneath her, raising her toward him again, and held her as the blows were repeated, until all at once he gave a deep hopeless sigh, and the throbbing pulse began.

Slowly they sank upon the bed and were still, until he began to slip out of her. She quickly reached as if to capture him, and heard him laugh softly as he moved away.

When she turned over he was standing looking down at her. They looked at each other intently, and when he smiled she smiled in reply, luxuriously content. Everything evil which had happened between them during the night and early morning had been vanquished.

His smile disappeared, and he spoke quietly, "Arabella, you must listen to what I'm going to say. When they find us—and they will—you must run to join them, calling your name, and Raoul's. Don't stay with me. You will save your life if they recognize you. Nothing can save mine. Promise me this."

She sat up quickly, shaking her tangled hair, looking away from him at a silk curtain on the opposite wall. "I promise nothing. How do I know what I will do—if it happens?" She gave a slight bitter laugh, glancing sideways at him. "Leave you? Do you think so?"

"If you don't, we'll both be killed. In a fight, anything can happen." He seized her shoulders and brought her up to face him. Then he shook her hard, for she stared at him rebelliously. "Arabella!" She turned her head aside, and he let her go. "I'll find some way to abandon you."

"You will?"

"You must do it." He touched her shoulder. "Give me your promise."

Her eyes looked into his without flickering—a steady defiant stare. "Is that likely? If I can't leave you now—if I couldn't leave you that night in the forest—tell me, how could I leave you then?"

◙ CHAPTER FIFTEEN ◙

When Robert had gone to attend the animals, see that their fodder was sufficient, their water fresh, to curry their coats, Arabella stood with some plan in mind, but then slowly sat down again. Why this fatigue, when it was only late afternoon?

Sitting on the bed, wondering why she was not in the tub, revivifying herself with the cool fragrant water, she grew unhappily aware that it was less likely to be the aftermath of last night's killing of the man and horse, or even her own mad impulse of killing the gypsy, than it was one more symptom of what his daily examinations had so far failed to discover. If something living was growing inside her, it was not yet large enough to be felt by his searching fingers.

These examinations, as he began them, affected her like a form of lovemaking, but when the pressure upon her belly became hard, the probing of his fingers deep, she must force herself not to beg him to stop.

Now she walked to the tub and seated herself cross-legged, languidly splashing the cool water.

I'm not afraid of the damned potion, whatever it does to me. It can't be worse than what would happen to us if I didn't take it.

Next time, we'll be careful. Lemons are plentiful in this country of his, and he says that half a squeezed lemon performs miracles.

Unless it interferes with our pleasure.

Having bathed, brushed her hair, and applied the decorations of kohl and henna, she tied a gold tissue scarf beneath her armpits, letting it fall free to her ankles, opening down the left side.

Having no idea how much time had passed, she glanced through a slit in the curtain, and saw that the sun had disappeared from their thickly wooded encampment. The gypsy was currying Caliph, who stood with imperturbable patience, staring straight ahead, alert for any hint of danger.

Arabella returned to the bed and awoke only when she became aware that she was lying on her back, her legs spread wide, her feet on the floor, and the gypsy knelt between them, gently inserting two fingers into her.

After a few moments she asked impatiently, "Do you feel anything?"

He shook his head as his fingers explored deeper, looking questioningly into her eyes as his other hand began to press low upon her belly. She breathed deeply, as he had instructed her, and braced her hands against the wall behind her head.

The explorations continued with slow relentlessness, until she gave a gasp of despair and anger, thinking that she was beginning to hate him for these daily incursions.

"I'm sorry. It's the only way to be sure."

He ceased prodding her belly and his fingers moved gently, beginning to rouse pleasure where, only a moment before, there had been intrusive pain. He withdrew his fingers slowly and she sighed deeply, relieved to have the procedure over for that day. She closed her eyes, and felt him parting the lips, touching the moist petals.

"The color is changing." He paused. "Like the inside of some seashells. Beautiful."

That made her angry. "Beautiful." She sat up. "Why don't you give me the damned stuff and get it over with?"

She stared at him for a moment. But the tenderness, and

his look of compassion, regret, defeated her and she threw herself backward again, one hand across her eyes.

He caressed her, gently, but she was scarcely aware of what would ordinarily have produced a quick response of excitement. "We must wait until we're sure," he said.

"Until you're sure." The caresses continued, but she was not to be so easily recompensed for the pain.

"Another twelve days or two weeks. Until then it's not safe to try."

She was silent for some time, and at last gave a heavy sigh. "I'm more or less crazy just now."

The caresses stopped, and he was silent. She sat up to find him seated on the floor, facing sideways from her, his elbows on his drawn-up knees, hands clasped lightly between them. His eyes were slightly narrowed, with the familiar expression of concern, considering their possible plan of action.

He will find something to do. He'll go outside, unless I stop acting this way. He's doing what he must, even if it hurts me a little. No more than he hurts me sometimes when we're making love.

She leaned across the edge of the bed and touched his hand. "Robert—"

He looked around quickly, studying her as he had this morning. She smiled and leaned a little nearer. "I know you must do it. I should pretend, at least—"

"Come here." He pushed her slowly backward, her legs embraced his shoulders, and he was inside her, moving swiftly. He raised himself above her, and as a sudden thrust went deep and hard, she found him watching her, alertly aware of her changing expressions, her face showing curiosity as he drew slowly back, an increasing anxiety that she would lose him. When he removed himself she gave a protesting sound and fell silent, looking up at him, wondering at the seriousness of his face, as if something of extraordinary significance were happening to them, while he stroked her several times, then placed himself just inside her and waited, poised above her.

After some moments he entered very slowly, prolonging the process as if he had found a way to extend all of himself into that glowing warm length, slowly tilting her backward, placing her feet upon his shoulders until his body was above her as he pushed deeper, waited, watching her face, and then deeper. "Shall I stop?"

"No, not even if I beg you to—" He tilted her body further, shortening the length she could offer him, and her arms flew outward in wild protest. "No!"

He hesitated, then began to draw back. She opened her eyes and he was still watching her, with an intensity of concentration greater than she had seen before. "Is it too painful?"

Arabella had no awareness of what her face was showing him, but her hands moved beseechingly over his chest. "As deep as you can—"

He moved to the outer rim, then began to slip into the widened passageway of her body. He plunged inward and at once she felt the pulsing beats. His eyes glittered and she saw a strange mirthless smile on his face, transformed by whatever he was experiencing, while her legs clasped about his shoulders in her need for a more prolonged sensation of painful glory and despair.

The throbbing ceased, she felt his body wet with sweat, and drops fell from his face. He remained with her, although he had softened, and after some time the slow throb throughout her body stopped, and she was looking directly at him, finding him alertly watching, extraordinarily intent.

He did not often speak while they were making love, but now, in a voice so low she could scarcely hear, he said, "This is a selfish indulgence for me. Everything comes apart at once. The quickest, strongest relief—can you endure it?"

"I want it, too."

He tilted her backward a little farther, his body bent to bring him deeper, and she felt him harden. She closed her eyes and would have covered her face, but he seized her hands and held them apart as he pressed downward.

"Oh, Jesus—kill me, then—kill me—"

He did not hear her or had no longer any ability to heed. If he was causing her pain, perhaps that was a necessary part of this mutual immolation, for now her body had been pressed backward, her knees touching her shoulders as he forced himself into her from his kneeling position, moving very slowly, until she began a wailing protest and would have struck at him had he not held her hands.

She felt that her body had been divided to give him access to everything inside her, and still he forced himself deeper. She was sobbing with intense pain, a pleasure as intense, the two commingled in some atavistic crime, his claim upon her, her surrender and protest against what he seemed to be doing, slowly, inexorably putting her asunder.

And then the slow pulsing began, and he let it take its reluctant course without moving.

When finally she looked up she found him still watching her, his eyes narrowed, his mouth opened slightly at a deep intake of breath, and a powerful shudder passed across his shoulders, communicating throughout her body.

He began to release the heavy hold he had upon her, easing her legs downward, until finally with some weird sense that hours had passed and she had no idea of where she had been or what had been done to her, she found herself lying as she had at the beginning, on the edge of the bed, her feet on the floor. He knelt before her, his head on her breasts.

Are we insane? He never did that to me before. He never did it to anyone else, either. He killed me, and then decided to let me live, after all. And here I am, back from wherever I've been.

Gently her hands stroked his hair, and found it wet. His head moved slightly, his mouth touching her belly; he was silent, holding her breasts.

This is all a part of what happened last night. It hasn't

been so easy for him to forgive me. Everything he's done to me since has been because of that. Now it's over. He's solved something and I'll never know what it was.

They awakened simultaneously, having fallen asleep, still in the same position. They looked at each other quickly, as if meeting after a long journey they had not expected to end with another encounter. He stood slowly, and then bent, took her face between his hands, and kissed her mouth.

Other than those few minutes, he had not slept for more than twenty-four hours. Quickly she moved to the other side of the bed and he lay beside her, holding her in his arms, and they were promptly asleep.

◉ CHAPTER SIXTEEN ◉

Arabella awoke reluctantly, after what seemed a long struggle to emerge from unconsciousness. The gypsy, dressed in his usual way, stood beside the table, eating from a leg of capon he had brought earlier in the day.

He was not looking at her and did not immediately become aware that she was watching. He continued to eat slowly, laid down the leg bone and pulled off the other, all the while gazing intently toward the end of the wagon, as if he saw something there of interest and concern.

It was an expression not very different from one she had seen on the King's face, when he was considering how to defeat an enemy, to take revenge for an insult, to bargain for an advantage in that eternal game of chess which was the content of his life. And just so, the gypsy had looked to her many times before.

But the gypsy could laugh, as the King had almost never done unless in derisive mockery of some rival's embarrassment or defeat. And the gypsy could smile, a free honest smile of a man with nothing to conceal, nothing to wish undone. She had seen few such smiles from him recently, and heard little of that laughter.

All at once he became aware of her looking at him and glanced around swiftly, almost accusingly. She sat at the edge of the bed, leaning slightly forward. "Is it morning? Night? Have we traveled? Are we going to?"

Now he smiled, that whole free smile she had been longing for. He came to her and presented her with the capon leg. "We slept about four hours." He nodded toward the rear of the wagon. "I buried the bloody clothes in the forest. Now I'm going to take Odysseus and go to see if the man Caliph killed is still there. That will be a clue, at least, as to whether or not he was alone."

"There may be other men. Don't go."

His smile was gone and he looked down at her seriously. "Did I do too much to you?"

"No."

"When you're done eating, put out the light. I'll be gone no longer than—"

The lock snapped and Arabella sat for a moment, then dropped the capon leg, drew up her knees, folded her arms across them, and began to cry as she must have been longing to cry for weeks, perhaps since the first day she had seen him squatting beside the campfire, both of them completely free for the last time.

When she could cry no longer she ate a little more, washed her face, found that the silk sheets had dried, after being soaked with his sweat, and went to sleep.

She awoke suddenly, terrified, thinking that someone was trying to force his way into the wagon, and then remembered that Caliph had made no sound. The gypsy came in. "Oh! I was scared. I'm becoming a coward." He glanced at her as he locked the door, and was once again preoccupied. "Was he still there?"

"He was gone. The horse was there. It will take a determined crew to get him off the road. Two or three men, judging by their footprints, had dragged the man a few feet, but the tracks stopped in the dirt road beside the tracks of horses' hoofs. They went off the road, into the ravine, and disappeared in the forest. I might have been able to follow them in daylight, but I'm not going back. I saw two mendicant monks, no one else."

"Spies?"

He laughed. "No. Monks. They spoke the language of

this area. I tried three other dialects, one from the north, and a little Latin. Their stupidity was real."

He stripped off his clothes, kicked away the sandals, and stepped into the tub, washing away the horse's sweat and dust from the road. "We'll stay here tonight and tomorrow. Whoever they were, they'll have gone on by then. It's near midnight."

He was drying himself as she approached him, drawn by nothing more than his presence. She was surprised to discover that everything he had done had still not completed what she needed from him.

Last night's near encounter with death—which instead of being the death of a stranger, might have been the death of either or both of them—had increased the need for continuous affirmation that they still lived.

He knelt upon the bed, spreading his knees for balance, and brought her downward with a swiftness and force which made her catch hold of his shoulders, as if to steady the universe, which threatened to reel away beneath her. Her ears had begun to ring, as he held her about the waist, raising and lowering her with swift increasing violence.

She clutched at his shoulders, nails digging into his flesh, her teeth clenched with the determination to remain silent.

They were both aware of which positions brought her an acute, brief pain. Yet at times he needed the force, the fierce energy, perhaps even the anguish her face showed him. For each time they assumed such a position he watched her carefully.

If the pain lasted more than a few seconds, he released her enough to ease it. Then he pressed her down upon him again. But this time he continued steadily, without pause, determined upon whatever pleasure he needed at this moment, and when all at once she cried aloud in protest he closed her mouth with one hand, muttering in Romany. The swiftness and fierceness continued another minute or two, and then he moved no longer, but held her hard upon him as the quickening throbs began.

139

Slowly, growing gentle, he released the pressure, stroking her back, caressing her breasts. "Forgive me if I hurt you." His face was somber, and he stared past her. "I hope to God I'm not doing this to you because of—"

"Because of what happened last night. Maybe you are. Maybe you would have done it anyway. For all the other reasons." She put her mouth on his, but found his lips immobile, while he continued holding her upon him, and though he had softened, he had not left her. "Once more," she whispered. "Then we'll sleep."

He laughed softly. "It's not that easy."

She began to move slowly, her arms holding his shoulders, and as she moved she felt the responsive hardening. Presently there was that same exultant seizure of her body, the hard downward thrust, but this time there was no pain, only the glory of their being once again in harmonious rhythm.

His eyes closed with the intensity of concentration; the look of a man being put to the torture was on his face, the striving for the completion of whatever he might have left to give her, or perhaps the discovery that, after these past twelve hours, there was nothing left to give.

Slowly, almost imperceptibly, the pulsations began, and he held her as if she were trying to escape. In a few moments he had slipped away.

They looked at each other questioningly, finding mutual reassurance, both of them finally cleansed of what had happened on the roadway the night before, and earlier this morning, when he had found the knife. All traces of her guilt and his suspicions had been banished.

"When did you leave?"

"A little after daylight."

Arabella had awakened sometime in midmorning, as she judged by pushing a curtain aside. She had slept about eight hours, and would have been glad to sleep longer, but she wanted to be bathed and perfumed when he returned from reconnoitering and buying fresh food.

He placed the food on the table and turned to look at her, observing her with unusual care, as he did now each day, as if one more day would give them some final evidence, even though they knew there was evidence enough. Then, satisfied that she was rested and happy, feeling no ill effects of yesterday's rough usage, he continued laying out their breakfast, and they sat to eat, silent for several minutes.

"You saw no one?"

"I saw a few farm men. The woman at the farm could tell me nothing. I believed her. It's easy to know when they're lying."

"Yes. I remember the women I saw when we visited the farms." She smiled. "Why is it only the nobility who learn to lie so easily? Almost in preference to the truth?"

"And the gypsies." He was picking up the plates. "We'll stay here today. Tonight we'll start south again. I won't have any reasonable confidence until we reach the sea."

"Even then?"

"Probably not." He rinsed the plates, saying that he would tend the animals, change the water in the tub and ewer. "Sleep, Arabella. You need it."

She got up quickly, challengingly. "I look tired?" She went to the mirror. "I know it. And nothing, nothing at all ever made me tired before." She turned pleadingly, but he was wrapping the food to keep it fresh for the next meal.

When he started to pass her to go outside, she touched his arm and he stopped. "Yes?"

"Can't you give me the medicine now? We know. There isn't any doubt—"

"There's still time for something to happen. I won't put you through needless suffering—and it is suffering—worse than you can imagine."

"I'm not afraid."

That was only partly true.

Her Royal Highness was not afraid, but Arabella was in terror of this ordeal and convinced she would not live through it, whatever the gypsy told her.

This superstitious conviction that her death was near had made her feel that whatever she might need to complete her life she must have immediately.

And what was it she wanted? The gypsy. The feelings he induced when he was inside her, when he caressed her, when he touched her lightly.

And a sight of the sea, a sight she had yearned for a long time, although she could not remember when it had begun. Perhaps one night, or several, in the Great Hall, when they had heard travelers talk of the wonderful things to be seen in the world beyond the castle keep.

But most of all, the gypsy, giving of himself, taking what she had to give him, and sometimes more than she thought it would be possible to give.

"Why—tell me, please. Why do I need you all the time?" Her voice was pleading. "It seems to be over, as if there were nothing more I could want, ever again. And then so soon, I do. Can you tell me?"

He touched her face. "Why this wish for a final satisfaction? Part of the wonder of love is that there is no final satisfaction. I told you long ago—"

"That it never ends, while there is life."

"Do you wish it would end?"

She gave him a quick glance of horror. "My God, no!"

CHAPTER SEVENTEEN

She looked at him with admiring reflectiveness. In the white burnoose and headgear, nothing to be seen of his body or the three sheathed knives strapped about his waist, he could, perhaps, be mistaken for an Arab.

He smiled questioningly.

She approached and laid one hand lightly on his chest, dreading his venture into the first seacoast town they had reached, still some distance away. He would ride Odysseus and stable him out of town. Horses, he had assured her, were more memorable than men, for horses were to be coveted if they could reasonably be expected to run a few kilometers without foundering.

"Your skin is brown against the white—darker than I realized."

"Dark enough to pass for an Arab?" He seemed to think the disguise a necessary game.

"Your eyes—so blue—"

"Some Arabs are blue-eyed. The Crusaders didn't take quite everything with them when they left the Holy Land."

He was well supplied with coins of the King and Guise, and hoped to learn if there had been inquiries for a gypsy traveling alone with three horses and a dog.

They had been moving south for several days, after leaving the encampment where they spent two days after the horseman had been killed. At last they had reached this land of his, of which she had yet only a glimpse. They were not near enough to see the sea.

These were the towns where he had spent much time from the ages of four and five, sometimes with other gypsy boys, sometimes with his stepfather, but often alone. He was confident there would be old acquaintances. She suspected, but did not ask, that he had also visited these same towns during the four years he lived with the Countess.

"There are men here I can trust," he had told her. "They think of me as one of them—above all they hate outsiders—men from the north—from the King's country."

Arabella heard this with a shocked surprise, and unexpectedly reverted to old loyalties. "They hate us? But why?"

Robert smiled. "Men from the north hate the southern provinces. You know that."

In another moment he would be gone, and she felt again that clutch of panic.

He is taking Odysseus. What if he's leaving me? He could solve everything only by going away from me. He would know where to hide in these seacoast towns if he were alone.

He smiled at her seriously, and perhaps read her mind quite well, for she was watching him eagerly, hungrily, as if she must forget nothing about him, should she not see him again.

He kissed her, gently disengaging her arms as they began to move about his neck, shaking his head to let her know this was not the time. The door shut, the lock snapped.

She heard him speak to Caliph, and as she ran to the window he mounted Odysseus with the swift leap which never failed to impress her high standards of horsemanship. They disappeared among the trees, and she waited, hoping for another glimpse of them, but at last turned away.

She picked up her favorite lute, sat beside the table with the instrument across her legs, and began to pluck at the strings, then to sing softly a favorite song of the troubadours—

a song of the north, sung for them at night in the Great Hall.

The music was not as distracting as she hoped, yet she continued to play. She had less fear that he was in danger, for she believed he had an uncanny instinct for sensing danger and protecting himself, than that the Countess might see him, for they must be near her husband's domain.

Not today, perhaps. Yet if they remained here, one day they might pass on the street and recognize each other.

He must be even more beautiful than he was four years ago. Of course he is—he was sixteen. Now he's twenty. He's a man, no longer a prediction, but a reality. She would want him more than ever.

And the gypsy?

He had told her that his life had depended so little upon others, he could not imagine jealousy. That was before he brought the young squire to her.

It was Arabella who depended upon him—not only for how he made her feel, but for her life. That was a heavy burden to have given a free man who had never anticipated that his freedom could be lost, much less willfully abandoned.

Yet whatever she might have said to him would have made no difference if he had not wanted her enough to take the chances he had understood so well that night in the forest.

Now, he was in hiding. Unless he found a way to get rid of her, he would have to remain in hiding the rest of his life. She knew as well as he did that the King's memory did not flag or forgive.

The northern song she had been singing changed. She had begun a song of the south, one he had taught her, a song of love, sorrow, renunciation, and as she sang, slowly and softly, the song seemed a prediction.

The Countess was a southerner. That was how she happened on to the gypsy encampment beside the sea. She had gone out to ride—no doubt looking for a small, safe adventure.

Like me. The first day I saw him. Women always prefer small, safe adventures—but Robert is not able to provide that. To be with him is to be in danger.

Yet if he met the Countess again, she would shelter him. Lies to her husband would be easy after four years. He was a troubadour, he spoke the language of the province, and he sang its songs.

Neither the King's nor Guise's emissaries would look for him with her. He could live in safety.

That Arabella would never leave him was not all she must consider. He could leave her—with some excuse of going to buy information, as he had done now—and never return. And if she should, somehow, find her way back to her own country, if her father should forgive her, she was no longer able to live as she had before, waiting for the future to happen. Small, safe adventures were no longer part of her character, if they ever had been.

I must give him that choice, to go to her, to find a way to send me back—to the King. After I've taken the potion.

The song trailed away, she fell silent, gazing at the silk carpet which covered the floor.

She set the lute aside.

He knew this as well as I did. He knew the danger of taking me with him long before I would admit there was danger. He knew it before he promised to be at the tournament and he kept that promise because of what he called the gypsies' peculiar sense of honor. If he wants to leave me—

She walked to the mirror, her confidant and ally.

Leave me? I don't think so.

When he opened the door she was still brushing her hair and wearing a long cloth-of-gold coat, sleeveless and opened down the front. She glanced around swiftly.

He gave her an answering glance as he passed her, hanging the burnoose on a hook, stepping out of the trousers and discarding the shirt and sandals and belt with its three

146

sheathed knives. He stood in the tub with his back to her, soaping his body, and she thought it best to wait.

He stepped out and turned, drying himself, running his hands through the curly blond hair, matted by the Arab headgear. He spoke softly, and she moved nearer. He might have been ashamed of the news he brought, for there was a slight ironic, angry smile. "Men were there, inquiring—less than two weeks ago. Three of them one day. Two another. They know who they want: a blond blue-eyed gypsy, driving a dark red wagon with three horses and a dog."

"No woman?"

"The King knows I would keep you out of sight, and he would never demean himself by admitting that he was looking for you."

"No. I'm incidental to his need for revenge. How does he want you?" She left the implication unspoken: dead or alive?

"They both want me, it seems. The King wants my head. Guise will be satisfied with my heart."

Arabella gave a quick outcry, then, seeing the look of warning, turned her back. "Maybe he will forget?" she suggested at last. "In time?"

"Do you believe that?"

"No. He never forgets even imagined insults. He will not tolerate having his power challenged."

"I knew that, too."

She went on, as if he had not spoken. "But I wasn't thinking of the King—that first morning when I saw you beside the campfire—looking straight at me as we rode toward you." She smiled a little, a tender, sorrowful joy on her face. "As if you had been expecting me for a long while. Had you?"

He turned away, getting into his clothes. "The animals need water and food. I'll be back soon." He went out.

Arabella continued combing her hair, and now and again peered through the slit in the curtain to see him carrying water, talking to Caliph in Romany, stroking his animals

147

with affection and a kind of confidentiality, as if they were all involved in the same conspiracy and understood the nature of it quite well.

When he opened the door she spoke his name in a clear steady voice, intended to command his attention. It did. He watched her carefully, with no change of expression.

"We're in the vicinity of the Countess's domain."

"I know that."

"You would be safe there."

"Yes."

"Then—go. Find someone to take me back. I can persuade the King to forgive me—at least not to—" She paused, looking away, for the anger on his face was different from any expression she had seen before. Something of contempt was in it, too.

"He won't kill me." She looked at him, her face as cold and unforgiving as his had become, as if this mutual predicament, this shared danger in their lives, had at last made them enemies. Then she smiled a little. "The Countess will have three or four children by now. Her belly will be streaked, and she won't be able to hold you inside as tightly as before. As I can." She laughed, a laugh which sounded strange even to her. All at once it stopped, for he was smiling without humor.

"You are barbarous, Arabella. No. I won't leave you. Don't talk of it again." He moved toward her, and the smile had changed, being now without anger, without challenge. He touched her breasts lightly, lingeringly. "That's all." He nodded toward the bed. "Now—lie down. I'm sorry, I'll try not to hurt you."

She lay on the edge of the bed and as he knelt before her, she braced her feet on his shoulders and closed her eyes against this painful daily invasion, which had never yet seemed to have any natural connection with the pleasures which had made it necessary.

As two fingers entered she gave a light sigh of pleasure, but then very slowly he probed deeper and his other hand pressed upon her belly. She clenched her teeth and all at once caught hold of his hair. He continued for what seemed an interminable time, probing, pressing, and when she thought she could endure it no longer, the pressure stopped, his fingers moved slowly outward, and he was stroking her, giving at last that quick turn of his knuckle which had made her gasp with astonished delight that first morning as she sat astride Solomon.

"I think so. A few more days."

He moved back, stripping away trousers and shirt, and was again kneeling before her, leaning across her body, kissing her mouth, stroking her hair, as if he longed to make some retribution for the pain he had caused, and the greater pain to come later. Her arms held his shoulders and her legs clasped his back, although he had not entered her.

"One day you must leave me," he said quietly. Her eyes shut in denial. "You must leave me when they find us. And they will."

"You won't let them."

Slowly he began to move into her. "Yes. They will. They will."

Then he was silent, entering her swiftly. He began to move at the remorseless pace which meant that his patience for this contest with himself had reached its limit of endurance. Arabella heard her voice, a sound of near delirium; her fists pounded his back, and softly she begged him to make this first time last a long while. Then, as often as he wanted, however he wanted, for as long as they had energy and will.

⬛ CHAPTER EIGHTEEN ⬛

Arabella awoke with a sudden alarm. The curtains on one side of the wagon had been pulled back and brilliant sunlight filled the wagon. The gypsy was not there.

She went to the window, and looking out caught her breath sharply, afraid the vision would disappear. It did not, and spread beneath her, some distance away, shone the blue sea.

She began to laugh with joy and some mysterious sorrow, as if she had come to the end of a very long journey and discovered there what she had hoped but not dared expect to find.

The gypsy was currying Saracen. She had gone to bed near daylight, having ridden Saracen to this new encampment.

He turned, and all at once gave her that free magical smile, which had filled her with wonder when she first saw it.

He unlocked the door. "Come outside—wait—" He took a burnoose from a hook and wrapped it about her, leaped the three feet to the ground and lifted her down. They stood together, Arabella breathing deeply the heavy rich fragrances of this southland, so different from the smells of the trees and flowers and grasses of her early life.

"There it is," she whispered. "Your sea. This is what you've told me about. This is the land you love."

She moved here and there, smelling a flower, plucking a great red bell and fixing it behind one ear, running her hands across the wet grass, and came back to him, her eyes shining. "How beautiful it all is. New trees, new flowers, new smells. All of it—somehow like you." He was watching her, smiling, but once again there was that slight sadness in his eyes, his knowledge of what she had yet to endure.

If only I could make a gesture, vanquish that look from his face forever. Make him as he was before he knew me.

For several minutes they stood silently, gazing toward the flashing water.

"The traveler said the water is like silk on the skin—like no other anywhere on earth—" She looked at him eagerly. "We'll go in tonight?"

He glanced at her, and although she knew he was about to tell her it was dangerous, this country more populated than the northern forests through which they had traveled, she would not tell him what she was thinking: Each day was one day fewer when she could be certain of going into the sea, of making love, of doing anything at all.

She did not doubt his skills, but neither had she any longer the conviction that her life was a gift nothing could take away.

"Tonight," he agreed. "Late. We'll ride down on Odysseus and Saracen. A single gypsy wagon near the sea would attract attention."

He had, she knew, come to hate the perpetual caution as much as she did. Perhaps more. And but for her, he would not be thinking in terms of caution.

"Come, let's have something to eat. I must leave you for a while."

He lifted her to the wagon doorway, then leaped up and stood beside her, turning the lock.

She had long ago stopped resenting locked doors, realizing that there was no countryside which, however empty it looked, was necessarily unpopulated. And although it seemed impossible anyone could penetrate Caliph's patrol, the gypsy's forethought was unfailing.

"Leave me? Again?"

They sat across the table, eating remnants of yesterday's food, bread and cheese, drinking clear, fresh water, looking at each other with the careful concentration which occurred whenever they were face to face.

Arabella had thrown aside the burnoose, slipping a sleeveless red silk coat over her naked body, and now he reached across, closed his hand over one breast and clasped it gently, his thumb caressing the nipple. He pressed a little harder and she knew what he was waiting for: the day when that thin fluid would flow.

He pressed a little more firmly, and after a few moments, as his hand carefully manipulated her breast, she began to feel a wetness, but did not look down.

"What do you feel?" she asked.

"I'm not sure."

"I am."

"Another day or two."

"Robert—" She leaned forward. "Promise me that when it's time you won't tell me the night before."

"I won't—I wouldn't have. Come here, Arabella."

She went to him and he took her between his legs, while his mouth closed over her nipples, sucking gently, then harder. Arabella brought herself down slowly astride him, but all at once he moved her away and in two quick strides had backed her against the bed where she lay as he knelt, moving into her swiftly, moving more and more swiftly until presently she heard a low sound of pleasure.

Last night and once again, each encounter ended more quickly, and now he slipped away. He stood looking down at her, smiling a little, shaking his head slowly in a kind of disbelieving wonderment. "Well—"

She lay on one side, comfortable and luxurious as a cat, smiling. "Well?"

"I heard news of a gypsy encampment—I want to find out exactly where it is. I'd rather that we be there—" She understood that he would rather be there when he gave her the medicine.

He walked to the back of the wagon, and she followed him. She wanted to ask how long he would be away, but since he had no more idea than she, said nothing, only touched his hair as he slipped on the burnoose, then covered his head and turned to kiss her. But after a few moments he stepped away, disengaging her arms.

"Arabella, this is something we must know about. We must." He pulled the curtains together. "Keep them that way. There are more people in this part of the world."

She pushed aside the curtain only enough to see him galloping away on Odysseus, without a glance or wave, only a few parting words in Romany to Caliph, who watched him, then began his routine of pacing around the wagon, pausing to sniff the air, alert to sounds she could not hear, following the overhead flight of birds too high for her to see. Ptolemy and Saracen, on long tethers, had fed and found a shady place to lie.

After gazing for some time toward the sea, she adjusted the curtain and went to look at herself in the mirror, discarding the coat and gazing at her breasts, as if their increased size, the tracery of blue veins, could answer once and for all the question of whether she must drink the potion.

Or perhaps the question had been answered.

The night before, as he examined her, she had watched his face, and after several minutes had seen an expression in his eyes, a look of concern and conviction. She had asked no questions.

And this morning, had there been any of that fluid she had been told would appear around the end of the third month of pregnancy?

With an irresistible curiosity she pressed one breast gently with her hands, and in a few moments a fluid like a tear ran from her nipple.

Arabella released herself quickly. "Oh!" But then, not convinced, pressed the other breast and soon there came a seeping fluid. She grimaced and turned away, faintly queasy. "Ugh." She dipped a cloth in the tub and wiped herself carefully.

Of course that's why he wants to be near the gypsy camp.

Not, she believed, because he expected to need help, but because they would have to remain in one place for several days. She trusted him to take care of her, and did not doubt he would perform those responsibilities as efficiently as he did everything else the gypsies had taught him.

"Every gypsy child," he had said, "is taught the gypsy lore of medicine. We learn to cure the afflicted with herbs and potions, to produce abortions and deliver babies, to amputate a finger or a leg. And how to kill in secrecy and silence. We must be able to care for ourselves. Outsiders won't touch us."

When she had bathed and combed her hair, painted her lids and palms and the soles of her feet, she rummaged in one of the chests and brought out a pair of crimson silk Turkish pantaloons, a thin silk shirt, and a green vest embroidered with pearls.

Taking up the lute she sat beside the table, bent her head, and plucked a few random notes—gypsy music, strange music, melancholy and defiant, with a profound sensuality.

She tried to guess how far he had ridden these past three or four hours and when he would be back. She was careful not to draw the curtain far enough to attract Caliph's brisk attention, but could not resist gazing toward the glistening water, thinking of what it could be like when she immersed herself in it, floated upon it, as the travelers had told them could be easily done, so long as one did not struggle.

It would be, she decided, something like that first morning when the gypsy had made love to her. She remembered the night before, trying to imagine what would happen between them the next day—as now she tried to imagine what it would be like to give herself up to the water, plunge into it naked, invite it to invade her body.

Her imagination failed, as it had failed that night, thinking of the gypsy while she lay motionless staring into the dark, waiting.

Now I have him. And there's nothing more I want. Once this terrible medicine is over and done—once we can stop fearing the King and Guise.

A thought occurred which caused her to set the lute aside and begin peering from each window for sight of him. It was late afternoon and the wagon was so hot that a film of moisture covered her face and body.

The Countess.

Love is jealous, he had told her. And jealousy closes the world.

It does.

It has.

If only he had made up some lie to explain where he had been—or said he had lived with the gypsies until he was sixteen.

But then—how would he have explained where all this came from?

The wagon, with its silk Persian carpets, its swagged cloth-of-gold ceiling, its silk sheets and gold and jeweled goblets and plates; the chests filled with embroidered skirts and coats and vests; jewels for the neck and ears and ankles. The walnut-sized emerald between her breasts. A fortune was there, nothing less. No lie would have explained all this, and she would have continued to insist upon the truth until she had it.

He says he will never leave me, and I must believe him. But he could die because of me—if we are unlucky one day or night—

155

She heard a sound and moved the curtain. He was riding fast, so swiftly that Odysseus was foaming. He slid down, tethered Odysseus, the lock snapped, and he was there. Not with the Countess after all.

I'll never think of that again.

And he was smiling, the same free wholehearted smile he had given her earlier that day. "The camp isn't far. Two nights' journey, more or less."

◈ CHAPTER NINETEEN ◈

It was a little after midnight when they set off down the steep hillside path, not the one the wagon had traveled, but rock-strewn and heavily wooded, difficult even for Saracen and Odysseus.

Arabella listened soberly, scarcely able to concentrate upon the strictures he outlined, absorbed in her deceitful plan of going into the water naked despite his warning of possible encounters with strangers who, in this part of the world, never slept, day or night.

No, she would not ride ahead of him. Yes, when they got there she would walk Saracen, not gallop him, on the beach. Yes, she would return to the wagon without argument when he told her they must.

He had also told her that his plan was not to drive into the gypsy camp the first night they arrived but stop on the periphery. The next morning he would go in alone, well supplied with gold coins, to introduce himself and explain the reason for his need of protected privacy for a few days, the need for hot food, and the greatest need of all: lies. No one answering to his description was or had been there— should inquirers pass through.

She did not like to hear of these meticulous plans.

Two more days. Two more nights. Some hours in the encampment. And then the time would come. She had two or three days left of freedom, and a life she could depend upon to be hers.

She was not convinced she would be able to expel the invader from her body, potion or no, and despite a guilty suspicion that this thought was disloyal to the gypsy, she could not think of the tiny growing creature in any other way. A usurper of Arabella's freedom and perhaps her life.

But she would not tell him she expected that once the process began so also would begin her last few hours of life. She pretended there would be nothing but the usual cramps, somewhat more blood, and that in a day or two she would be Arabella again.

While he had been making the horses ready, she had remained in the wagon, and with a monk's cloak wrapped about her had slipped off the Persian trousers and shirt and vest, covered her head with the hood and was out the door and astride Saracen while he was locking the door.

They proceeded in silence, the horses swaying slowly with the uneven path which was occasionally lost. The closer they came to the sea where they could hear its murmurous sounds, the faster her heart beat.

What can it possibly be that is as exciting as I'm imagining? I feel almost as I do when he's about to make love to me. What would it be like to do it in the water?

But of course, once he saw her spring away from him and plunge into the sea naked, the best she could hope for was a few minutes, diving beneath the surface to hide before he caught her and sent her back.

At last they reached the bottom of the hill and he began to ride a little faster, although he did not summon her to come abreast of him, only glanced around now and then, keeping a watch for other travelers.

The sea was still, the waves touched the rock-strewn shore with light sounds. Arabella followed obediently, watching the sea, breathing the air deeply, taking it into her lungs as if it had some life-giving force, then opened the front of the cloak to let the warm air flow over her body.

He glanced around, saw her in the bright moonlight, and reined in his horse. With a triumphant laugh, Arabella kicked

Saracen in the ribs with both feet, lay flat along his back and neck, urging him to run, run as fast as he could, and flashed by the gypsy without a word, a glance, a wave of farewell.

But not for long. He did not call out, for he had warned her that whatever happened they must not speak, and that if they should encounter anyone she was to follow him, whichever direction he took, without question or delay.

She did not look back but continued to kick at Saracen, urging him faster and faster, and heard Odysseus gaining.

Exultant with joyous apprehension, she hauled Saracen to an abrupt stop, hanging onto his mane so that she would not slide down his back, and contrived the maneuver so unexpectedly that Odysseus had galloped past her as she dismounted, throwing the cloak aside and running toward the sea.

Whether it would prove deep or shallow, warm or cold, she did not know, and then she was splashing into the water, surprised at first by its chill, then all at once ecstatically engulfed, sunk beneath her depth, making the movements of spreading her arms and pumping her legs as he had instructed.

The sensation on her skin, the water seemingly rushing in to fill her body, was embracing as she had not imagined. She gave herself up to it with joyful abandon.

When she saw him he was only a few feet away, running to plunge headlong into the water with great strokes, coming toward her.

As if they had agreed to play a game she laughed aloud and moved away from him as quickly as she could, delighting in the water's pools of warmth and coldness, the gentle motion of the waves. He was near enough that he could soon catch hold of her, and she dove beneath the waves, keeping submerged until her lungs seemed ready to burst, emerged to take a new gasp of air, and felt her feet upon the sand. There he was, reaching for her as she moved away, at a maddeningly slow pace, for the water dragged at her, as if to make her its captive.

"A little longer," she whispered, "a little longer." How many times had she made that plea, in another kind of restless bed.

All at once he had hold of her arm, a firm hold, and then was carrying her out of the water, her body clasped against his wet shirt and trousers, while Arabella threw both arms about his neck, begging, "Take me in there—in the water. I want to know what it would be like. Please, please—"

He set her on the rocky beach, gave her a light slap on the buttocks, but as he went to retrieve her monk's cloak she had eluded him again and was astride Saracen, starting up the hillside at a gallop, wet hair blowing and tangling around her face and neck.

She galloped on. In a moment she heard Odysseus's hoofbeats, and while Saracen struggled to make his swift treacherous climb, she clung to his mane with both fists, encouraging him with the same endearments she used when she stroked him at night. And still the gypsy had not called or spoken.

Is he angry? Will he punish me? He can only forbid me to go into the water again. Surely he knew what would happen. How could he have expected anything else?

At the wagon she slipped off Saracen's back and stood waiting for him to arrive a few seconds later, to unlock the door, and climbed in before he could help her. She stood rubbing her wet hair with a woolen cloth and heard the door slam. She backed away and heard him stripping off his wet clothes. They could not see each other.

All at once she laughed. "Now—whatever happens—I know what the sea is like. It's as the traveler told us. It feels like silk on the skin. It's glorious." That was the word the gypsy had used the first morning to describe what he would do to her if he came again the next day. He came no nearer, and she stood still. There was a long moment of silence, before she asked softly, "Are you angry?"

She felt him move nearer. "I've never been angry with you. You mistake concern for anger."

"We can't spend the rest of our lives being concerned."

"If we hope to stay alive, we must."

Their bodies came gently together, as if by some calculated prearrangement in the dark, and her arms went around his shoulders, her mouth against his neck. "The sea is possessive," she told him, as if at some remarkable discovery. "It would have liked to drown me."

With a deft motion he pressed the back of her knee and eased her to the floor. Still holding him with both arms she gave a long shudder as he moved into her, retreated to her body's rim, and was back with a swift force. It seemed to her they had never left the sea, that their bodies were moving with the waves, flooded by each other.

Arabella remained passive, motionless, one arm thrown across her eyes, and with each lunging drive her body shuddered.

During the past three days, there had come a need so continual that the time he must spend with the animals, reconnoitering the countryside, traveling in search of news, created a deprivation more painful and serious than before. There was reassurance that the world held only when they came together with quick force, near to rage springing from nowhere, as if each were determined that this time they would appease for that clawing urgency.

He finished swiftly, and drew away. Arabella closed her legs to preserve the deep throbbing in her belly, and her hand stroked his back, for he was sitting up, his head bowed, one hand run through his wet hair. Whatever he was thinking he was not going to tell her.

Presently he got up, lifted her to her feet, and lighted a candle. He took hold of her arm and turned her to face him, narrowing his eyes, looking at her with that searching expression she had seen frequently, as if he would know once and finally the components which had gone to making this young being he had in his care.

Just as quickly he let her go, the riddle solved or not, she had no idea. No better solved, she supposed, than she had solved the riddle of what it was composed the gypsy she had been with for three months, most of the summer; even though she could no longer remember having ever lived without him.

Somehow I must have known he was there that morning Maria and I and the others went galloping over to inquire what news a gypsy might have for us. Not much, I supposed, until we drew near enough to see what he looked like.

Her first response had been astonishment.

He exists? This man exists? Let me look at him more closely.

Now he gestured and she knew it had come around again, the time for that daily examination, since he had gone off that morning without having performed it. The last two or three days the probes had not been so prolonged, nor so painful—as if he had, finally, found what he had known he must one day discover.

She lay on the edge of the bed with her eyes shut, drew in a deep breath, and his fingers pressed into her, the palm of his other hand probing low on her belly with steadily increasing pressure. Then it was over. She sat up, giving him a quick inquiring glance, but he stood and went out to make his final nightly survey of their surroundings.

Arabella rinsed the salt water from her face, thought of how she must wash the salt from her hair the next day, and told herself in despair that once it was over, this ordeal of the potion, he would never want her again.

Looking into the mirror and finding a sorrowful expression she shook her head to dismiss the thought. She had learned that about him long ago. Whatever was animal or human was an inevitable part of the world, causing him no disgust, no dismay, no rebellion that things had not been otherwise ordered.

It will make no difference to him, once it's done.

But to me? How will I feel about myself?

Would she feel what she had taken for granted for as long as she could remember, perhaps since the first page had touched her with wonder and delight—that she was always and to everyone a woman of an unquestionable desirability.

He came in, smiled and nodded, as if to signal that the night was quiet, the world in order. He blew out the candle and lay upon the bed, flat on his back, as she knelt above him, felt his hands take firm hold of her breasts and slowly urge her body downward, until he had filled her. She heard herself give a gasping sob, then began to cry bitterly as they moved together, swiftly and eagerly, as if to be done and then, as quickly as might be, to begin again.

❧ CHAPTER TWENTY ❧

For two nights they moved closer to the gypsy encampment, and each night, as gaily as if no ordeal waited at the end of this journey, Arabella rode for three or four hours, slept soundly, and woke in Robert's arms, after he had found a place for them to remain secure during the day.

She was dismayed when he had told her of the need for a purgative before the abortifacient—to be administered in heavy wine so that when it took effect she would be less conscious of what was happening.

"I'll be with you. And the purgative will do its work with no help from you. In a few hours, you'll awake and wonder if it was a hideous dream."

She had looked away.

And while it's happening—you will have to take care of me. Someone was always with my brothers or sisters when they were—

She grimaced with incredulous disgust that now this ugliness must be his responsibility. "You will hate me after this. You'll think of it every time you look at me."

He had smiled, shaking his head in wonderment. "How little you think I can bear."

He awakened her in the early-morning darkness, standing beside the bed, extending to her a goblet: "Drink this."

The wine had been strong, strong enough to mask the taste of the purgative, strong enough that she had only a vague recollection that once she had swallowed it he had picked her up and carried her out of doors.

Later, when she tried to awaken, she found it difficult to come out of a drunken stupor. At last she opened her eyes to see him seated beside the bed, watching her with a look of tender concern. No disgust, no contempt. Perhaps it had not happened.

Perhaps he had not carried her out of doors—she had not squatted naked over that hole dug in the ground, groaning as the pains stabbed again and again, the entire contents of her bowels exploding in one liquid stinking burst after another. Was that what had happened? Yes.

She closed her eyes, ashamed. She sighed with humiliated resignation, and felt tears of pity for herself streaming from the corners of her eyes.

"Arabella—" His voice was gentle, as if not to disturb her.

After a few moments she spoke slowly. "I feel as if my head had turned to stone. A stone that aches. Whatever you gave me—my God, the wine, I remember that—" She looked at him. "Is it over? Is it gone? Am I rid of it?"

She had become aware that although she was naked and the white silk sheet drawn only to her waist, she was clean. He had washed away all traces of the effect of the purgative, and her body was perfumed. He ran one hand across her hair.

"No, my darling. It isn't over."

All at once she remembered the tearing, ripping pains as she squatted there to let the purgative do its fierce work. She remembered crying out in protest at the pain while he knelt before her, holding her shoulders fast, and then remembered nothing more until this moment when she lay, looking at him pleadingly.

She had some vague sense of becoming briefly aware that the wagon was moving, leaving behind her scene of disgrace and foulness.

He had told her that after the purgative had done its

work, he would move to the outskirts of the encampment, where he had spent much of the day before with the gypsies, making arrangements for their stay.

She sat up slowly, found that her head throbbed and the stone remained inside it. She had expected it would disappear, that it was an illusion. Perhaps it was real.

He took a few steps to the back of the wagon and returned holding one of the golden goblets of the kind from which they had drunk the first glass of wine, and every glass of water or wine since then. Now, it looked like a menacing chalice, containing not the end of her pregnancy, but the end of her life.

"It's time. You must drink this."

"So soon? Can't I wait?"

"No. Drink it now."

He had told her there would be little wine in this. Nothing but the potion itself. And he had warned her that the agony must be endured without any palliative. She must be able to push hard, expel everything inside her. When it was over, he would give her laudanum, the pain would end and she would sleep, remembering nothing later. All those promises seemed neither truthful nor important as she looked at the goblet.

"I don't think I can drink it—so soon."

"It's been four hours. You must."

She took the goblet, reaching for it slowly, holding it with both hands between her breasts, looking down into the slightly reddened color of the liquid.

After several moments, unable to make the decision, she said softly: "I kept hoping something would happen. But now that it's time—I don't want to give him up." She continued gazing into the liquid, as if she might find reflected there what would happen to her once she drank it.

"Drain it quickly, all at once. It is bitter."

"I know. I must. We must."

She glanced at him swiftly as she raised the goblet, and saw him make a furtive sign of the cross. She tasted it, more bitter than she had expected, tipped her head back and drained it in a few gulps, then tossed the goblet onto the floor and covered her face with both hands. "There. It's done. Now—"

She gave him a swift accusing glance as he knelt beside her, and there was a slight scornful smile as she repeated his gesture of the sign of the cross. "When was the last time you did that? Outside of church?"

He glanced away, embarrassed, although the gypsies professed the religion of whatever country they were living in. "Never."

She stared at him accusingly. Memories of pleasure did not occur. Only the past few hours of shame and suffering, and the hours yet to come of greater shame and greater suffering.

"What do I do now?"

"Wait."

"For how long?"

"Not very long."

They fell silent, watching each other carefully, as she continued to sit on the edge of the bed, staring at him. Finally she closed her eyes, found that the stone inside her head had been dissolved, and after some unknown time, several minutes, half an hour, all at once there came the first clenching cramp, low in her belly, and she gave a surprised outcry at having been taken by surprise. She bent over and pressed her hands against her belly, hoping to force the pain away. Instead, it grew stronger.

He took hold of her elbows, and although she began to protest he raised her slowly and carried her a few steps to where she saw, with a dull sense of dread, a birth-stool had been placed. As he helped her lower herself upon it, she noticed with bitter amusement that beneath it, waiting for the blood and that product of their hours together, was a familiar porcelain basin, a basin beautifully decorated with Arabic script, another prize brought from the Holy Land by some dead Crusader.

She sat, legs apart, knees high, bent forward, clutching her belly as another pain began to move inside her.

As if she had been through this before and knew what to do, she began to push with all the strength of her muscles, no longer concerned that her face was twisted, ugly with pain and despair, aware of nothing but the need to rid herself of what her body had treacherously hidden, a cocoon deep inside her which would grow and grow, until at last it came forth to make its clamor in the world, to hinder their freedom of movement, to let them be captured and killed. And it—the gypsy's child—killed with them.

As the pains swelled and diminished, as she pushed and strove, clenching her fists until the nails dug into her palms, through the pain, through the mighty effort she must make again and again, she heard her voice repeating: "Oh, Holy Mother of God, help me, save me, save me, help me—"

The pains came with increasing ferocity, causing her to clench harder at her belly in futile self-protection, until when she had begun to hope that she was pushing the intruder out, the pains subsided, leaving her strangely tranquil, uncaring.

Gathering strength from the interval, the pain clenched her again and she threw her head backward, eyes closed hard, while still the despairing words went on: "Save me, Mother of God, help me—"

She believed now that she was alone. She did not see him kneeling before her, holding her shoulders so that she would not fall, and all at once, after what seemed an endless time of pain and effort to rid herself of that internal incubus, she fell into sudden despair.

The pain ceased as her muscles ceased to work. Let it die inside me. Then I'll die, too. I can't do more than I have.

She opened her eyes and looked at him fiercely. "I can't do it. I won't do it. I'm going to die."

He stared at her steadily. "Again," he said softly. "Again. Harder. Harder. You must—" He gave her shoulder a light shake.

She closed her eyes, sighing, as once again the clenching pain began to gather, growing in strength. Her mouth pulled downward and the cords of her neck stood forth with the effort not to scream. All at once he shook her hard, then harder. Her head bobbed helplessly back and forth as he continued to shake her, for she had turned white and felt herself slipping toward unconsciousness, a cool wetness covering her face and body.

"With all your strength—" he commanded, and when she looked at him his face seemed to reflect the expression of crazed desperation she felt on her own.

She yelled at him. "Let me go!"

All at once, with fierce determined intensity she clenched her muscles, clenched tighter and tighter, as if she could by force of will subdue the pain, and pushed downward, heavily downward.

Her head fell forward, resting upon his chest, then pushed hard against him.

Something inside her, everything inside her, dissolved in pain, and it seemed her guts began to pour out. She tried to reach between her legs to force whatever it was back inside, but his hand caught hers, and as he held her wrist she had a glimpse of her hand dripping blood, empty. She had not caught hold of it.

A sound as of churchbells rang in her ears, she heard herself give a pleading sob and then, with a distant sensation of having been granted freedom from her body, dropped into black, dense unawareness.

When she saw him next, and she had no idea if hours or days or possibly weeks had passed, she was lying in bed, the sheet drawn to her waist. She became aware of a warm wet bandage swathed about her hips and passing between her legs. She lay silent, eyes closed, hearing the soft sound of the lute, a low murmurous sound, as if he did not want to awaken her suddenly or, if she preferred to sleep, not to awaken her at all.

For some time she lay with her eyes closed, listening to the lute, and slowly became aware that there were other sounds, children playing, men's and women's voices, horses neighing, dogs barking, all of it taking place outside the hot wagon.

She knew now what had happened. She was free, they were both free. It had happened when she had thought it never could—and yet she was afraid to ask a direct question, afraid to find that perhaps all her guts had come out with whatever it was she had given up.

She began to tell herself that she must know, she must force herself to speak, to discover if it was possible to speak.

She turned her head and opened her eyes slightly, to find him watching her, his face serious, noncommittal, telling her nothing she wanted to know. He played for a few minutes longer but when she began trying to speak, he laid the lute on the floor and bent toward her from where he sat on the low stool.

Carefully, as if she might rebuff him, he touched her hair, the side of her face, and withdrew his hand. He smiled a little, as if to convey some silent message that all was well.

"It—happened?"

"It happened. Yes."

She was silent again, still afraid of the answers to any questions she might ask. When she found courage her voice was no longer a whisper, but still so low he bent near. "Was it all there? Complete?"

"Complete."

"Complete—" She repeated wonderingly. She tried to visualize what it might have looked like. A miniature human being. "Fingers—and toes—" She gazed at him questioningly.

"Yes."

She thought about that. Fingers and toes. It seemed a miracle that during those months she had been producing inside her, with no design on her part, that small creature which had been forced from her body against its will—very

170

much against its will or she could not have felt such pain. The creature had come forth complete, a head, legs, arms, fingers, and toes. There was another question, although it was some time before she could ask it.

"Was it a—"

"A male."

She looked away, and gave a light sigh. "Yes. I've always known it."

And now all that she could think of to call that uncompleted creation of theirs, which had given her more joy and more pain than she had imagined possible, was that dubious word of negation and contempt—"it."

"A male—"she repeated, looking not at him but at the cloth-of-gold ceiling. "Yours." She turned her head away, closed her eyes, and felt her throat tear with a protesting sob which remained silent.

It seemed she had known since the first suspicion that she was pregnant that what had been given her by him must be a male.

But a male no longer. No longer anything. A bloody amorphous pulp buried somewhere on the outskirts of this gypsy encampment, in some place she had not even seen. His country, his people, having nothing to do with who she was or who she had been before she knew him.

After several minutes she turned her head toward him. Tears continued to gather in her eyes and she touched them with her forefinger apologetically. What was there to cry about? It was over. They had made the decision because no other decision was possible. Now they might, after a few days, continue their fugitive travels.

"How long have I slept?"

"You've been sleeping for almost twenty-four hours. I awoke you twice to give you laudanum and some broth. You don't remember?"

She made a grimace. "I remember the laudanum—bitter. After that I remember only—dreams—beautiful colors—" She traced a vague pattern with one hand. "Moving, changing shapes, beautiful beautiful colors—" Her eyes closed slowly, hoping for a return of the colors. But then, as he began to stand, she spoke, without looking at him. "Don't go away. Please. Where are you going?"

"To get something for you to eat. It's time—"

"Not yet. I can't."

She was silent again, and he continued to stand motionless until all at once her eyes opened, large and black in her white face, and she gazed seriously and steadily at him, searching for courage for the next words.

"Will you ever want me again?"

His eyes narrowed quickly, as if at the painful flash of a bright light. She looked at him, feeling herself to have become irreparably ugly to this man who valued beauty as she did. Finally he said, "Yes." He added, reluctantly, "Of course. But you know that. That will never change."

She closed her eyes again. It was what she had known, perhaps since the night they had met in the forest. His love for her was not accepted as a benediction, but a threat. Still, he had no defense against it.

❧ CHAPTER TWENTY-ONE ❧

She awoke in darkness and for a few moments lay motionless, wondering where she was, who was with her. With difficulty she awakened further, and that brought a sense of bewilderment and a beginning fear. Slowly she moved her hand across the bed, and touched nothing.

He's gone. He's left me, now that I'm rid of—whatever it was that came out of me.

She experimented with trying to speak and her voice asked pleadingly, "Robert?" She did not expect an answer.

Then he was sitting on the bed beside her, kissing her face, holding her consolingly in his arms. "A bad dream?"

"A dream? I suppose. But I couldn't find you. I reached for you and you weren't there—"

He kissed her mouth gently. "Go to sleep. I was sleeping beside the bed—on a pile of carpets. It's comfortable, and I didn't want to disturb you by moving. There. Sleep."

"Without you? How can I?"

He stroked her forehead slowly, saying that the laudanum still held claim over her, and she fell asleep magically, slipping into drowsiness from which she tried to tell him something, failed, and disappeared into a deadened slumber. He had given her a few sips of the bitter laudanum last time she awakened, for the cramps were still active.

The next morning, telling her she had slept for most of thirty-six hours, he went to bring food.

In the distance she heard the early-morning sounds of the encampment, voices calling, an occasional verse of song in a high quavering female voice, laughter and shouts of children, horses and dogs, and the sounds were comforting. She lay waiting for her belly to clench at her again with one of those final spasms of resentment at the treatment the medicine had put her muscles through, but felt nothing.

At last she got up, very carefully, as if moving about, crossing the floor, were all new arts to learn. She felt light as a cat, and seemed to have little control over what her muscles did. She was relieved that they were able to act without instruction, for although the heavy effects of drugged sleep were nearly gone, she was neither alert nor confident.

She knelt beside the tub of fresh water to wash her face and scrub her teeth, routines which he had obviously performed for her several times.

The bandage was still swathed about her hips and between her legs, a somewhat artistic creation she might have thought, had it served a different purpose, but she found with relief there was little blood, which was almost dry. It had been changed while she slept. How many times? The others were buried somewhere.

He's had to do everything for me, as if I were the newborn baby—not the one we did away with.

How could he have brought himself to do it?

But if something had happened to him?

I would have done whatever was necessary.

It was impossible to imagine him helpless, sick, damaged. He had been made to some standard of perfection, and was meant to stay that way.

Drying her face she looked into the mirror and saw her skin white, her black eyes too large, and although there was no vivacity, what had happened a day and a half ago had not changed in any essential the way she looked.

You're still Arabella. He will love you again—when he can.

174

There seemed no urgency. The prospect was remote.

Out of some self-consciousness, because of the bandage, she found the cloth-of-gold coat, wrapped it around her and tied it with a red silk cord depending long silk tassels.

During the day he came and went, advising her to sleep as much as she could—without the help of laudanum, and told her the wagon was being repainted that day and she was to keep the curtain securely closed. Dark red, black, and purple, this time, like three others in the encampment.

Yes, there had been inquiries here a few weeks ago.

"A few?"

"Three or four. Don't think about it. Don't think about anything but yourself."

She gave a soft uncertain laugh. "Myself. Just now, I'm not sure who that is."

"You will be." They had finished eating and he stood, then bent to kiss her mouth lightly. "A few days. You're very strong, Arabella."

The next night, as it was growing dark, he covered her with the monk's cloak and hood and they went out so that she could see the newly painted wagon and make her acquaintance with the animals again.

Odysseus and Ptolemy and Saracen, and finally Caliph, had been taken away separately, each for two or three hours that day, and although she did not ask, she imagined they had returned slaked and well gratified, a condition which might have to last them for some time.

She stroked them, talked to them, and laughed aloud when several children drew shyly near, speaking to her in Romany. The gypsy bantered with them for a few minutes, then dismissed them, and they went obediently.

They walked a little longer, and she was surprised to find that she was weaker than she had expected, so they returned to the wagon.

"How far are we from the sea?"

"About eleven kilometers."

"When I'm well—can I go in the water again? I'll promise not to do what I did before."

"Of course you can. But not for another five or six days."

Five or six days meant that he considered she would not be fit for any kind of activity which made a demand upon her strength and endurance, and that meant another five or six days before he would make love to her. She was surprised at the relief she felt to know her energy and resilience would not be tested.

Still, enough vitality had returned that her need for the reassurance of his body began to assert itself slowly and tentatively, and they watched each other carefully most of the time they were together.

Looking at him earlier that day, working with the animals, joking with two dark little gypsy boys, she had at last turned from the window.

When we finally can, will I remember what to do?

What difference does it make what I remember? He will know how much he can give me, and whether or not I can give him anything in return.

The next morning early he left to ride Odysseus to the nearest town, the first such absence since she had taken the abortifacient five days before.

He wore the clothes he had worn in some variation almost every day since she had first ridden to his encampment— faded blue linen Turkish trousers, pushed up on his calves, faded striped cotton shirt, open to the waist, the wide braided belt of soft red leather holding three sheathed knives, without which he never left their camp, and seldom even the wagon, and leather sandals on his bare feet.

It was what most men wore when they were not dressed as knights, squires, monks, or Arabs from across the sea. Nothing about it to attract attention, she thought, since these trips gave her inevitable qualms, but for his manner of standing, moving, sitting his horse, the graceful power of

176

body, the blond hair and clear blue eyes, the look of command which drew alert attention from men and women alike. There was no means by which he could hope for near-invisibility, to pass as one more man in a crowded street of men; and cloaks, whether a monk's or an Arab's, made no difference, since those men neither walked nor rode nor moved their bodies with the same fluent rhythm.

She smiled wistfully. "Everyone will say: Who is that? Where did he come from? Just as all of us did that first morning."

He kissed her briefly and carefully, stroking one breast, his hand enclosing it for a moment. Then he left quickly. Perhaps an idea had occurred which it seemed best not to consider.

And as she watched him mount Odysseus and start off at the usual swift canter, the same idea occurred to her, but did not persist.

The sun was not yet high, and finding that she was still half asleep she fell presently into deep sleep, that curative sleep which he encouraged, but no longer prompted by laudanum or wine.

The day passed in a somnolent dream, between sleeping, bathing, eating, occasional attacks of panic for his safety or—once again—his possible defection to the Countess, that fear she had supposed gone forever.

She washed her hair and bathed, relieved that the bandage was no longer needed, applied the cosmetics and smiled to see Arabella glow again, dressed in a low-hung silk Turkish skirt, transparent silk blouse, and short vest, the emerald between her breasts.

I look as if he could do anything to me. But he can't. Not yet.

She was seated late in the afternoon beside the window, plucking at the lute and singing a soft gypsy lament, singing words in Romany he had taught her even though she could remember little of what they meant, when he came gallop-

177

ing toward the wagon, gesturing to various children, dismounted quickly, and ran to the wagon. His manner announced that he brought news.

Arabella looked at him quickly, set the lute aside, and stood, but had some fear of asking what he had learned: Were they safe? Was there danger? Were they still being sought? She dreaded the answers, and preferred to wait for them.

He nodded, as in reply to some unspoken question, unbuckled the belt and put it aside, and bent to wash the dust from his hands and face. Then he turned and looked at her, half-smiling, as if the news he brought was not so very serious, after all. Perhaps he was growing impatient with bad news, or the foreboding of it.

"It seems they're deployed north, east, south, and west."

"Oh." Arabella gave a sigh, closed her eyes, shaking her head slowly, and sat down. "You talked to many men?"

"Yes. And they all told me the same thing. They weren't lying. And they didn't want money. They think the men from the north have no right to invade their land with their feuds against one of their countrymen." He sat on a stool near her, leaning slightly forward, knees widespread and elbows on his knees, his hands falling loosely between them. "When we leave here—as soon as it's safe for you to travel, another day or two—we'll reverse direction. Back toward the east. That's where the biggest towns are and we might be harder to find in or near a city. They might least expect us there."

Arabella watched him silently, trying to keep her face expressionless, but there was a sick despair at the pit of her stomach. No relief, no release, no moment free of fear.

He went on, speaking in a low reasonable voice, as if discussing not their lives but a projected outing to view a new terrain they might enjoy. "Or, of course—they might think a city the most likely place for us to hide." He smiled, as if all this had become a matter of indifference. "Since we

178

can't know—we can only try. I know Marseilles well. Every street and byway. If they can find us there—they can find us anywhere." He took her hand and held it gently, stroking the palm, gazing at it reflectively. After some time he asked: "Arabella?"

At last she said, not accusingly, but in a tone of wondering dismay: "You've always known this. You said it would be possible for me to save my life—but that nothing could save yours. And yet you let me come." He looked at her, his eyes moving slowly over her face, her body, then back to meet her straight stare again. "Why?"

"I've told you why. I wanted you. I thought I had a good chance to outrun them." He stood, impatiently pacing the length of the wagon two or three times, and turned quickly. "Arabella, listen to me—and then, no more discussions. I lied to myself, yes. But then, I have always cared very much about living, and I think not much about dying. I made the choice most consistent with the rest of my life. There's nothing more I can tell you."

He stood before her while she continued to sit, looking up at him, more filled with fear and doubt than ever before. At last she said softly, "We've been gone three months and a few days. I would have thought—" She hesitated, unable to refer to the man who pursued them as her father. "I would have thought the King and Guise would have given up the search."

Robert smiled slightly. "Such men do not give up the need for revenge. Did you ever know the King to forgive an enemy—real or imaginary?"

She looked away. "No. I suppose I thought once he understood I was not coming back, he would let me go. I was treated differently from my brothers and sisters."

After a time he squatted on his heels before her and took firm hold of her wrists, saying: "Arabella, look at me. Listen to me. If we are found—when we are found—no, no protests, listen. When we are found—you must leave me—

run to them and convince them you didn't go of your own will. The King will believe you, or pretend to. That's what he needs to believe. Promise me."

She twisted out of his hands and he let her go easily. They stood and faced each other. "But when they see you? Is it likely he will believe I didn't go of my own will?" She smiled.

"They won't see me." He was looking at her incredulously, unable to comprehend her refusal to accept what was inevitable. "Don't you understand that? They won't see me. The King won't."

"Maybe," she agreed, thinking of the Countess.

"No. Not because I will leave you. There will be nothing left of me to see. Nothing recognizable, at least."

She stared at him, trying to see the picture he had shown her, then gave a high uncanny cry, descending down the scale to a sob, and threw herself upon her hands and knees, pounding the floor with her fists, screaming, "No, no, no, no, no—"

⊛ CHAPTER TWENTY-TWO ⊛

Arabella awoke to find him asleep beside her. They had left the encampment two days before, and by traveling at night and remaining secluded during the day, had retraced their course.

It was still early, probably not later than seven, she guessed. She got up carefully, making sure not to disturb him, and peeked between the drawn leather curtains to see the animals on long tethers, cropping the grass which grew along a narrow stream, Caliph nearby in his perpetual stance of distrustful watchfulness. She returned to the bed and stood looking down at him.

Eight days. It happened eight days ago. I'm well. I'm strong. And he still treats me as if I'll break into little pieces if he touches me.

During the past two days, as her need for him increased, he continued to insist "a few more days."

"How many more days?" she had demanded the night before, when they were about to begin traveling. "Anything," she pleaded. "Anything at all. Do something to me. Let me do something to you. I cannot endure this complete separation from you any longer."

For the past two days he had caressed her body, and when she took him into her mouth he made no objection, though he was able to prevent her from forcing that final pleasure from him. At the end she looked at him helplessly.

"You don't want it?"

"Wait a little. We mustn't do anything that will make it more difficult for you."

"But this is making it more difficult for me."

Now, looking down at him, lying on his back, legs apart, slightly engorged, which was how he slept, as if his body prepared itself even during sleep, or perhaps his dreams prepared him, she began to feel an ache of longing, more intense than she had felt since that morning eight days before when he had awakened her with the offered goblet.

What had followed, the agonizing cramps she had expected would kill her before she produced that prize of love which must be expelled from their lives, seemed so remote it might never have happened.

She looked at him with helpless longing—the light curls of blond hair across his chest, in his armpits, a thicket about his groin—and at last lay beside him, clasped him gently with her hand and began to move her hand upon him, feeling the quick throbbing life, looking down into his eyes as they opened, then filled with light and pleasure. His arms went about her eagerly and, with one of those maneuvers accomplished so quickly she was never quite sure how it happened, her legs were apart, his body lowered upon her, and he entered slowly, gently, then stopped.

Her arms surrounded him, and her hands in his hair pulled his head backward so that she could look at him. He was moving carefully, while her legs clasped his back and she tried to force herself closer to him. But she could bring him no deeper, for he held her motionless.

The slow luxurious movements, inside her a small distance, manipulating her with his fingers, then entering her again, a little deeper, soon produced almost the same greedy desire of their most violent encounters.

Whenever she looked at him, his eyes were closed, either the better to concentrate on his own sensations or the better to control his needs for deeper penetration, swifter and harder movements. Now and then she made a quick movement, but he held her fast while he went slowly into her and out again, sucking her breasts until he had lulled her into a languid acceptance of this much pleasure and no more.

Some time had passed before he moved away, went to the window, and sliding the curtains aside saw the full-shining sunlight.

"It's near midmorning."

Arabella lay with her chin upon her arms, her body full of warmth and gratification, and smiled at him. "At last I feel alive again."

He closed the shutters and stood beside her, and she took hold of his hand. "Come back to me. I feel as if I'd been without you for all the time since the world began."

"Later—"

She sat up, taking her hair in both hands and lifting it above her head, stretching, then realizing that he was dressed, ready to go out the door, she sprang up, alarmed at the prospect of having him leave.

What he had told her three days before was there every moment, and she maintained a running fight with herself not to speak of it, not to think of it. Yet every time he left, even while they had been in the encampment, she had felt a sick sensation of danger, something which brought her near panic.

"You're going?"

He laughed. "Of course. We need food. The animals need attention."

Arabella went to the window to watch him, and when he disappeared, having saluted each of the horses and explained his errand to Caliph, she closed the curtain. All at once she was filled with a sense of life and energy, realized that she was hungry—found only an orange and a piece of cheese—and set to work to bathe and refurbish Arabella and to make up the bed, the only chore she had been found competent to perform.

When he came back she was dressed in a new combination of jeweled silks, decorated with henna and kohl, and sat playing the lute, singing one of the songs the troubadours had sung in the Great Hall, a song of love and renunciation which had always seemed to her ridiculous, although very pretty for its melody. Renunciation of anything had never suited Arabella's philosophy.

I had the beliefs without any idea of what it could mean if I took them seriously. Well—I took them seriously. Here I am.

She looked up, smiling joyously as he entered, and went to take one of the bagfuls of provisions he had bought at a farmhouse.

While he washed, Arabella set out what appeared a feast—not the rich, heavily spiced stews of lamb or beef they had eaten at the gypsy encampment, but good fare from a competent farm cook—half a dozen squab, wrapped in vine leaves and roasted over an open fire, a goat cheese so fresh it was scarcely firm, grapes and oranges and lemons which she piled into a gold bowl. There was rough dark bread, a thick slab of smoked ham. Arabella rubbed her hands gleefully as she contemplated the still life she had created.

He stood drying himself, watching with a look so amused, so tender, that she walked slowly to him.

"What did you hear?" she asked hesitantly, for by now her optimism had begun to suffer from repeated injuries.

"Nothing. No one's inquired for a gypsy, a wagon, three horses, and a dog—or anyone at all. Not anywhere near here, at least."

She knelt, taking him into her hands. "Let me—just once."

He bent and lifted her gently. "Later."

Later, when they had eaten, she supposed.

But when they had eaten he left the table, saying that it was midafternoon, he must attend to the animals, bring fresh water, and he was gone.

I cannot make him do what he doesn't want to do. But he will, he will. He'll do it because he won't be able to help himself.

Yet, it seemed, he was able to help himself, and no smiles, no caresses, served to change whatever plan he had.

They went to sleep in the afternoon, since they must travel that night, and when he had slept five hours he awoke, telling her in the darkness: "It's late enough. Time to set out."

She threw herself upon the bed, furious with frustration. "You said 'later.' How much later did you mean?"

"Tomorrow, sometime—if we're careful."

"Careful?" In the dark she was aware of feeling more anger than she would have felt if she could have seen him. There was a glow in the wagon as he lighted a candle and she looked up to see him beside the bed, watching her soberly, almost sadly. She took his hand, kissing the palm. "I know you're protecting me. But I don't need it anymore. Let me at least—"

She moved quickly, taking him between her hands, and was gratified by the quick springing of blood, hardening him, and he made no protest as she took him into her mouth, filled with an excitement so intense that she was on her knees, pleading with him. "Let me have just that much, let me—please—"

Whether it was the pleading or his own need for release, the throbbing began, and the stream filled her mouth. When it was over she found herself exhausted and was grateful when he drew the sheet to her waist, leaving her with a long kiss.

She was not so strong as she had supposed. Several hours later, when the wagon had stopped moving and she awoke to find him asleep beside her, she kissed him carefully, and slept again.

With everything else he knew about her, he also knew how ready she was for any activity which would demand of her the kind of self-abandoned energy they gave to their lovemaking.

When she awoke next he was gone, but there was fresh water in the tub and drinking vessel, Odysseus was not in view, and Caliph stood with his head raised to sniff the air for aromas which might hint of danger.

Two or three hours later he returned to find her seated in the tub, her hair speared with jeweled Chinese pins and fastened upon the top of her head, her eyes closed, as if she might have been there a long time, but for the smoothly made bed, the table laid for their meal.

She looked at him with a brief questioning, was reassured by a nod, and then he was stripping off shirt and trousers, kicking the sandals aside, and getting into the water facing her, spreading her legs and holding her ankles beneath his arms. He entered slowly, watching her expressions. Her smile disappeared and there came that first quick alert waiting apprehension, something of desperate eagerness, and something of fearfulness. The conviction of her physical invulnerability was not complete.

Slowly, carefully, he placed himself against her, then moved into her. She tried to bring him deeper, but he allowed only a brief penetration, a withdrawal to her body's opening, a return no deeper than before, and presently Arabella was sighing with a new uncanny pleasure, a responsive clasping and unclasping of her muscles as he continued the slight penetration, the withdrawal, until at last he moved deep inside her and she felt the throbbing of his release.

They remained motionless for some time. Then he stood, bringing her to her feet as they looked at each other in silence with the shared sense of having at last experienced familiar joys, however gently administered. Arabella was convinced that now the days of abnegation were ended.

But again it proved impossible for her to plan what was going to happen between them. He was soon dressed, and with Arabella in the sleeveless cloth-of-gold coat they sat across the table, eating slowly, now and again smiling, as if at the accomplishment of some conspiratorial achievement.

He knows now that I'm healed.

Not a tinge of blood had appeared in the water.

He can't still be afraid of hurting me.

But the fatalistic sorrow she had experienced again and again these past several days took unexpected hold, insinuating itself into the midst of her joyous rediscovery of the pleasures their love conferred.

It will all happen again. I'll be pregnant again. I'll have to take that potion again.

They had talked about that possibility once, a few days after the abortion, when she asked despairingly, "How can I go through this again?"

"You never will."

"But we'll forget—we'll put off doing anything—we won't want to do anything—"

"Now that I know your body's calendar is accurate, if you miss three days I'll give you a few spoonfuls of the potion, and the bleeding will begin with a few cramps, no more pain than you've been accustomed to. No more than you can tolerate."

If that should prove true, and everything he had told her before had come true, then: Yes, I can tolerate it. I can tolerate anything, if I can have him when I need him.

Eating slowly, they watched each other, reading each other's minds, she was sure. For while she was determined that later he would be deep inside her, as deep as he had ever been, she suspected that he was planning on evading her upon one pretext or another: setting out early that night, perhaps, for there was a new moon and the day had been cloudy. It would be dark earlier than usual. And in the meanwhile he would find things which must be done out of doors.

❧ CHAPTER TWENTY-THREE ❧

By midnight it had begun to rain, hard enough for the sound on the roof to wake her, and she felt the wagon jolt to a stop. She knew from the backward-and-forward movements that he was unharnessing the horses, leading them to shelter, covering them and Caliph with the woolen leather-topped blankets kept in a box beneath the driver's seat. He entered quietly and undressed, but when he lay naked beside her she felt that his flesh was chilled.

The wagon was unaccustomedly cool, and she stepped across him and went to one of the chests, lighted a candle, shielding the light so that it would not disturb him—for he often fell asleep the moment he was in bed—found a cashmere blanket, spread it across the bed, and was moving over him when his hands touched her breasts and he settled her upon him, slowly, deeper and deeper, until at last they were profoundly close.

She raised and lowered herself, his hands about her waist guiding how far she might descend, how quickly or slowly she might move, until there was the warm sensation of spreading ease throughout her belly and his pulsing seemed to fill her. Presently he slipped out and she was lying beside him, her hand enfolding him as he softened slowly, and they were asleep.

When Arabella awakened she was aware of being alone. He usually left while she slept, to reconnoiter the neighborhood, bring water, tend the animals, and visit farmhouses to buy food and ask questions.

Now she guessed that although it was dark beyond the drawn curtains and rain struck heavily upon the wagon, it was midmorning, and for several minutes she was still, trying to reconstruct a dream, or memory.

As he was getting out of bed he had slipped inside her, gently, carefully, her legs and arms had closed around him, there had been only a few strokes, the prolonged throbbing, and in a few moments he was gone.

The two encounters, unexpected and unhoped for, had left her with a richness and gratitude, and when she began her morning preparations she was still reflective, moving carefully, as if to disturb nothing of what he had left her.

But the mirror showed her a surprise. Her face was sorrowful.

What is there for you to be sad about now? The pain and fear of the potion belong to the past, and if I hope to keep sane I won't think of the King, or Guise.

Yet a kind of numbed despair was taking hold of her, a sense of emptiness, and she admitted at last a sense of irreparable loss.

She had not been aware, since that day when it seemed her guts were being torn loose, of thinking about what her body had discarded.

Now, as she looked at herself, she heard the gypsy's voice, very low, speaking the words he had said when at last she had roused from the effects of the laudanum and begun to question him:

Complete.

The tiny creature had been complete.

Yes, fingers and toes, he had replied to her unbelieving question.

Two tiny hands, curled into fists, appeared before her and she stared at them incredulously, as if she might reach forth and touch them. Miniature feet, a miniature body, perfectly formed, a finished human creature, eyes opened wide, mouth beginning to smile.

A male, he had said, when she asked another question.

Yes, I've always known it—yours.

She turned away from the mirror, hoping that would stop the tears, and was angry with herself.

What are you crying for? You didn't want it. He didn't want it. It happened because we forgot. We cared too much about being together to take those precautions he told you about. Then why, in God's name, cry when there was no choice to be made?

Yet, as she emerged from the tub and began to rifle through the chest she continued crying softly, gently, until all at once she dropped to her knees and was crying uncontrollably. Now she no longer cared if he should return and find her abandoned to this rage of inexplicable grief. The loss had returned to her as something infinitely desirable, never to be recovered.

She was still crying when the lock snapped. He stopped, looking at her seriously, closed the door and came to her, taking careful hold of her shoulders. "Arabella—"

The sorrow was absurd. They were in flight from those who would kill him. She stood up, as he removed the heavy rain-soaked cloak and hung it on a peg.

"I know—" he said. "At least I think I know."

He had a large sack in one hand, and he dropped it onto the table top. Arabella stepped toward him, put her arms about him and her head against his chest. He held her closely. After a long silence she whispered, "Do you ever think of it?"

"I think of it. Of course." He held her closer, stroking her hair, then moved slightly apart, studying her seriously. "To feel sorrow is natural. Why are you ashamed? It was alive, it was ours." He shook his head. "There was no choice."

Arabella shook her head. "I want you. Nothing more.

Ever—" She looked at him searchingly. "Such a long word—Ever—"

He bent his head, turning her body so that her head rested in the crook of his elbow, and placed his mouth on hers, finding her scarcely responsive at first, still somewhat distant, in that country of sorrow which was perhaps more imagined than real, or if real, only briefly so. And then she was holding him as his hands moved over her, waves of warmth and longing moving with them. He sank to the low stool beside the table, drawing her with him, and moved swiftly and deeply into her.

He was holding her firmly about the waist, and when she would have forced herself to envelop him more deeply, would not let her. She moved quickly upward and down again, trying to heighten the sensation by surprise. She bent her head to his shoulder. "Please, please. Don't keep me from you any longer." She tried once again, clenching her teeth with the effort to exceed his determination to hold her slightly above complete penetration. She struck at his chest and shoulders with her fists.

"Don't force me to give you what you should not have yet—"

She leaned back, closing her eyes upon the slow luxurious sensation of his movements, another giving of himself, slowly, and when at last he was quiet he let her sink down upon him.

She looked at him, her eyes glistening, and smiled. "I can't force you to do what is against your will."

"Yes, you could—because I want it, too."

"Then why—"

"You know why."

"Nothing will make me whole again but feeling you all through me." Her hands touched her breasts, belly, passed along her arms and down the sides of her legs.

"Later."

Then, as if he spoke from one part of his mind and acted

from another, his fingers touched her carefully, his knuckle pressing so that she gasped in dismayed surprise and delight, and as his fingers continued to caress her he was saying, "I'll give you enough—more than I should."

He began to move slowly, then with a steadily increasing speed, as if experimenting with her tolerance for intensity. Unexpectedly he forced her downward with a hard swift movement, and so quickly there seemed no break in the continuity he stood, backed her toward the bed, and again was inside her.

"I won't be tired. What if I am? What difference does that make compared to this?"

"None."

He had straightened his arms and she found him watching her without seeing her, blinded by the intensity of that anguished concentration which accompanied each expulsion of violent energy.

With a heavy sigh, he lowered himself full upon her and they moved together with the swift rhythm of what seemed to have last happened many years ago. The muscles of her belly stretched wide, and she heard those ungovernable sobs which broke from her when the pleasure had become, as he had warned, nearly unendurable, when the boundaries of her body seemed ready to disintegrate, so that she would never again be able to piece together another Arabella. The sobs continued, as did the rending of her muscles, but he did not pause, did not seem to hear her, and perhaps had ceased to be aware of her as separate from himself.

The swift movement eased but continued deep and purposeful, while she held him as if otherwise they would lose each other, as surely as if death had taken them unaware.

At last he was quiet, or nearly so, kissing her gently.

Her legs clasped his back, her arms held him, though there was not as much strength as she had had before. When the final pleasures had ebbed and he was still she began to move slowly beneath him; there was no possible end to the gratification she needed from him now. He moved slightly, kissing her, and as she felt him growing harder, his hands beneath her buttocks to bring her closer, make her more open and accessible to him, he gave a swift powerful thrust, as if to push everything inside her out of the way to make room for him.

"Robert, we're going to kill each other this way some day."

He continued holding her against him, tilting her backward, and thrust into her with great intensity, the reward for what they had both endured since she had drunk the potion, ten days ago.

Two magical effects had been produced by the potion. It had rid her of what she could not keep. And it had made them more valuable to each other. No time could be long enough for the pleasures which, as his face showed her in brief glimpses, caused him a pain akin to her own.

Which is Robert? Which is me? What am I feeling? What is he feeling? Are we the same person? Has it happened as I knew it would one day? When he tries to leave me, will he find it impossible?

She gave a moaning cry of protest as she felt him begin to throb, and at last he left her, slipped away, soft and spent, although he was still lying upon her, braced on his elbows, looking down at her with curiosity and some strange expression of regret.

Presently they were lying side by side, holding each other's hands as if they had gone for a congenial walk, and for some time they remained with eyes closed, subdued, speechless.

Finally, surprised, he said: "It's stopped raining."

Arabella said nothing, preoccupied by the sensations of completion which spread throughout her body, a throbbing of the blood in her legs, a pulse beating steadily beneath her navel.

After a few more minutes he sat up quickly, and she let

him go, watching as he slid back the carved wooden shutters, pushing aside the leather panel, letting in a strong midafternoon sun.

Quickly he got into his trousers and shirt, stepped into the sandals, and as if at some unexpected discovery, unwrapped the food he had brought three hours before. He laid it out on the table, glancing at her questioningly, and without sitting down began to eat. "I've neglected them." He nodded toward the window. "Those blankets are hot. The earth is steaming."

Arabella jumped up and came to peer out, surprised by a momentary dizziness.

He tore off a capon leg, offered it to her and they ate greedily, silently, concentrating on the scene out of doors, the three horses, standing patiently, weighted by their rain blankets, Caliph, having freed himself of his, alert amid the tall grasses, where a smoky mist was rising from the heating earth. The sun was strong and their eyes narrowed against it.

Then, with a kiss, a swift movement of his hand over her breasts, he was gone.

She continued to eat slowly, watching him with the animals with an interest as intent and admiring as if this graceful, affectionate performance was something she had never seen before. Setting aside the capon leg, she stretched, and it seemed that every muscle in her body had been kneaded by magic fingers.

She walked to the tub, noticed that the door stood ajar, and looked out. She could see Saracen, perhaps waiting for her to stroke him, as she had not during the past ten days.

Quickly she took one of the burnooses from its peg and threw it around her. The gypsy let nothing happen by accident, and so this was an invitation to come out of doors. He had told her earlier that they were in a place so isolated no one had driven that overgrown path for months.

She walked slowly down the steps, exhilarated by the air, the smells of the earth. The gypsy looked around, smiled and nodded, and she went to stroke Saracen's neck, speaking to him in the confiding voice she had always used with him. There was a bargain between them, and now Saracen rolled his eyes at her expectantly:

Where have you been?

She laughed. "I'm back. I'm with you again."

CHAPTER TWENTY-FOUR

She put her head against Saracen's, stroking his muzzle,
but then slowly let her arm fall.

"Later," she told him apologetically. "I'm a little
lazy now." She smiled, as if he would understand that
excuse, but as she stood looking at him from one side his
eye rolled and fixed itself balefully upon her. "I'll make up
to you for everything, Saracen. I promise."

Her back was to Robert as he knelt beside Caliph, who
stood sniffing the air while his master brushed his sleek gray
coat.

The gypsy had been right. What she had demanded,
what he had given her, had left her not tired, not pleasantly
listless, but exhausted. "We'll ride a little later," she told
Saracen, moving slowly away from him.

"Not tonight," said the gypsy, without glancing around,
and she began to think she was free to do as she pleased, and
she knew what it was, something she had been longing for
ever since they had reached this warm southern country of
his. "The ground is soft. We'll wait until tomorrow night."

"You heard that, Saracen?"

A weakness washed through her. She threw the monk's
cloak onto the wet grass and stood naked for a moment,
arms outstretched toward the sun. "Tomorrow," she
added.

Then she was lying flat on her back on the cloak, eyes
closed as she felt the sun's hot bite upon her flesh. The

196

gypsy glanced around and she looked at him, smiling. "Someday," she said softly. "Someday—when they've forgotten us."

He returned to grooming Caliph and her eyes closed.

I'm not lazy. I'm tired. More tired than I've ever been. He gave me what I begged him for and I feel as if I've evaporated into this mist.

Languidly she lifted one arm, as if to take the mist into her hand, and let her arm fall again.

She closed her eyes and did not wake until she found she had been wrapped in the cloak and that Robert was carrying her into the wagon. The sun was low. She must have slept three or four hours, and the effect was at once restorative and further debilitating.

When he laid her gently upon the bed, bending over her for a moment, she looked at him, longing to explain something important, but unable to think of the words. Instead her arms reached about his neck, her legs parted to welcome him, and for a brief time she lay motionless, eyes closed, while he moved gently and slowly, an embrace not so much of sensuality as reassurance: the only sure refuge they had discovered during their long journey. Then he left her, kissing her lids, telling her to sleep.

"I'm going to get water and reconnoiter the countryside."

She looked at him with an effort, tried to lift one hand, but her eyes closed and she was once more asleep, carrying with her into that other land the day's treasures.

She awoke sometime in the night and found him beside her, profoundly asleep. Finding that sleep was not yet done with her, she let it take her again.

When she awoke again he was lying on one side, his head propped on the heel of his hand, watching her. "I did too much to you yesterday?"

"Yesterday?" she inquired vaguely. "Yes, yesterday." It seemed a very long time ago.

The exhaustion was gone, her arms went about his shoulders and she began to kiss his neck, his face, and then she pushed him, unresisting, upon his back and was astride him, taking him between her hands as if she held a sacred object, and began slowly pushing the red-purple bulb inside her, pressing herself downward until her body had yielded its full length to him.

His eyes closed, his lips parted, an expression uncannily beautiful to her, the sudden beginning of that last expulsion before he began another period of days without any culmination or release.

All at once he gave a low protesting sound, as his movements slowed. He kept his hands upon her breasts, turned her swiftly upon her back, and drew away from her gradually, saying softly, "Go to sleep. I must leave you for a while."

"Good night—if it is night—"

After three more nights of travel they were approaching the seacoast and Arabella, who had ridden each night and felt again strong and vital, had begun to talk about going into the sea. The memory had remained vivid and exciting, the smell of the salt water, the chill and warm passages, and the exhilaration which followed.

"We've heard no word of searchers for days."

"We've been in isolated areas."

"You've heard of them in other isolated areas. One place is as likely to be safe or dangerous as another."

"Probably. But not certainly, Arabella. One cannot trust entirely to luck."

"Oh, I can," she had assured him, cantering Saracen beside the wagon. "I've been lucky all my life."

There was a pause, and with dismay she imagined his expression—surprised, then incredulous, finally stricken.

"So have I," he said at last, and his voice had a heaviness she had not heard before. "So have I," he repeated, and she sensed that her remark, impulsive and arrogant, had spoken to him painfully of the predicament where past good luck was of little use to him now.

He had never reminded her that she had begged to come with him, casually putting aside every warning he had given, which had now come true. There was nothing he had not foreseen, and nothing she had been willing to foresee.

Even so, the mystical conviction that now they were free of their followers, recalled by the King and Guise, she preferred not to examine too closely.

What had once seemed a dangerous game they could win with skill and patience, now appeared as what it was: Their lives, at least the gypsy's, were forfeit in this game, whichever way it was played. Once begun the conclusion was foregone.

Unable to live from moment to moment with this knowledge, she had contrived to banish it, replacing it with a shining sense of euphoric conviction, a grasping after sureness and finality. That was what she expected to find in their lovemaking: Refuge and forgetfulness.

I am lucky. We are lucky. Two people born to good fortune. The King knows he cannot bring me back and has forgotten me.

The thought was absurd, and she stopped thinking of that, too. She thought of the moment she was living, and the one to come, and even the next day, seacoast town or no, seemed a vague distance in time and space.

They were traveling toward Marseilles because that was the only place where he could be sure of getting accurate information.

"The farm people here are greedy and stupid. Given money they will tell you anything. In the seacoast towns I know many men who will tell me the truth."

Two nights later he found a place of concealment on the outskirts of the town.

He returned not long after midday to tell her there had been no recent inquiries, no one looking for anyone in at least two months—men's memories became vague beyond that time; they were too preoccupied with the confusion and opportunities of the town itself.

He had rented a brick barn belonging to a prosperous farmer, not far from the town's periphery, and by means of a large outlay in gold coins and a plausible lie or two had it for their use. He had told the owner he was waiting the arrival of a stolen shipment of wool to arrive from Corsica. Wool, it seemed, was the least likely commodity to arouse any farmer's cupidity. Let the thief have his stolen wool, was the attitude the earlier farmer, and this one, had taken to the proposal.

"If I'd told him I was an honest merchant, he'd have been sure I was lying."

Arabella laughed joyously, for the great dream seemed about to come true: She would see a city, not a village.

"Let me go with you."

He hesitated a moment. "It's too dangerous."

"Must I live in this box for the rest of my life because it's dangerous to go out? Must I live this way another month? Another—"

He looked at her quickly, his eyes slightly narrowed. "No. I've no right to demand it of you any longer—for any reason."

They traveled to the farmer's barn and settled there for the night, the gypsy warning this farmer, as he had the other, that Caliph trusted no one but his master, and Caliph was trained to kill at the slightest provocation.

Arabella spent the night restlessly, eagerly awaiting the anticipated excursion. She protested when the gypsy left not long after sunrise to reconnoiter once again.

"We'll go this afternoon, if there's no news."

"You think they've come in the last few hours?" When he laughed, so did she. "I know. They can come any time."

She wanted to reassure him that her guardian genie, her good spirit—something or other—had promised them safety, but she did not, less from fear of his derisive laughter than from the fear of wounding him, since as between them the risks had never been and could never be fairly distributed.

When he left, she went about her usual routine, dressing in transparent jeweled and embroidered silks, since the burnoose she must wear would conceal her finery. She held the face veil across her nose, gazed at herself disapprovingly and tossed the veil aside, shaking her head at the thought of going out of doors in such a mask.

It was midafternoon when he returned, bringing a meat pie purchased from one of the vendors, and as they ate Arabella's heart beat with the excitement of the projected trip. From time to time she gave a soft exultant laugh.

"I can't believe it. Marseilles. A city, isn't it?"

"Not much larger than the castle, when it's crowded for the tournaments, or after a battle."

Wrapped in burnooses, they observed each other: His was white, covering his head, hers black, and above the face veil she looked at him with dismayed mockery, as he said: "Everything concealed—but your eyes. You could scarcely be more noticeable if you were naked."

CHAPTER TWENTY-FIVE

He paused at the doorway to deliver a last bit of advice. "Walk directly behind me. They'll know we're not Arabs if you don't. And I make a dubious Arab, at best." He smiled slightly, for even with his browned skin and the contours of his face half swathed by the Arab headdress, he was unmistakably north European. "Keep one hand touching my back and let no one pass between us. If anyone tries, kick my ankle. If I move suddenly, follow without hesitation. If I run, keep up with me."

"Keep up with you?"

"You can. The streets and alleys are crowded." He unlocked the door and they stepped into the brilliant midafternoon sun. "Whatever happens, don't speak. Your northern tongue will give you away. The Arab women are supposed to be silent out of doors, anyway."

As they walked, as quickly as she could follow without running, for it was never wise to be languorous or off-guard here on the seacoast, they passed few people but farm women with baskets laden with vegetables, or laundry on their heads, wagons coming from town loaded with produce, and ragged children and beggars who approached at every step.

Arabella kept her eyes down, except when she could not resist a quick glance to see what was around them, and the gypsy gave no alms, which would have indicated that he carried money. He sent the children and beggars away hastily, with a few words in rough Arabic, and they went, intimidated by his height and agility.

As they reached the town, its houses built so close across the narrow streets it would have been possible to climb from one into another, Arabella could not resist peeking, finding that it looked here on the outskirts much like the villages she had known. But as they entered the town proper she found it so much larger than anything she had seen before, noisier and dirtier, stinking of piles of refuse, offal flung from butcher shops over which starving dogs and cats fought, that it took on a bizarre unfamiliarity.

The variety of humanity in all its diverse ugliness and occasional radiance astonished her, and as they came nearer the city's heart it seemed the populace was being drawn together by magnetic force to some indeterminable point of general congregation, where traffic on foot or horseback, and the occasional hand-carried litter of a lady, came to a virtual standstill as draymen and squires bellowed and blows were exchanged with fists or staffs.

She had imagined they might encounter men dressed in the King's gold-and-red livery, or the green-and-silver of Guise, prancing along on their shining horses, lances upright, pushing the crowd aside as they did in the villages. But the gypsy had assured her that if such men were in the town, she would not recognize them.

"They won't be dressed to advertise their errand."

A fine lady passed on horseback, blond and blue-eyed, dressed as Arabella had once dressed. She wore brilliant blue silk and was accompanied by four squires on foot, wearing striped blue-and-red jerkins and red tights. As she passed she looked straight at the gypsy with disbelieving surprise, and smiled dazzlingly.

Arabella's heart gave a quick uncertain beat: the Countess.

Although he had not told her where the Countess lived, she knew that by the time he was fourteen he had spent much time exploring this city and others in the vicinity.

That lady was not the Countess, of course, since her

squires had not worn her green-and-yellow colors. Only another predatory woman, struck by the gypsy's startling appearance, hoping for a small adventure such as he must have offered many of her kind during the past four years.

In a few moments they had passed the lady and her entourage, but even so Arabella was compelled to glance back, and found the woman turned in her saddle, still gazing longingly after him.

The streets absorbed her attention again, for although she had seen nothing she had not seen in the courtyards or the villages which clung for protection to the walls of the castle, there was so much more of everything that its emotional force became far greater.

"There is little the town can show you that you haven't seen."

And it seemed that living at her father's court had made her worldly wise very young.

It was as if she had seen all this long ago, but for the nearby sea, which was visible from any street corner and could be smelled everywhere. Yet the town had a vehemence and enthusiasm which was new to her. For these people did whatever they did, with furious gusto: fighting one another, beating a horse or dog or a child, riding bareback into a hostile crowd that struck at their animals. Men and women alike were armed with a variety of weapons and used them freely upon one another, upon the animals attacking them or those refusing to move out of their paths.

Arabella gazed upon these scenes with the cool indifference cultivated long ago toward outsiders. Those she did not know had no real meaning for her, beyond curiosity.

No pity or sentimental empathy was aroused by the sight of lepers swathed in rags, mendicant monks, cripples and maimed, or men and women missing eyes and teeth, arms and legs. Although she had never seen so many monstrosities gathered together in one place, still she had seen them all, at one time or another.

She took pleasure in watching the acrobats, performing

on a wire strung above the level of the heads of the crowd, somersaulting and dancing, men and girls capering; and the jugglers amused her with their tricks of swallowing fire and breathing it forth from mouth and nostrils, to the screams and laughter of the audience. She laughed with ironic amusement, having no faith in the veracity of their skills, just as she had laughed when they appeared in the Great Hall. Her tutor had explained how it was done.

A caged tiger caused her to tug at the gypsy's burnoose. They paused to watch it pacing, but despite its beauty, its evident ferocity in captivity made her uneasy, and they moved on, finding themselves outside a large wooden building, probably intended for the warehousing of overseas merchandise. A naked woman swiveled her hips, shook her big breasts, then turned her back upon the crowd, bent forward and clutched her widespread ankles with either hand. She peered at them from between her legs, offering the first customer a free encounter with what she had just shown, and disappeared inside.

Another woman began a similar dance and the gypsy started to move on. Arabella touched his back, whispering, "Let's go in."

"You've seen it all. So you've said."

"They may have something new."

He shrugged and they entered the large building. Inside she noticed that but for the female performers there were few women among the crowd, and they were taking customers one by one to small booths along the wall.

The place stank of animal manure, dead fish cast upon the shore nearby, and the stale sweat and bandages of half a hundred men. It was dimly lighted and the gypsy muttered at her to stay close, lean against his back, and tell him if anyone touched her. But the men were not interested in a concealed Arab woman.

There were enclosed stalls, making it necessary to pay a fee to witness the performance, and as they stepped into a small crowded enclosure, where Arabella drew shallow breaths, since the air itself seemed full of foulness and disease, the first dancer they had seen was lying on a table, legs spread. The first customer drew away and the second promptly entered, pumped industriously a few times, groaned his satisfaction, and was as promptly replaced by a third. Arabella glanced around and found twelve or fifteen men waiting their turn, their opened trousers showing their impatience.

The gypsy glanced at Arabella, questioning whether she had seen enough of that act, and she nodded toward the next enclosed stall, where a woman knelt and a man, fully dressed, stood inserting himself into her mouth. He, too, was quickly satisfied, and as the woman spat into the straw which covered the floor, another organ was thrust into her open mouth. This woman also had a line of uneasy customers and Arabella noticed that once the act was completed they usually returned to the end of the line, vigorously preparing themselves for the next encounter.

It seemed that each individual in the vast building, each customer and each female who served them, might have been alone, without self-consciousness or seeming awareness of onlookers.

The gypsy glanced again at Arabella, a slight questioning smile on his face, as if he understood quite well her determination that nothing in this wicked city by the sea was going to surprise or dismay her.

She nodded toward the next stall which they entered to find a naked woman squatting, bent forward, over a fully dressed man who lay beneath her, penetrated through the anus by another man, and she seemed as indifferent to what was being done to her as the others.

In the next booth a woman lay at the edge of a low table and a large dog was inside her, making his movements with more evident excitement and pleasure for both of them than any display they had seen so far. They watched for a few minutes, but the animal was not to be gratified so quickly as the men. They moved on.

A great hairy creature, looking to Arabella like the ugliest man she had ever seen, stood with his long arms chained to poles, his legs chained apart, and a naked woman was roped to him, moving quickly back and forth upon him while he grunted with satisfaction.

Arabella glanced at the gypsy with a grimace, and he whispered, "An orangutan. None of them visited the castle?" He seemed amused they had found something to which she was not indifferent, but quite amazed.

"Never. But how—oh, well—" She shrugged, still certain that nothing could disconcert her. A slight surprise, perhaps, no more.

The next exhibit displayed a naked woman with a dildoe strapped about her, copulating with another woman. Arabella had seen this before too, when some itinerant performers had set up a stall near one of the villages and she had gone to watch with her maids-in-waiting.

There came next a fat woman, her billowing flesh half concealing a dwarf who climbed bravely upon her and inserted himself with confidence. A woman with a pony, his forehoofs thrust through rings hanging from the ceiling, completed the program.

The gypsy paused at the door with a slight mocking smile. "Again?" She shook her head and they walked into the sunlight.

Most of it had been familiar, but like the town itself there had been so much more at one time. The room had been so crowded, the men so repulsive, so many of them sick or maimed, the women so ugly, that Arabella was eager to forget it.

"Can't we walk out on the wharf and look at the ships?"

They walked slowly, Arabella in back of him, holding firmly to a fold in his burnoose, but nevertheless being jostled by men who were careless or drunk. Yet nothing happened worth starting a fight over. The crowd, seemingly at a constant level of high readiness for action, turned against whoever aroused its animosity as with one accord. It was best to be silent, since they could not be invisible.

Great and small ships lay along the wharf, being loaded and unloaded by men staggering under the weight of great bales. Men stood gossiping, leaning against the posts. There were galleys, captured from the pirates of the African countries, riding empty while their crews had perhaps been sent below to sleep, or given leave to visit a house like the one they had just left.

The smell of the water was strong, and a brisk wind whipped their burnooses about, making them hold tight to their headdresses. At last they stopped near the end of the wharf, where great birds swooped into the water and emerged bearing flopping fish in their bills, to settle nearby and tear their prey apart.

By some unspoken rule they did not discuss what they had seen. They understood what to talk about and what to ignore. He began, instead, to point to where the countries of Africa lay, beyond the sea's horizon.

"In that direction lies Tunis." He raised his arm, passing his hand in a half circle and bringing it to rest, while she gazed into the distance, squinting against the glare from the water. "Morocco." His arm moved again. "Algeria. Egypt."

"The only places where we might be safe—if we could get to them."

They had discussed these possibilities long ago. "But we can't. I've thought of every possibility. There isn't any real chance of making it alive—for either of us."

She was quiet, reflecting, not thinking of her own needs for the moment. "You could go back to the gypsies?"

"I tried to find them once—about six months after I'd left. They were gone. No one knows where the gypsies go when they break up an encampment. Anyway, I had left them. I had no right to return—to them, or to another tribe."

"Your peculiar sense of honor." The same which had sent

208

him, in Guise's armor, to the tournament because he had impulsively promised he would be there.

"Maybe."

They fell silent, staring across to those lands which promised freedom from their eternal vigilance, their eternal fear of discovery—the unending flight.

She turned to him. "Should we do it? Get out of the country—any way we can?"

"How? Before I could sell everything, we'd have been discovered. That kind of merchandise does not go unnoticed in any market. If we abandon it, we'd be marked out for what we are—Europeans—before we took ship. I would be killed. And you would be sold to a man who owned a house like the one we've just seen. Maybe to a man who wanted to amuse himself by finding out how slowly he could kill you." She looked away, shocked. "Yes, it happens. Often. That's something you were not told of?"

"No."

There was a scream, high and piercing and prolonged, in a man's voice. Arabella started, both hands covering her ears. "My God, what is that?"

There had been other screams, not so piercing, not so terrible, other howls, while they stood talking, but they had seemed to come from somewhere halfway up the wharf. She had been too engrossed in thinking of the possibilities of their leaving the country to separate those sounds from the general noise.

Yet she had heard such cries, such screams and yells of anguish, when the men were brought into the courtyard after a battle, and she and her maids-in-waiting had looked from their windows, too high to see clearly the faces of the men who protested at the sawing of a leg, the sewing of their guts back into their bellies.

He did not answer but stood listening, as the scream was repeated, and his face had turned grim and angry, as she had never seen it.

"What are they doing?"

He had begun to walk and she followed him, asking him again and again as the screams of protest and pain tore the air and caused even the men on the wharf to pause in their gossip or their traffic to and from the ships, listening, exchanging surly glances, then going on.

He walked more swiftly, and she was half skipping to keep up with him. As they drew near a building below them on the sand, a barnlike structure on stilts over the water's edge with closed doors, the cries and screams grew louder, never ceasing.

"Tell me!" She seized his arm and he stopped, speaking to her over his shoulder, so as not to attract attention by the sight of an Arab talking to his woman in public.

"You don't want to see that," he said quickly, and began to walk on, but again she caught his arm.

"Why don't you want me to?"

"This is not a thing for you to see."

"I want to know if it's true, what the traveler told us in the Great Hall, that there is no evil ever invented that can't be seen in the coast towns. We were allowed to see everything."

He turned angrily. "You would not have been allowed to see this."

❧ CHAPTER TWENTY-SIX ❧

Another scream rose, trembled for several seconds, descended in a louder scream, and suddenly stopped. She looked at the gypsy for a long moment, her eyes wide, shining with horror.

"It's known as The House of Dead Men," he said slowly. "They are alive and suffering beyond their endurance. "They will be dead, all of them, in a few hours."

"How can such a thing be?" she whispered.

"Come. Don't stand here."

She hesitated, started to move away with him, then began to walk toward the wooden structure. "I can endure looking at anything." She glanced at him sideways, for as she moved he stayed beside her. "Anything," she added fiercely. "I wasn't taught to be a coward."

He paid the man who opened the locked door, and they entered a large dark room, so dark, but for an occasional pitch torch, that it took a few moments to accustom their eyes.

The smell was overpowering, making her choke, and she put her hand against her mouth. The stench of dried and fresh blood, excrement, sweat, the pitch from the torches, began to gag her.

Men stood grouped about pens enclosed with metal bars to keep their prisoners inside. There were several such enclosed cells along the sides of the room, each with its spectators—she saw no other women.

Arabella moved slowly toward one of the pens and peered between the heads of the men gathered in front of her. The gypsy was behind her, holding her against him to keep her from being touched.

There inside were two men, recently blinded, their eye sockets bloody, fighting each other with short double-bladed knives, slashing at arms and faces, groins and chests. Their bodies streamed blood. They fought savagely, screaming continuously but never pausing as each sought the smallest advantage.

Arabella shut her eyes and tried to move, but the crowd was dense, the watching men silent. But for the screams of the men in combat, the room had an uncanny silence. No sounds from the audience but an occasional grunt, as of satisfaction, participatory cruelty.

In the next pen two naked men fought with nail-studded clubs. Each had beaten the other's groin to a bloody pulp. They staggered, lurched, struck again and again, and as one began to fall the other raised his club feebly, and brought it down upon the other's skull, falling on top of him, struggling to inflict one more blow.

Arabella had begun to tremble uncontrollably, and a retching began, making her clutch her throat in an effort to keep the vomit from erupting. The gypsy turned her toward him swiftly, and as she covered her mouth to keep back the vomit, she noticed in every face around them an intense concentration upon the two men fighting with clubs, a fierce expressionlessness but for their eyes, glazed and stupefied by a gluttony of loathing, a rapacious need to see ever greater pain inflicted and endured.

All at once she was vomiting, and the gypsy propelled her swiftly through the crowd, pushing men aside. They were allowed to go, a distraction scarcely noticed.

Outside she raised the face veil, bent forward, and vomited violently for a minute or more. When she stopped he urged her to the water's edge where she walked in and bent over, vomiting as he splashed water over her face and burnoose. It seemed the vomiting would never stop, bringing up everything inside her.

She was still trembling as she leaned against him and he held her close. After two or three minutes they began to walk toward the street, pausing at the edge of the crowds where she struggled not to vomit again.

All at once she covered her face with both hands, sobbing, and she continued sobbing, unaware of herself, of him, of the crowds they had entered while they walked slowly onward.

As if emerging from unconsciousness, she found they were once again on the outskirts of the town, and there she stopped, lifting the face veil, and vomited again.

Weakened and empty, she walked on, following him, remembering that they must not attract attention, although a woman vomiting in the streets had surprised and interested no one. She was shivering violently, despite the heat of the day, still lingering as the sun descended over the sea.

They made the trip back to the farmer's barn slowly, for she trudged after him with a great effort to make each step, as if she had grown old and feeble. Her hand continued to touch his back, though now they were passing few people, most of them again farm women with baskets of vegetables or laundry on their heads.

As they entered the darkened barn, comparatively cool, Caliph, smelling the vomit, came as if to inquire after her health. She leaned against the wall, eyes closed, and thought she would never move. The gypsy picked her up, carried her to the wagon, and laid her upon the bed, and there she remained inert while he stripped off the veil, the burnoose, the silk clothing, the boots, and when at last she looked at him she was relieved to see no accusatory or secretively triumphant expression, only concern and sorrow.

"Get into the tub," he told her softly, and when she tried to move but could not, he carried her there, stood her in the cool water, and washed her carefully from head to foot, three times, as if performing a ritual ablution.

As he dried her with a soft cloth she whispered, "Who were those men—killing each other?"

"Prisoners of war. Pirate captives sold to the owner of the house."

At last she moved toward the bed and he covered her with the sheet and a silk carpet, for she continued to shiver, spasms passing over her body.

She kept her eyes closed, trying not to think, but all at once, sensing that he was not beside her, sat up, her heart pounding with the fear that she was alone.

He had undressed and was throwing their clothing out the doorway. He had lighted a candle, and then stood in the tub, washing.

"Oh. Thank God. You're here." She lay down again with a sense of overpowering weakness and relief.

Dressed again in trousers and shirt and sandals, he came to stand beside her, lightly touching her chin. She looked up reluctantly, but neither spoke, fearful of intruding upon the dark privacy of remembered horrors. They encountered each other's eyes with a bleak questioning to which neither received an answer. Still, she had an answer of sorts: his reason why they did not take ship for another land.

"The animals need food and water. Will you be all right?"

She nodded and did not look up until she heard the door open, and then she looked at him anxiously, in terror at being left alone. He nodded and disappeared, closing the door.

After several minutes, telling herself she could not continue to lie here shivering, something must be done, although what or why was not clear, she went to search one of the chests, brought out a large square of embroidered gold tissue, and tied it around her, beneath her armpits, then began to comb her tangled hair.

She was afraid of the mirror. What would she find on her face? A reflection of what she had seen, engraved there forever? She felt that by her insistence upon going in to The House of Dead Men, she had committed an unforgivable sin.

All at once, interrupting the blank stupor which enveloped her, he stood in the doorway. "I'm going in to town—to ask if anyone noticed us, if there've been inquiries—"

She nodded, and he came to her, touching her hair, stroking it slowly, watching her with deep concern.

She had no apology to make for her insistence upon entering The House of Dead Men, and he offered none for having taken her there. She would have continued to insist. Finally, they would have gone to silence her.

He left without touching her, without kissing her, as if by mutual agreement, and she sat at the table, took up the lute and strummed it listlessly. From time to time she turned cold and began to tremble, afraid the morbid sickness would once again well irresistibly into violent vomiting, and her energy and concentration centered upon preventing that.

She laid the lute aside and leaned upon the table, pressing the knuckles of her fists against her eyeballs, pressing until there appeared flashes of color, wildly merging, erasing the images she could not endure.

It was quite true that she and her brothers and sisters had been permitted to see everything. They had witnessed much cruelty and suffering, at the tournaments, after a battle, but it had not been inflicted by enslaved men or prisoners for the purpose of giving pleasure to others. The tournaments, the battles, were a part of the great game of power and challenge which constituted life for the court and its retinue. Men were injured and killed by their own choice, not for another man's enjoyment.

She had not eaten since early morning. Now she listlessly peeled an orange, ate a section, and put it aside. Time passed, but she had no sense of how long he had been gone. The door opened and he was there again.

"Yes?"

"No one has been seen who seems, at least, to be looking for us." He shrugged, walking toward her. "For whatever that may be worth."

He stood beside her for some moments, perhaps waiting for a sign, some indication of what she wanted from him. Then all at once he turned, kicked aside the sandals, put off the trousers and shirt, and in another moment was asleep in that position of self-abandonment he often took, arms behind his head, bent knees spread and ankles crossed, breathing deeply.

After a few minutes Arabella went to stand looking down at him with a surge of painful protectiveness and some deep sense of pity and yearning toward that perfection of face and body, more precious to her than ever before. Her throat ached with a welling of love and terror that one day she might lose him. The fear was no longer that he would leave her, but that he might be taken by force.

She shook her head in swift warning reproach against such thoughts, unknotted the scarf, and fitted herself carefully into the spaces he had left, taking care not to touch him, and almost instantly slipped into a sleep from which she awakened sometime later, slowly, feeling his hand moving over her breasts. But as she reached to enclose him, he picked her up and she realized that he was dressed, saying as he carried her to the door, taking a burnoose from a peg: "We're going to the beach. It's long after midnight. No one should be there."

Saracen and Odysseus were waiting, saddlecloths on their backs, and they rode out of the barn and set off at a gallop in the moonlight. All at once she felt free of the ugly memories, as if many years had lapsed since this afternoon's experience.

Tall pines grew near the shore and they tethered their horses. Arabella flung the burnoose upon the sand while the gypsy undressed, and they ran toward the water.

"There was a gypsy encampment here once, years ago," he told her as they paused, Arabella testing the water.

"The one where you lived?"

They walked in, then plunged forward, side by side, and

he kept her hand in his, swimming with one arm. He had taught her how to kick her feet and legs.

"One I visited. Stay close to me. There are shallows and depths." He dove deep, while she flung herself backward, floating, and presently he was beneath her, buoying her upon his back. She laughed aloud, joyous and confident again.

No one had seen them in town. No one was looking for them. The euphoric sense of having triumphed began to return.

The water was cool and they moved strenuously, coming together and parting, again and again, their hands exploring as if this dimension of the water had given new shapes and dimensions to each other's body. Her legs clasped about his waist, he slipped into her and out with the movement of the water, until the entrance and retreat had built a strong undeniable need.

"Let's go onto the sand. Make me clean again, Robert— make me forget—"

They ran to the beach, Arabella throwing herself upon the burnoose, lifting her arms as he knelt, clasping him as he entered her, and the shudder passed between them, leaving them lying clasped together, waiting for a return of his energy. After some minutes he began to move, penetrating her deeper, withdrawing with slow deliberation, reentering with a swift movement.

She drew a luxurious sigh as he began to move with surging power toward one more profound pleasure. It came all at once, and they grew slowly still. The memories, she supposed, had been obliterated.

CHAPTER TWENTY-SEVEN

She awoke slowly, with a sense of something hideously wrong with the world, then remembered The House of Dead Men. She got up and pushed back the leather panels.

He was there, in the darkened barn, currying Odysseus. She noticed fresh food on the table—a cold roast capon, a bowl of fresh white cheese, a loaf of hard-crusted bread, grapes and oranges—and since it had not been touched he was waiting for her.

Sensing her watching him he glanced up, smiled, and presently appeared in the doorway. She went to him, seeking comfort. He held her gently as he had the night before, when they returned from the sea expecting to sleep, but instead, surprised by the need for the reassurance of each other's body, had lain together until dawn. This sureness of naked contact, with all its powerful sensitivities, had become the single trustworthy reality.

He moved her away to look into her face, raising her chin, and when she closed her eyes defensively he held her again. "Don't think about it."

"It comes back."

"Think about—think about—oh, God, think about anything. Come, it's time to eat. Think about food."

They sat opposite each other, eating slowly, watching each other with concentrated interest, but as she was about to approach he stood suddenly.

"I'm going in to town. I'll walk. If there's no news—we can go in this afternoon. Do you want to?" He spoke tenderly, almost sorrowfully, as if he were offering a sick child an outing which might distract her.

She smiled with delight at the prospect of another trip into the exciting city. "Oh, yes! The streets are an adventure in themselves." They would enter no more closed buildings.

He kissed her, smoothed his hand slowly over her body, but changed his mind. "If we start that, there'll be no excursion this afternoon."

She watched him cross the floor and leave the barn, Caliph following him to the door, his invariable ritual of farewell, for which he received a confidential stroking of his head. When his master had disappeared Caliph stood a moment, evidently lost in thought, like Arabella, and then both of them resolutely set about their respective responsibilities, Caliph to patrol the barn, Arabella to smooth the white sheets upon the pile of feather beds; then to bathe and wash her hair, afterward setting to work with kohl and henna and perfume.

All the while she tried not to remember what she had seen, and when sharp pictures threatened she shut her eyes and pressed her fists against them until blurred flashes of color made them vanish.

Two hours or more passed until she was satisfied with the way she looked, and she smiled in the mirror as she combed out the long, curling dark hair.

Once they set out upon their excursion she would be concealed by the black burnoose and face veil, but now she wore a thin yellow silk skirt, low on her hips, an opened white and gold silk shirt, and the emerald as always between her breasts.

She took up the lute and began to pluck it, expecting she would presently find a song to sing.

Instead there came another sharp vision from The House of Dead Men, and with a cry of protest she let the lute fall, closed her eyes, and pressed her fists against her eyeballs.

Why did he let me go? Why didn't he tell me what I would see?

Because you were determined to see it, whatever it was. You'd be begging him today to let you see what it was he thought too terrible for you to witness.

He had not reminded her, and he never would, that the only way she would believe she could not endure seeing it was to let her see it.

The door opened quickly and she started, her heart pounding intensely.

The gypsy paused, looking at her, and seeming to understand what she had been thinking, closed the door and stood against it. For several moments they were silent, as if each waited for the other to speak of what they had seen.

"Yes?" she asked finally.

He made a gesture, still standing as he had entered, measuring her carefully. Perhaps what his four years with the Countess had once been to her, The House of Dead Men printed in her memory was to him: a cause of distrust between them which must be resolved, one way or the other. He did, she knew, blame himself for having let her go.

"No one has been looking for us. No one, at least, has asked any of the men I talked to."

Arabella gave a triumphant laugh. "I knew it."

He went to the table, quickly peeled an orange and began to eat it. He glanced around at her, still standing in the same place, wondering about this negative news. For she knew the gypsy was no more convinced by negative evidence than he would have been by positive evidence of searchers.

Of course he was right. The men who were looking for them might have discovered that in this southern province they learned less from questions, or money, than might be discovered by some other means.

He walked toward her, holding out one hand, as in supplication. She put her hand into his, as if they were about to begin one of the stately court dances, and as she moved slowly toward him, he went step by step away from her, seating himself on one of the stools and drawing her to stand between his legs.

Then, after this slow quiet interlude, there came a quick abandonment of apprehensions, and she held his head close, his mouth against her breasts. Her legs moved apart and with a swift jolting movement he forced her down upon him, producing uncanny surprise and a rising ecstasy as he moved her steadily upon him.

His movements were swift, purposeful, remorseless; his hands crushed her breasts, and when she looked at him his eyes were closed as he sought that needful finality, releasing them from whatever misgivings had taken hold. He sighed heavily, and a spreading web of pleasure moved throughout her belly. The movements slowed, his hold upon her breasts became gentle, and as she began to kiss him his mouth was quiescent. At last she felt him slip away. But he did not release her, only bowed his head upon her shoulder, while her arms encircled his shoulders, her lips moving across the curly blond hair. The dangerous moment, if there had been one, had passed.

After several minutes of silence she felt him begin to stir against her. He raised his head, looked at her questioningly, then slowly smiled. His hands around her waist lifted her upright, and when she began a soft protest he shook his head. The next moment he was taking down the burnooses, the black one for her, the white for him, rebuckling his belt with the three sheathed knives, and Arabella let him wrap her close, fasten the face veil, and stuck out her tongue as she looked at herself in the mirror.

"Ugly, ugly," she said.

"That's the idea. Come. It's growing late. And be sure your fingers touch my back every moment." He looked at her gravely. "Don't lose me for an instant."

"No."

221

Even two kilometers from town there was heavy traffic on this day, women with baskets, farm wagons loaded with produce; pages or squires, riding ornately caparisoned horses. A blonde lady rode by, the same they had seen yesterday, Arabella noticed, dressed in vermilion silk, surrounded by her retinue, and again she turned in her saddle to watch the gypsy.

But jealousy was gone from Arabella.

If he left her, it would not be for a woman.

She was replete, warm throughout her body and filled with the energetic buoyancy he gave her.

Walking behind him, skipping now and then to match his rapid pace, the fingers of one hand placed lightly within the folds of his burnoose, she thought of what she had said that first morning when she had gone to him to learn the great secret: Now the world is mine.

He had looked at her with vague alarm, as if he had produced a greater effect than he had intended, and the memory made her smile.

The world is mine. Yes. He gave it to me.

As they entered the town she began to look, as furtively as possible, at the passersby in the crowded narrow streets, and to her amused surprise the town's entire population seemed to have changed overnight. They passed men and women and children dressed in outlandish clothing from every nation bordering the sea.

And riding at the wharves there seemed a new flotilla of craft, flying different colors, while men heavily laden rushed back and forth over the gangways.

He took the main thoroughfare, away from the wharf they had walked down yesterday, and although they were jostled she stepped nimbly to one side and the other, following him with alacrity, until all at once he paused where a large group had gathered about some musicians and acrobats.

Yells of admiration or derision came from the crowd as jugglers dropped knives, flame swallowers set their hair afire and had to be soundly beaten for their own good. The crowd took a rowdy delight in mishaps of every kind, encouraging them with shoves at the acrobats when they had attained their most precarious perches. They threw garbage into the musicians' horns, trampled upon one another's feet, but took care when they were near the gypsy, for he was taller than they, those squat southerners. Arabella gazed at them with fascinated contempt for their ugliness.

There was a sudden commotion, a moving surging moment, a simultaneous outcry from the crowd, which drew back as with the instinct of a single animal. The gypsy seized her wrist, then her shoulders, and began pushing her ahead of him, thrusting the heel of his hand beneath the chin of any man who got in his path. Arabella glanced around to see a mendicant monk lying on his back, a dagger thrust to the hilt in his throat, eyes staring sightlessly, the blood spurting from his neck and mouth. There were yells and a general scramble to escape.

The gypsy propelled her into an alleyway so narrow the upper stories nearly touched. Men passed them warily, clinging to the walls.

Out the other end he pushed her so swiftly that she was forced to run, then grabbed her wrist and dragged her. She was no longer aware of anything but a blur of distorted faces, shouts and curses.

Abruptly the gypsy stopped. Arabella struggled to breathe as they paused inside a dark doorway. She heard him speaking in Romany to a man who stood there, got a reply in the same tongue, and began to run again, pulling her along.

Even when they had reached the highway out of town, he continued to drag her by the arm while she floundered, lost in the burnoose.

Now and then he glanced back. "Faster. Can't you run faster?"

A few shouts from passersby on their way toward town demanded to know what the excitement was, but the gypsy ignored them.

He unlocked the barn door, and Caliph, sensing a danger

Arabella had not yet comprehended, came at a loping gait to meet his master, who stroked his head but paused for no explanation, opened the wagon door, and pitched Arabella inside.

He threw aside the white burnoose, and she noticed a stain of blood on it, saw that his shirt was slit, and blood oozed slowly from a knife wound.

"You've been hurt—"

He did not look at her but pulled off the trousers and shirt and began to rummage in one of the chests, bringing forth the yellow-and-green tights and mail-lined yellow-and-green jerkin he had worn as the Countess's squire.

He got into the tights, fastened the jerkin, and strapped the belt around his waist. She noticed it was missing one of the three knives—left in the throat of the mendicant monk. He brought out another and fitted it into the empty sheath, opened the door and might have left without a word, but she placed herself before him. "You can't go back!" Her arms spread across the door.

He pushed her aside, but then, as she seized his arm, stopped and looked at her incredulously. "He wasn't alone. There was another with him—"

"You can't find him!"

"He can't hide from me—not unless he's gone—and he wasn't sent to run from his quarry. I'll find him."

"How?" She was still cinging to him, her back against the door. "How?"

"Men will tell me. Those two—monks—were from the north. Their faces and their voices gave them away—"

He moved her aside, gesturing her back from the opened doorway and went out, locking it. As she ran to the window he was across the floor, then a few words to Caliph in Romany, and he was gone. Arabella gave a high cry of protesting despair and threw herself upon the floor, curling her legs close to her belly, covering her head with her arms.

▣ CHAPTER TWENTY-EIGHT ▣

S he remained curled in a self-protective ball, and presently began to cry. The sobs came uncontrollably and could not be stopped. She would never see him again.

The knife wound near his left nipple had destroyed at an instant her faith that the gypsy was a species of supernatural being, immune to ordinary human accidents, immune even from death itself.

She had held this superstition from the first morning she had seen him, squatting beside the campfire, the sun on his curling blond hair turning it the color of gold—looking to her more deity than man.

Now that he had been wounded anything could happen to him. He could be harmed, as ordinary mortals were harmed. He would die one day, as ordinary mortals had died before her eyes—during tournaments and battles, from sicknesses that swept over the healthy and, in a few days, they were dead.

And since she could imagine no life without him, this recognition was a double condemnation—her death, as well as his.

The warning of the old gypsy woman returned: Let her beware of love.

Love had seemed easy to avoid, as she studied the young men who lived at the castle, the visiting nobility who came and went; travelers from lands far distant. Her designated fate had never been to marry for love, but for the Crown's aggrandizement. And so she would have done, knowing there were compensations to be found wherever her fancy struck.

Lying on the floor without energy or will, she was indifferent even to what her reliable oracle the mirror might tell her. It had betrayed her into euphoric confidence too often.

When he had been gone an hour or two or three, she still lay with knees curled close to her belly, arms folded to cradle her head. She had cried for so long she was unable to stop. Now and again she stroked the silk carpet with nervous gestures, as if seeking comfort.

Remembering she had heard that a sensitive dog could know when his master was in danger, even to knowing whether he was alive or dead, she got up and peered into the darkened barn.

Presently she discovered Caliph, gazing alertly toward the outside door. As she studied him she could discover nothing different in his stance, in his expression, from any other day when he had waited for the gypsy's return. And she turned away.

She thought of lying on the bed, but rejected that to lie again on the floor, curling inside herself. And she was there, staring without expecting to see anything, when the door opened, the gypsy entered, paused momentarily, and Arabella sprang up, seizing his arm as if he were trying to escape.

He held her gently, perhaps because the wound was still painful. Then he put her aside, lit a candle, and turned to find her with her hair tangled, her face swollen and streaked—no Arabella he had ever seen before. He looked at her for a long quiet moment before he took her into his arms, stroking her hair and back, kissing her face and swollen lids.

"You think I can't defend myself?" He moved her away a little to look at her, and his expression was amused, somewhat puzzled. "You thought I would be killed?"

"Oh, no," she whispered, as if it were a desecration to speak the words aloud. "But they might have been many."

"This time—they weren't."

He pulled off the tights, stripping them down like a layer of skin, for once they had been sewn while on him to assure the proper stylish fit. She looked at him in helpless admiration, telling herself that his beauty alone should protect him.

At last she found courage to ask, "You found him?"

"I found him."

He had thrown aside the soft leather boots and tights and was unfastening the mail-lined jerkin. His voice was matter-of-fact, as if she had asked if he had found food, or a new hiding place—not a man to kill.

"Someone told you?"

"I had no need to ask. He was where I expected he would be." He made a slight grimace, tossing aside the jerkin, and she saw that the blood had clotted, although it was still fresh and dark red. He examined the contents of the medicine cabinet.

"In the cathedral. Praying. Probably with conviction." He extracted a jar, and with a wad of clean cotton cloth wiped the wound.

She wanted to ask where he had killed him, but remained silent. He glanced at her with an ironic smile.

"What difference does it make?" he replied to the unasked question. "I killed him." He took a length of white linen, tore it into long strips, applied it to the front of his chest, and Arabella wrapped it tightly, tying the ends and folding them flat.

"Two of his men dead in one day. The King drives a hard bargain." He picked up a pouch he had thrown aside and balanced it in his hands. "Coins. They were hidden in the cassock."

"The King's. And Guise's."

He tossed it onto the chest, nodding. In a few moments he had dressed in white linen Turkish trousers, and this time, to conceal the bandage, pulled a high-collared white shirt over his head.

He went to feed the animals, bring fresh water, and

227

Arabella prepared to look once again as much like herself as possible. She washed her face and, remembering the restorative powers of a bath, stepped into the tub, washing herself with perfumed soap.

She had, all at once, a reassuring happiness, something near to joy because he was there, essentially unhurt.

He has no fears. He would have, if there were reason.

Or wouldn't he let me know?

She was standing drying herself when he appeared in the doorway. An hour or more, she supposed, had passed while she sat half-stupefied in the tub.

"It's dark," he told her. "I'm going back. They may have had companions, and I must know if there's news."

Intimidated, for he seemed no more agreeable to her protestations for his safety—to him not safety but cowardice—than the King had been, setting out on a campaign. Even so she placed her hands on his arms, but kept silent.

"Men are killed here every day. Trouble thrives in the seacoast towns. Men with scores to settle—with life, or with other men—"

"Please—"

"Arabella—" Something in his tone, or perhaps something not in his tone, silenced her. "This is my country—my people—not theirs—I won't be long—" He was gone, and once again she watched as he bade Caliph goodbye, and closed the door.

She tied the long gold-embroidered scarf beneath her armpits, sat down to pluck at the lute, and presently began to sing one of the melancholy gypsy songs he had taught her.

At the sound of the door she was on her feet, expecting some new disaster. He smiled, shaking his head.

"Either there was no one with them—or the men of the north have learned it isn't wise to ask questions here."

Arabella walked toward him, having prepared her speech while she waited. "Robert—" She paused, and her heart was beating a hard fast rhythm. He looked at her, skeptical.

"Yes—"

"You must give me a promise. Will you?"

He looked increasingly wary. She moved nearer and their bodies touched.

She spoke rapidly. "Promise me that if we are found you will kill me before they do."

He stared at her, then all at once seized her shoulders and shook her hard several times. He spoke through his teeth, angry as she had never seen him. "Stop talking like a damned fool. You're going to live. You're going to live—whatever happens—"

"Not if—"

"They don't want to harm you. They want to take you back—"

"I won't let them."

"Arabella—we've spent less than four months together, four months out of a lifetime. You'll forget me in a year. Four months—" He gave a sharp snap of finger and thumb. "Nothing."

"Nothing? Nothing, Robert?"

He turned away. "You must think of it as nothing. In time, you will forget me. Now—" He glanced at her again, suspiciously, as if she might begin some new drama. "I've told the farmer the stolen shipment has arrived. He's been well paid and he's glad to see me go. He thinks I may cause him trouble—he might be tortured to tell someone where I've gone—if the shipment were valuable enough. He has only my word that it's wool, and he doesn't believe me."

"When do we leave?"

"When I get back. We'll turn off the main highway and head up into the hills—there are places to hide. But I don't want to be too far from town, so I can ride there for information."

She said nothing, since nothing would influence him, and she gazed at the floor as he spoke, intimidated by his anger, stunned that he should have told her their four months together had been nothing.

He touched her face, his mouth brushed hers, and he gave her a long steady look, asking her not to cause him new guilts and new anxieties. She smiled tentatively, and with another quickly brushed kiss he went out.

The journey into town produced no news, and he made ready for them to leave. He had told her she could not ride that night, and advised her to try to sleep, despite the roughness of the terrain they must travel.

She untied the scarf, carefully folded and replaced it in the chest, and lay on her back, stretching her arms and legs and drawing a deep sigh, unable to resist the alluring fatigue of youth.

There was a sense of relief that he was not there. For when he came to sleep, the next morning, the hours would have mended the tear in their feelings.

The road was deeply rutted, the wagon pitched precariously, and she awoke from time to time, but could not stay awake. Whenever he came to sleep he did not wake her, and when she saw light at the edges of the leather panels, he had gone.

He's still angry.

She got up and moved the curtain cautiously, letting in a stream of sunlight filtered through what must be a shadow of overarching trees. The horses, Odysseus and Saracen and Ptolemy, grazed on long tethers, and Caliph gnawed a bone with a good piece of meat on it.

He had been up long enough to reconnoiter the neighborhood.

She was cleaning her teeth when he came in, bearing an iron pot, steaming and fragrant as the stew he had been preparing the first morning when she and her maids-of-honor had come upon him.

She gave him a wary questioning glance, not certain if the anger had lasted, but he smiled, nodded toward the steaming pot, and while she finished washing and slipped on the cloth-of-gold coat, he was ladling stew into two bowls.

They began to eat, hungrily. It was midmorning, and there had been nothing to eat, no time or inclination to think of food, during the past twenty-four hours.

They looked at each other as they ate, unwilling to speak of what had happened—the two men dead, the wound on his chest, his savage anger when she had begged him to kill her if they were found.

After a while she reached across, slowly moving aside his shirt. There was no bandage, the dried blood had been washed away, and there was only a slit in the skin of his breast. She touched him wonderingly, not near the wound, and tears came into her eyes, but she blinked quickly to keep them from falling.

She returned to eating the stew and kept her eyes down, gazing into the bowl as if its contents were of profound interest. She must cause no further alarms or disturbances.

The reddened slit convinced her there was true magic in the gypsy's salves and potions. Or perhaps the magic was in the blood of the gypsy himself. That omen she took to be a good one.

But even so she distrusted her belief in luck, her faith that life was on her side, and warned herself not to think beyond the moment as they sat there, facing each other, the forest surrounding them, the animals at peace in the sun.

"We traveled for long?" That seemed a safe question.

"About six hours, and that was because of the road. I took a long route to a place I remember above the sea. I'm going in to town, I'll take Odysseus and leave him with the man I spoke to yesterday. I want to find out—" He stopped, and went on eating, watching her carefully, as if his steady stare would prevent her from protesting.

She looked at him, giving only a slight nod of agreement.

There was nothing to question, since he must learn what he could, and if he learned nothing—even so, they knew now they could take no satisfaction in the absence of news. There had been no word yesterday morning, either.

Yesterday had not vanished during the night, but intensified in meaning and future portents.

At last Arabella, longing for peace and a return to their easy intimacy, smiled a little, not a bright gay smile, but a smile asking for a return to their closeness. It was less a plea than an offer.

He replied with a slight answering smile. After a few moments he reached toward her and slipped the coat from her shoulders, closing his hand over one breast as his thumb caressed the nipple.

She stopped eating, waiting, and remained silent as he continued stroking her breast. He went on eating, intent on prolonging the time before they came together, looking at her breasts as carefully as he had ever looked into her face.

The color of his eyes had deepened, a sign she had recognized the first morning, and she leaned slightly toward him, as he went on stroking her, slowly, thoughtfully. Her eyes closed.

Enjoy the small pleasures first, Arabella. I'll give you everything you want. Only now, wait—

She understood what his hands were telling her, lulling her into a trancelike state where every sensation was heightened, the lightest touch of his fingers leaving in their wake an awareness of her beauty, as if the movements of his hands had power to delineate the way she looked to him.

As he came to stand beside her, her head tipped backward and her arms closed around his hips. He took her breasts in both hands, moving them gently as a sculptor molding clay.

When it had begun to seem he would do nothing more, and the pleasure had become so intense all sensation seemed concentrated in her breasts, he brought her slowly to her feet, and began backing slowly away. She followed him, her hand in his, as if they moved across vast spaces of a dream.

CHAPTER TWENTY-NINE

S till with that dazzled sense of having no control of what was happening or might happen, she again closed her eyes as he lowered her slowly to the bed, knelt before her, and was swiftly inside her. Holding her buttocks he brought her astride him and they faced each other, his eyes questioning the vague look of pain and uncertainty while he forced her steadily downward.

She gave a sound of wondering despair as the muscles in her belly went into spasmodic movement, her hands clutching him as if to save herself from unknown dangers. The spasms continued stronger, more threatening, and her voice broke into dismayed sobs, followed by a surprising kind of laughter, a laughter of terror and triumph. Her hands caught hold of his hair while the spasms ebbed as they had begun, leaving her vaguely aware that he had disengaged himself.

She began to kiss his face in protest and despair, while his hands, which had with such gentle slowness molded her breasts, seized them forcefully, pushing her backward, and without warning the long slow prelude had turned savage. She tried to free herself, caught by the fear that this was real rage, no longer kept in control by underlying concern, that he might injure her, perhaps kill her without knowing what he had done.

Her nails raked his back and she bit deep into his shoulders as each thrust jolted her body. All at once it was over.

His mouth touched hers in a kiss which asked forgiveness for whatever madness might have taken him. He made no further movements, although she held him, kissing his shoulders where she saw the marks her teeth had made, surprised and ashamed they were so deep. Her hands stroked his back and as she held them away from her there was blood on them.

The brief angry moments seemed to have obliterated everything remembered since the afternoon, less than two days ago, when she had demanded to see The House of Dead Men. The memories of torture were gone. The man killed in the streets yesterday—the mendicant monk lying amidst a shouting, jostling crowd, the hilt of a knife standing erect in his throat; her terror when the gypsy had returned to kill the other man, and his anger when she had begged him to kill her if the searchers ever found them. If such things had happened they had been demolished and they were at peace again, a peace gained during the unforgiving moments when they had sought to obliterate not only dark memories, but their need of each other, the continual discovery that the last encounter had not been the end of all desire.

They knelt on the bed, looking at each other as if neither understood what had happened. Something, it seemed, outside themselves, had responsibility for that precarious wildness.

He touched her breast by way of apology for the pain he had caused, and went to the tub, where he stood scrubbing himself, gazing intently at the floor, and seemed to have forgotten her.

Presently she came to examine his back. The red welts left by her nails made her shake her head in wondering dismay.

That's what we do to each other. And whatever it is, it's never enough.

She stood before him, silent, seeking that brief glance of mutual reassurance which followed their violent lovemaking. He smiled, and very quickly was dressed again, reaching for one of the mendicant monks' cloaks.

"I'm afraid I'm too tall to make a believable Arab—to anyone who's looking for a blond gypsy masquerading as an Arab."

At the door he kissed her forehead lightly, a kiss chaste and contrite. She stood motionless, longing to ask him not to make that foray into dangerous territory.

She watched as he threw a saddlecloth and stirrups over Odysseus, stroked the other animals in his signal of hail or farewell, and with a brief salute in the direction of the wagon, disappeared through the thick forest of trees.

Arabella continued to watch long after he had disappeared, but when Caliph began his round of pacing the encampment, she turned to familiar responsibilities, smoothing the bed with its sheets marked by the blood she had drawn.

She bathed, and as she began the tedious process of combing her hair, she watched herself in the mirror.

Her breasts ached, but purple marks had not begun to appear, and the warmth in her belly reminded her that the need for union grew more domineering as the indications of danger multiplied. There was no other means of forgetting the truth of their situation, even briefly.

She got into a Persian skirt, red with gold embroidery, a transparent yellow silk blouse, and a sleeveless vest, the green color of the emerald between her breasts.

She guessed he had been gone at least four hours, but the time had no meaning, good or bad, for he would traverse the town street by street, alley by alley, talking to men he had known during the years he had lived in the surrounding countryside.

She sat plucking at the lute, the door opened, and he was looking at her with a slight smile. The smile told her, so she wanted to believe, that he had discovered nothing to alarm them.

He tossed a sackful of food onto the table and began to

unpack it. The lamb stew, delicious in the morning, had turned tepid and greasy, but it would please Caliph, who exhibited, upon opportunity, a dainty palate.

"I talked to every man I could find." He unpacked a slab of roast pork, smelling of herbs, a hard strong cheese, a round loaf of bread, and a cluster of red grapes. This was their next meal, when time came to eat it.

"No one heard anything unusual or saw anyone more unusual than the general population."

"Then we can go into the sea?"

"Later. After midnight. Come out. It's time you got reacquainted with Saracen."

Down the pine-forested hills to the sea along a narrow pathway, they traveled in single file. No moon shone through the trees, and they proceeded slowly.

They tethered the horses loosely to pine trunks some distance from the beach, left their clothes there, and ran eagerly into the waves, Arabella throwing the burnoose off beyond the reach of incoming water.

She stayed close to him, obediently silent despite her joy at the feel of silky water on her skin.

They came together and drifted apart with the movement of the sea. He held her wrist and swam, towing her with him, pumping the water with his legs when they got beyond their depth, and turning back to shore until they stood waist deep.

He dove and came up beneath her, clasping her around the waist, and as Arabella threw herself backward, he swam with his legs holding her hips.

Presently they came together in deeper water, and as Arabella spread her legs to enclose him, he slipped inside her, moving her back and forth with the slow movement of the waves.

She sighed softly. "Every time—it's different—I never expect what happens, the way it feels—"

He moved away, dove beneath her spread legs, swam a little distance away and then back to her, seizing her hand and bearing her along with him as he swam. Their bodies touched, held together, parted.

At last the water began to chill them, and they waded ashore. He dried her with the burnoose, then dried himself while she wrung water from her hair and twisted it into a long coil.

"Quick," she whispered. Each moment they were not together was a moment lost to the eternal ocean of time.

He spread the burnoose on the sand with its thick covering of pine needles, and entered her quickly, sending a kindling pleasure flashing through the interior walls of her body. A few movements, and there was the pulse beating, giving a sense of miraculous relief, as if the deprivation had been long.

The slow movements continued for an indeterminate time, while her head tossed restlessly from side to side, pleading for something more intense, more demanding for both of them. Her hands flung outward in a gesture of exasperation and hopelessness, clutching at the folds of the burnoose.

With his hands beneath her knees he rose above her, plunged so deep that there were streaks of pain. She clenched her teeth, waiting for her muscles to accommodate him. The movements were swift and hard, with the violence which built in both of them once the first gratification was complete, yet it was never all they wanted.

He drove on until there came a sudden loosening of her muscles, as if some irreparable disaster had occurred in her body. Her fists pressed against her closed eyes and she began a quiet sobbing, begging to be saved from this ominous threat of disintegration. Not hearing, or not caring, he drove downward with increasing swiftness and force, but now she held him against her, afraid no longer, determined they would never again exist as two separate beings. Only one would be left of this encounter. Neither

Robert nor Arabella, but finally one whole self, perpetually joined.

She lay motionless, arms and legs spread wide, and at last he paused, withdrew to the rim of her body, waiting, as if asking permission to enter her, and for some time they hovered there, Robert waiting, Arabella silent, motionless.

Suddenly he thrust downward, and there came a flowing back of energy and desire. Her fingertips passed over his face, trying to read his expression in the darkness. His lips had drawn outward, his eyes were closed, and as she described his features with her hands he gave a low sound of despairing protest, the lunges came faster, and he was still, breathing as if he had run a desperate race against himself or a powerful enemy.

Slowly he lowered her body and lay for a time upon her. When at last he moved away his mouth touched her breasts, giving to each a light kiss, final benediction to that rough encounter.

He stood a moment, straddling her hips, then reached down and drew her upward to stand against him, her head upon his chest with a sense of weariness and renewal so intermingled she had no idea if she had begun to die or only just now come in to full life. His hands slowly, reassuringly, stroked her back. Then, as if becoming aware that there was a world somewhere outside them, he glanced upward.

"It's late. There's light in the sky. Come along." He picked up the cloak, took her hand, and they ran toward the stand of pine where Odysseus and Saracen waited.

In moments the gypsy was dressed, and as Arabella pulled on the crimson skirt and yellow shirt, he separated her wet hair down the back and tied it into a loose knot low on her neck, and wrapped the burnoose around her.

"Keep well covered. We've stayed too long. Quick."

Arabella vaulted swiftly from the cradle the gypsy made of his palms onto Saracen's back, and they started off, up the hillside toward the wagon. She halted Saracen and turned, looking back toward the sea.

He had ridden a few feet ahead. "Come, Arabella."

She joined him and for a few minutes they proceeded at a walk, the gypsy, according to his habit, glancing down the beach, up the hillsides, searching for anyone who might be in the neighborhood.

Presently he paused, gazing through the pines far down the beach, toward the east, where a vague rim of light showed along the horizon. Arabella followed his gaze. There were two riders on horseback, some distance away, dark figures, scarcely distinguishable.

"Are they coming toward us? Or going the other way?"

He was silent a moment longer. "They're coming toward us. Slowly." He kicked his horse into a faster gait with his bare heel, and Arabella kept Saracen beside him. When next he looked around, the men were approaching at a canter.

"It's early," the gypsy said, as if to himself. "Early for anyone riding on the beach."

He spoke reflectively, and she heard a sound of troubled concern. She said nothing. There had been too many meaningless reassurances from her, and she did not like to see the strangers, either.

"Let's cut around this way. We can put ourselves out of their sight, if they've seen us—or are looking for us." The horses turned, taking a path which led around the hill, farther down the beach, approaching nearer to the wagon.

All at once another horseman came into view, from the opposite direction, nearer than the other two, who were now galloping along the beach.

"There's an unusual traffic for this hour," he said. "Or—"

The gypsy kicked Odysseus into a faster gait, running up the hillside, holding Saracen's rein to keep her with him.

He stopped suddenly, throwing one arm upward in a sign of dismissal. "Go back. Caliph will protect you." He put two fingers to his mouth and she heard the piercing whistle. "Take the keys—"

He pressed the keys into her hand. She dropped them.

He gave a muttered curse in Romany, swooped down with one arm, leaning far over Odysseus's side, and swept the ground, searching, not finding them. Then he was upright again.

Another dark figure on horseback was approaching slowly and cautiously from above and to their left, pausing behind a pine trunk.

Down the beach, the two men had disappeared among the pines. The gypsy continued up the hillside and Arabella kept Saracen beside him. Some scrap of memory from The House of Dead Men flashed by.

I won't leave him. Whatever happens, they must not take him.

They had traveled some distance up the hillside, when the gypsy gave another piercing whistle, startling her, startling Saracen, so that she had to catch him roughly by the bit to keep him from bolting.

The gypsy spoke in a rough undertone. "Get out of here." Once again there was that piercing whistle.

The men down the beach reappeared, moving steadily and quickly nearer. The other two approaching from the opposite direction came forward with caution, pausing to conceal themselves. A fifth horseman appeared, some distance above them, moving down the hillside.

Caliph's bark sounded in the distance. Arabella had heard his voice only once, the night the man had been killed on the highway, but the sound was unmistakable. The bark came again, nearer, reassurance that he was in swift motion.

The gypsy turned. "Go that way—anywhere—get out of here!"

He had swung Odysseus around and was starting back down the hill. Arabella turned Saracen, following him. The men had left the beach and were mounting the hillside.

240

The gypsy yelled at her. "Get out!"

"I won't leave you."

He struck her hand, and she let go her hold upon Odysseus's rein. "Can't you see what's happening?" He gave Saracen a kick and a great blow with his fist. "God damn you—get out of here—"

Then he was galloping toward the two men coming upward from the beach.

Saracen reared back and as she pulled savagely at his bit he gave a shrill whinnying protest, prancing on his hind feet as she wheeled him around and started after the gypsy, who was no longer aware of her, all energy and attention concentrated upon these men who came forward out of the dawn.

Arabella followed, with no thought but that the gypsy must not be taken captive.

During the past few minutes the darkness had lifted. She saw the gypsy draw a knife, take aim, and the nearest horseman paused, then toppled to the ground, the knife through his throat. Still riding toward them, the gypsy shot forth a second knife, caught the man in the face, and as he fell, the gypsy was on the ground, snatching away the knives, seizing a broadsword from the first man, and as one of the riders from farther up the hill broke into a gallop, the gypsy backed against a broad pine trunk to confront him.

Arabella slipped from Saracen's back and started toward him. Caliph appeared, streaking by her, as another horseman approached at a gallop, and she saw that the other two men had appeared, one of them galloping with fixed lance toward the gypsy.

There were shouts of rage, shouts of alarm, although the gypsy was silent, engaging the new opponent, now dismounted, in a slashing combat of broadswords.

The lancer approached swiftly, and as Arabella ran between him and the gypsy, Caliph's teeth severed his horse's ankle tendons, the lancer toppled from his horse, and the lance drove through Arabella's right shoulder, through the gypsy's chest, pinioning them to the pine's trunk. The gypsy slashed across the man's neck and shoulder at the moment the other's broadsword cut through the gypsy's neck. She felt what seemed a blow as the lance was seized by someone behind her, struggling to pull it from their bodies and out of the pine's trunk. . . .

She heard, as from a distance, the sound of a doleful wail, Caliph's dirge as he took up a warning stance over the body of his master. The spear had been pulled free. Robert was lying nearby, upon his back, arms flung outward, palms up, the broadsword buried through his neck.

She was aware that he was dead, the other man dead, while all around were the sounds of men sobbing, and presently she realized that she was lying across a man's legs, his arms holding her fast against him, his head pressed to hers.

Through advancing and retreating waves of consciousness she heard a near sound of sobbing, sounds which came from the man who held her, kissing her face again and again, wiping away the gypsy's blood with his hand.

At last she recognized that familiar long-ago-loved voice, sobbing, repeating, "My beloved sister—my beloved sister—"

"Raoul?" The name was a whisper.

"Yes, yes—it's Raoul. I'm here—" He held her harder, sending a sickening pain throughout her body, and the sound of his voice grew so distant she could scarcely hear it. "Dear God, don't let her die—don't let her die."

"You came so far—" she murmured in wonder. "For this."

"Not for this! No! No! I came to take you with me. Dear God—have pity on her, save her from sorrow—save her from suffering."

The wild confused yelling of the men had stopped. There was uncanny silence, broken only by Raoul's sobbing and

Caliph's song of grief, rising and falling and rising in unchanging rhythm.

Bewildered by her brother's despair, his clutching her so close, his wild rocking of her to and fro, his sobbing and praying, she reached slowly, trying to touch the gypsy's hand as it lay palm upward, fingers slightly curled. The distance became vast, and she was forced to relinquish the effort.

"Raoul—"

"Yes, yes, I'm here—I've come." The sobs stopped his words.

She had wanted to ask him something of importance, but the question sank beyond retrieval.

"My beloved sister—Arabella—live, my dearest—live—"

There was something she must say. A few words. But before she could speak them they were gone. She tried to find Raoul's face. "Has it grown dark? Why can't I see you?"

"Dear God in Heaven, don't let her die!" He collapsed upon her, sobbing uncontrollably.

He doesn't know. He doesn't understand.

Once again she made an effort to touch the hand which lay not far away, no longer Robert's—no longer the gypsy's. No longer anyone's at all. But at last she gave up the attempt, and drifted far from Raoul, far from the gypsy, from the silent men, kneeling close by.

At last the question returned. "Raoul—" He bent forward until his ear touched her lips. "Raoul—who did we harm?" She saw his face as a darkened blur. "Anyone?"

She looked questioningly at him, waiting his answer. Then her eyes moved again toward where the gypsy was lying. A look of unseeing dazzlement came into them as her breathing stopped.

The kneeling men crossed themselves. Raoul held her more fiercely, kissing her eyes to close them, while Caliph's howling dirge went on rising and falling, rising and falling.

"Arabella—Beloved Arabella—"

The men chanted:

"Hail Mary, Mother of God, intercede for the soul of this sinner—"

"Mercy—mercy—have mercy upon her soul—"

"*Id quod maxime timendum erat factum est—*"